Lizzie -

CARLY MARIE

Igor loves driving Yuri insane *inside* the bedroom even more than outside!

♡ - Carly Marie ♡

Editing Services: Jennifer Smith

Cover: Tall Story Designs

This is a work of fiction. Names, characters, businesses, places, events, locales, and incidents are either the products of the author's imagination or used in a fictitious manner. Any resemblance to actual persons, living or dead, or actual events is purely coincidental.

CONTENTS

NOTE TO READERS

First and foremost, thank you Julie for helping me with translations. Russian is not an easy language to write when you're not a native speaker. That being said, by no means am I fluent in Russian and after writing this book, I don't it every happening. Russian is a complex language, made more difficult because there are often times no direct English translations for words or even the Cyrillic alphabet. Just because I used one spelling of a word does not mean that every instance of that word is spelled the same across the board.

Second, Yuri and Igor were created well before the war between Russia and Ukraine occurred. This book is in no means in support of the war. Yuri and Igor are simply two people, created before I ever thought they would fall in love and end up as MCs of this book. But here they are, and their story needed to be told.

And finally, here is a list of terms used in this book that many readers might not know about. Yuri is a coffee snob, so the first two are terms used to describe different preparations of a cappuccino. The rest are Russian words that may or may not be explicitly explained in the book. I tried my hardest to give direct translations of words as quickly as possible, but I probably missed a few here or there.

Cappuccino: one-third espresso, one-third steamed milk, one-third foam

Dry cappuccino: same as cappuccino except there's more foam to steamed milk in this ratio

Sosiski: breakfast hot dog/sausage

Mochi perkhoti: pee hole dandruff

Kozyol: a male goat who does stupid things

Da: yes

Krasivo: beautiful

Blyad: fuck

Solnishko: Sunshine (male)

Korolevsky: Russian Royal Cake... see back for more information on this cake, as well as the adventure I took in making it.

CHAPTER 1

IGOR

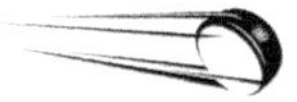

"M*udak*!"

Asshole.

I couldn't make out the rest of what Yuri was saying. My brain was still foggy from the anesthesia and he was speaking so quickly there was no hope of me figuring out what he was saying. It wasn't like my limited Russian would ever let me make out his rapid-fire speech.

A door opened and Yuri spoke faster. I only picked up the last thing he said, but that was because he'd paused for half a beat and spoken slower and with affection in his voice.

"Da, da, tebya lyublyu, durak."

He must have been talking to his brother, Danil. At least I'd never heard him call anyone else an idiot after saying he loved them. Since I was Latvian, my Russian was limited to terms of endearment and insults, but at least I could tell the difference... usually.

"Mr. Yurievich," a female voice said, speaking quietly. "I wasn't expecting you to still be here."

For a brief second, I forgot why I was in the hospital bed and moved to adjust myself, causing my hip to scream in pain and letting me know that I was not going to be moving for a bit. The doc had told me it was an outpatient procedure, but they'd also warned me that I was going to be sore as hell for a bit.

"Here, yes. Igor still sleeps."

The woman hummed. "I suspect he'll be up soon. His vitals are fine. Sometimes the anesthesia takes a while to wear off. He was starting to wake up in the recovery room. Kept talking about a puck bunny."

Yuri went off on a tangent in his native tongue. I picked up enough to know he was cussing me out and calling me names. He would never forgive me for sending the entire building looking for Puck Bunny at an away game. It was his own damned fault for forgetting the bear on the bus. I wasn't going to let his absentmindedness cost us a game—the bears were a good luck charm we all had—but the confusion and shock on the staff's faces when they discovered they'd been looking for a stuffed animal—not some random woman—for an hour had been almost as good as the red Yuri's face had turned when the bus driver appeared with the bear wearing tiny pink bunny ears.

I had no idea where he'd found the ears, but that bus driver would forever be my hero.

"I'm sorry, I don't understand. Should I get a translator?" The woman on the other side of me was trying so hard to be kind and I could hear in her voice that she thought she was missing important information.

"No translator needed. He is cussing me out in Russian." My throat and mouth were parched and my voice had come out like I'd been asleep for a month, not a few hours.

Had the last hip surgery been this rough?

"Igor!"

"Ah, welcome to the world of the living, Mr. Ozols. Your friend has been worried about you."

Yuri grunted. "Not anymore. Please, put him back to sleep. He is better when he cannot speak."

The nurse laughed in spite of her best attempts not to. "Sorry."

I still smiled at her, ignoring Yuri completely. "Water?"

She nodded. "Of course. I'll be right back."

The doctor had used laparoscopy to shave part of my inner hip down. There had been a bony growth from years of butterfly maneuvers on ice. I was certain the original surgery hadn't been this painful.

Before she'd left the room, I'd shaken the thoughts of pain away to turn to the man who should have been on his way back to Russia to visit his family, not sitting in a hospital room in Tennessee, and pointed a finger at him. "You're here?"

"I am here."

"You should be heading home. Your family."

Yuri shook his head slowly as he gathered his thoughts. I silently thanked him for doing so, my brain still too sluggish to be able to decipher Yuri's excitable and oft-butchered English. "No. I'm staying here. I am needed more."

He finished with a soft smile that silenced any rebuttals I'd begun to form. I didn't like giving up easily, so I gave a half-hearted counter. "What about your babushka's cake?" I'd heard enough about the dessert since Christmas time that I knew Yuri was looking forward to going home to have it. Hell, I'd heard so much about it, I could almost pronounce it, at least if I took a really long time and had a few practice attempts first.

"Babushka sent recipe." He lifted his phone and shook it gently. "Babushka gave it to Danil, told him to send it to me. Must learn to make it now."

My eyes widened as the nurse returned with a cup of water. "You cannot cook."

Yuri shrugged. "I cannot. Tap is a good cook, though."

Poor Tapio had somehow become known as the go-to baker in the last few months as well as a fantastic defenseman on ice. He'd taken the title as team chef in stride and with a smile, often joking that he needed to go home to make the latest request. As fantastic a baker as

Tapio was, I wasn't convinced he was going to be up for the complicated Russian dessert. From what I'd read about the cake, it was an absolute bitch to make.

The nurse handed over the water, waiting for me to take a drink before beginning to question me. "How's your pain?"

"Which pain?" I shot a wink toward my best friend. "He is a massive pain. Hip is a bigger pain for now."

Yuri's face showed surprise before he flipped me off behind the nurse's back, leaving me to fight a laugh as I focused on her. "We'll get you some painkillers before you get discharged, just not too many. You need to be able to use crutches today."

I groaned. Crutches were not fun. It wouldn't be my first time on them, but with my pending retirement from playing professional hockey, with any luck this would be my last.

"Svoloch' Schmidt," Yuri said with a huff.

My head bobbed in agreement. Leif Schmidt had delivered the collision that had been the final blow to my hip, and he really was a bastard. The surgery I'd just gone through had been a long time coming. The last season and a half I'd been babying my hip as much as possible, but being plowed into at full speed by a dirty hit from a brute of a player had been enough to sideline me for the last few games of my final playing season.

Schmidt's three-game suspension was little consolation when we'd ended up being eliminated in game seven.

The only thing that had gotten me through was that Tampa was going up against the team that was predicted to win the Stanley Cup. All I had to say about that was, *Washington better win it.*

The nurse looked between the two of us, then shook her head. "I'm just going to assume that I've missed something here and go on with my duties. The first one is to get you to the bathroom."

"Dammit." I knew it was coming, that always seemed to be the requisite for leaving the hospital following a surgery, but the last thing I wanted to do was hobble on crutches to the bathroom to take a piss.

Yuri snorted in a poor attempt to hold back a laugh while the nurse smiled sweetly at me. Instead of the normal teasing, Yuri spoke with a serious determination I rarely heard from him off ice, his accent sharp but the words clear. "I will help him."

The nurse gave the two of us curious looks, and her eyes finally settled on me, an eyebrow quirked upward. Before I could form a response, Yuri spoke again, his tone somehow more matter-of-fact than it had been before. "Igor recovers at my house. I need to know how to help him."

I blinked in surprise. This was news to me, but he'd said it with such finality, I knew that any possible argument I could come up with would fall on deaf ears. There was still a slight fog of anesthesia that made everything a little out of focus and parts of my brain not fully functional—mainly the part that should have told Yuri to get lost.

Instead of disputing Yuri's statement, I found myself nodding in agreement. The smile he gave me was something different than I'd seen on him before. It was an odd mixture of happiness and pride that lit his face up. He was already walking toward me, but my brain had gotten caught up in his smile and trying to figure out ways to make him smile like that more.

The nurse came to the side of the bed and put the rail down. "Do you think you can sit up for me?"

It took some help, but I was able to get to a seated position, my legs dangling over the bed with the nurse to one side of me and Yuri coming to stand to the other.

He turned his head to the side and studied me closely, then looked at the nurse. "How to?"

Her eyebrows drew together in confusion for all of a second before she figured out what he meant. Instead of answering him, she turned to me. "How do you feel? Light-headed? In pain?"

"Head's fine. Hip hurts but nothing unbearable."

She chuckled lightly. "Well, it is unbearable, at least to weight. No standing on it."

I'd heard the lecture numerous times. I'd been through a similar surgery on my other hip five summers earlier; there was a reason I had been putting the surgery off. I huffed, then gestured for the crutches. "Here."

Yuri looked at the nurse as though I might break, the

expression rubbing me in all the wrong ways. "I'm not a twig. I know what I'm doing."

My best friend recoiled like I'd slapped him, but his back stiffened before I could apologize. "No shit, Sherlock. You are hurt. We play hockey, get hurt. Over and over again, we get hurt. But you are my friend. I can worry."

Properly chastised and feeling like a complete fool, I managed a nod and a genuine apology. "I am an ass when in pain. Sorry."

Yuri's shoulders straightened but his back relaxed, a much more comfortable look replacing the grouchy one from a few seconds earlier. "Yes, you are an ass, not just when in pain. Ass or no, nurse says you must pee."

The nurse laughed, a cute, tiny sound that matched her petite stature and drew a sharp contrast to Yuri's stern words and commanding presence in the room.

"No weight on my leg."

She nodded. Her name tag read Amber, and I tried to commit it to memory for later when I wasn't in as much pain. As it was, crutches were being thrust into my hands and I needed to get to the bathroom.

I adjusted the crutches under my arms and planted my no-skid sock-covered right foot on the ground to support my weight while trying to remember the ins and outs of standing while on crutches. It had been a few years since I'd done it and the skill, while much like riding a bike, was coming back but was a little rusty.

When I wobbled, strong hands gripped my sides to

steady me. It wasn't the size or strength of the grip that let me know it wasn't Amber's hands around me; it was the familiarity of the hands around my waist and the trust I had in their grip that made my body relax immediately.

As teammates and neighbors for nearly four years, I'd spent countless hours with Yuri. We worked out together, spotted one another, chirped each other, and stood up to the homeowners association together. I was well acquainted with the way his grip felt. In that moment, knowing there was someone I trusted standing behind me, I felt more sure-footed as I lifted the crutches to make forward progress to the bathroom.

Amber hummed an approval as I finally made it through the door, Yuri never leaving his place behind me, though he'd dropped his hands from my waist after three steps. I was finally feeling confident as I closed the door.

I twisted and yelped in shock, my surprise making the sound a few octaves higher than I had known possible. "Yuri! Out!"

He shook his head. "Not leave. You must pee. No weight on foot." He shook his head again and pointed to where he was beside the sink. "I stay here."

"Dude! Privacy."

His only response was a grunt and to cross his arms. When I didn't make a move to hobble toward the toilet, he blew out a frustrated breath. "Igor Ozols, you have used bathroom next to me before. We change in same room. I have seen what you have in your underwear before. I have same stuff in mine. Go pee." He gestured for me to hurry up but gave a command in case I hadn't understood. "Now."

"There is a divider in the bathrooms! You do not stand to stare at me!" My frustration had my accent coming out thick, almost unrecognizable to me. If I wasn't careful, I'd slip into Latvian and Yuri wouldn't understand a thing I said.

"I will not stare at penis. Just here to remind you to behave. You are no good at that when not drugged. I do not trust you to follow nurse's directions on pain meds."

My mouth flapped open as I tried to come up with a response and I inwardly cursed the anesthesia still in my system for clouding my ability to make a reasonable argument.

Yuri rolled his eyes, then winked at me. "Igor, I do not want to jump your dick. Do not need straight-man's dick. I learned hard way, stay away from straight men. Besides, many women and men very happy to share a bed with me. Will not hook up with a teammate."

It definitely wasn't the anesthesia that had my brain unable to make a comeback. I hadn't even *thought* that before he'd said it. Yuri was openly bisexual and had never had a problem expressing his feelings about men or women. Though now I wanted to know what straight man had hurt him.

"That wasn't what I meant. I just... it is weird having anyone in the bathroom watching me pee."

"Says man who is naked in locker room." Yuri rolled his eyes. "Pee. Bathroom small, Nurse Amber will think we do something here."

I found myself laughing at Yuri's absurdity as I finally adjusted myself to stand in front of the toilet and lifted my gown. Between the billowy cotton hospital gown, my hand, and the sink separating us, Yuri wouldn't be able to see anything even if he tried, which helped me relax. What I did know was that Yuri kept his word. He was looking straight ahead, his head barely angled my way, just enough to see that I wasn't putting weight on my foot.

When I flushed, Yuri finally turned and reached for the faucet. "Not so hard, no?"

I managed to prop myself against the sink and flip Yuri off before washing my hands and drying them on a paper towel. He opened the door, that proud smile on his face once again. I couldn't explain it, just knew I'd never seen it before, but it made me feel like I'd won the Stanley Cup, not peed and washed my hands without hurting myself.

We made our way into the room, me hobbling slowly in front of Yuri, and finally back to the relative comfort of the uncomfortable hospital bed. Thankfully, it was only temporary.

The nurse grinned. "Great. I'm going to go let the doctor know you're up and moving, and he'll be in to talk with you and get you on your way soon."

Her smile didn't make me feel as triumphant as Yuri's had. I didn't have time to contemplate why that was because Yuri was settling himself in the chair beside my bed and looking at me expectantly. "I buy LEGO. Much LEGO. Giant ship." He mimed flying through the air, and I had to laugh.

"Of course you did."

Yuri shot me a bright grin, one without his right eyetooth. He usually wore a fake tooth when he wasn't on ice to hide the gap he'd acquired while playing in the Kontinental Hockey League in Russia. One of my favorite pastimes was teasing him about being the only goalie I knew missing a tooth.

Yuri also had an obsession with LEGO. He had an entire room in his house that was dedicated just to LEGO builds he'd done. While most of us spent our free time playing video games, Yuri rarely played with us. When he did, it was almost never one of the shooters that the team favored. He and our second-line defenseman, Brax, had made a tradition of playing a racing game before every game, but aside from those times, Yuri spent his extra time on LEGO.

"You help, da?"

I pretended to think about it but could already feel a grin spreading on my face. "Da. Of course." I'd found myself building more LEGO sets over the years I'd known Yuri than I'd ever thought possible, but the way his smile lit up when we completed a set made it worth my time.

"Yeees!" Yuri pumped the air just as the doctor entered the room with my discharge paperwork in his hands.

CHAPTER 2

YURI

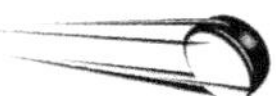

"Ozols!" I swore I'd barked his name in frustration more in the last five days than I had in all the years I'd known him.

Igor paused, bent over in front of the entertainment center, and looked over his shoulder at me. "Yuri." I'd gotten accustomed to his guilty smile the last handful of days. "You are home early."

It wasn't early. I'd only run down to the grocery store to pick up an order I'd placed two hours earlier. The store was barely out of our neighborhood, and Igor knew that as well as I did.

"I leave for fifteen minutes, go pick up groceries, tell you to sit your ass in chair and not move! What do you do? Move!" He listened worse than Boris had as a puppy. If the doctor told him to lie down, Igor stood. If the post-op instructions said zero weight-bearing for two weeks, Igor tried to limp around on his surgically repaired leg.

His refusal to follow directions had led to me putting the team's sports medicine doctor, Indy, on speed dial. Her contact had quickly shown up on my most frequently used numbers shortly after Igor came home from the hospital and was now my top contact.

Multiple times a day, I was texting her to ask if Igor should be doing what he was, and by this point, I'd come to expect the answer would be *no*. After five days, I knew the post-op instructions the hospital had given him by heart, but Igor was still pushing his limits, like bending at a severe angle to get the fucking game console set up instead of waiting three more minutes for me to get home.

"I was being careful." He batted his eyes and I was sure the innocent act had gotten him far with many of his hookups, but it wasn't scoring points with me. The only thing it was scoring him was my desire to put Igor over my lap and paddle his ass bright red. Though if I did that, he wouldn't be able to sit and would probably get into more trouble.

I looked at the crutch he was leaning against. *Crutch*, singular. The other was propped against the entertainment center while his angle was well over ninety degrees as he tried to change the game in the console by leaning precariously against the crutch holding him up. I'd been told more times than I could count that ninety degrees was as far as he should go for at least two weeks.

He was pushing his limits and my patience.

Pointing at him, I shook my head. "Not careful, Igor Ozols! You should not bend like that, you know that. Indy will yell." Not that he didn't deserve being yelled at. The man was going to drive me up a fucking wall. "You sit your ass in a chair. Move every thirty minutes. Move does not mean bend like... like... like... pretzel!" I wanted to throw my hands in the air in frustration, but I was holding the bags of groceries and had to settle on a nasally growl that my subs always knew meant they were a few seconds from pushing me too far.

Unfortunately, Igor was not a sub, wasn't mine, and definitely didn't know that the sound that had come from me meant I was over his antics.

Instead of learning his lesson or acknowledging that what he was doing was only going to set his recovery back, he stood gingerly, slowly taking the crutch he'd placed on the entertainment center, then righting himself fully. When he finally turned to face me, he had an impish grin on his face while he batted his eyes at me.

That time I dropped the bags and threw my hands in the air, cursing under my breath as I tried to calm myself. When it didn't work, I bent and grabbed the bags I'd dropped then headed to the kitchen, throwing a few extra curses over my shoulder as I went. "Zhopa! *Murdak!* Pain in my ass!"

The familiar clicking of his crutches followed me down

the hall and into the kitchen. "Zhopa? Yuri, what does zhopa mean?"

It figured he was more curious about the meaning of what I'd said than interested in apologizing for his disregard of his recovery. In frustration, I flung a cabinet open. "*Ass*. It is a nicer word than I wanted to call you."

"What did you want to call me?"

"Mochi perkhoti."

Igor leaned his weight against the counter. "Mochi what?"

"Perkhoti." I smirked to myself when I saw his blank expression as he tried to work the saying out. *Good luck, my friend.* There was no true direct translation of the insult.

His eyebrows moved into a straight line in confusion. "Perkhoti. What does that mean?"

I huffed as I tried to jam another can in the cupboard. It was overflowing but my annoyance made me more stubborn about making it fit. "I will tell you when you are older."

Igor grumbled something I didn't understand, not that I much cared, then began to pout. "That's not fair! You called me a name and I want to know what it is!"

The cans finally moved enough that I could shut the cabinet without things falling out, and then I folded the first bag up and placed it in the bag of paper grocery bags I had. I turned my attention to the next bag. "You figure it out, then tell me."

Igor stuck his middle finger up at me. "Shopah!"

It was a good thing I had already walked into the pantry to put some canned goods away because I was nearly doubled over laughing at his butchered pronunciation of *ass*. If he couldn't get the pronunciation of ass right, he'd never be able to remember *mochi perkhoti* well enough to look it up online. In the meantime, I was going to take a perverse thrill out of knowing it would drive him nuts until I told him.

Which I didn't plan to do anytime in the near future.

My cheeks were still warm from laughter when I made it back to the kitchen to put the last bag of groceries away. Igor hadn't left his spot and was scowling at the pantry door as I came through it. "What is so funny?"

"Nothing, nothing at all." I grinned. "You are just a pain in the ass. Again, I tell you no more trying to do things until you see Indy next week in person. You will hurt yourself, then bitch and moan that you are in pain. *Oh, Yuri, my leg hurts. I want to coach but cannot skate yet!*" I was pretty proud of my imitation of Igor.

Igor rolled his eyes at my statement. "Yes, Dad."

Letting myself growl was easier than allowing myself to show just how much I liked his agreement. Then again, knowing Igor, we were probably going to have the same argument the next day, if not later today. We'd had almost identical arguments every single day since he'd come home with me from the hospital. And inevitably, as soon as he decided to sit his ass back down, he'd end up bitching that his hip hurt.

I finished putting the groceries away without more commentary from Igor, a small blessing, then turned my attention to my best friend, who hadn't moved and was still pouting as he leaned against his crutches. Taking a small amount of pity on him, I let out a resigned sigh. "What game were you trying to load when I came in?"

Igor brightened before he shot me a mischievous grin. "*LEGO Batman*. I am bored, thought you would like to play too." He batted his eyes, knowing full well the LEGO game series were the only video games I was any good at. While most of the team wanted to play *Call of Duty* or *Counter-Strike*, I was the person that had never gotten into them. My gaming interests ended at the occasional game of *Minecraft* or *LEGO*.

Grumbling because I didn't want to admit defeat but knowing Igor had won this round, I inclined my head toward the living room. "Go. I will set game up. You will sit in chair and not move."

When Igor had told me he needed surgery, the first person I had called was my babushka. She had raised me and my brother while our mother and father traveled for work. Every year when hockey season ended, I was on the first plane back to Russia to see Babushka and Danil. Knowing that Igor would be recovering with no family near, I had been uncomfortable knowing that he would be by himself. I knew my best friend well enough to know that he would injure himself more if he was alone.

The words to tell her I wasn't coming home hadn't fully left my mouth when Babushka had hushed me. "Moya dorogaya rybka," she'd said, her soothing Russian a balm to my soul. Even her still calling me her darling little fish didn't bother me. "You must stay in America with your friend." She'd understood before I'd told her I felt like I needed to be here. "Your old babushka will be here next summer. I have no plans of leaving any time in the near future. You take care of Igor. He needs you more than I do."

She had been the reason I'd wanted to go home since I knew she wasn't getting any younger, but my heart was telling me to stay in Nashville and help Igor. Not just because he was my best friend, but because I knew I'd be happiest knowing I was being helpful to him even when he drove me insane. As long as I could remember, she had warmly teased me that I was always happiest when I helped people. She was the one who had pointed out that it was in my nature to care, sometimes too much.

Now that I was pushing thirty, I could admit that sometimes I did care too much. Sometimes I nearly tortured myself to help someone in need. Someone like Igor, who was my best friend and had no feelings for me but I still enjoyed helping him. I'd begun to live for the moments he'd give in and let me do something for him. It was a dangerous position to be in, and I knew that I was quickly approaching the point that I would need to have a serious conversation with my heart about not actually falling for the hopelessly straight man.

I'd sworn I was keeping things platonic, that I was just being a good friend and was not going to catch feelings for Igor, but I was starting to question if that line between friendship and a crush had begun to blur. The first inkling I'd had that I was in over my head had been at the hospital when I'd walked into the bathroom with him. Yes, I could have left him alone in there, but that would have meant I wouldn't have been right there if he had needed help. There were two things that turned me on faster than anything else—a bratty submissive and knowing that what I was doing was helping the person I was with—and Igor didn't have a clue that he was quickly becoming my kryptonite.

My need to please had been such a confusing part of myself that I'd desperately wanted to understand more about it. That quest had led me straight into the kink and BDSM scene where I'd learned so much more about myself than just my need to please people. Years later, I still hadn't decided if what I had was a service kink, but I had accepted that it was hardwired into my psyche. I'd also discovered that I was a Dom with a soft spot for bratty subs. The brattier the better, especially if they liked impact play as much as I did.

I'd never thought that kink would extend to a friend, but standing in the hospital bathroom with Igor, I'd quickly realized it did. It hadn't gotten better since we'd come back. He pushed limits and made me want to scream in frustration, paddle his ass, and fuck him into oblivion multiple times a day. For nearly a week, I'd found myself counting down the minutes until his last dose of meds for the day so he would head to bed and I could run up the steps to lock myself in my shower and use my fist to take care of my pent-up sexual frustration. For five nights, I'd made it no more than three minutes before I'd exploded all over the shower wall with an intense orgasm that had built throughout the day.

Every time Igor allowed me to do something for him, I found myself aroused. The arousal was only compounded when he argued about it first. Falling for a straight man never ended well, and I'd had to remind myself of that repeatedly each day. Not only were the feelings never returned, but it always led to heartbreak. Unfortunately, living with Igor was testing the friendship boundary I'd never had to work to maintain before.

While I'd been stewing in my thoughts, Igor had made his way to the living room and the time had come that I could no longer hide in the kitchen. I took a deep breath, then headed toward the living room too, willing my cock to behave itself and once again reminding myself that Igor was my friend, nothing more. There was nothing to the banter beyond Igor being Igor, the stubborn, obstinate straight man that had started to tick all my boxes but was also my friend.

I was fucked.

Thankfully, my dick behaved itself long enough for me to set up the game and take a seat on a different couch than Igor. My resolve to not get hard left the building when Igor looked over at me with a grin. "Thank you. I might have been trying to do too much. My hip hurts."

My groan was unintentional. Thankfully, I was able to play it off as annoyance that he had hurt himself by trying to do too much and not from the thank you he'd given me. Damn my kinks for forgetting boundaries.

"It is too soon for pain medicine." I glanced at the clock and sighed. "One hour. Pain medicine, then nap."

That drew a frustrated huff from Igor; however, he'd been sleeping a lot since his surgery. Between the pain and not being able to sleep well at night, not being able to move much anyway, and the pain meds that he was still on, Igor was usually taking at least one or two naps a day. The guaranteed space had become a much needed relief to my overactive libido.

Thankfully, he didn't continue to pout and managed to lose himself in our game until my phone timer went off and I made him get up to walk around. I headed to the kitchen for drinks for us. Before I made it, I glanced back to find Igor's leg on the ground as he went to take a step.

"Nyet!" I hadn't meant to yell at him, but the frustration of feeling like I had been dealing with an obstinate brat all week had finally gotten to me. "*Stubborn brat, you deserve punished,*" I said, muttering in Russian. My hands flew into the air in irritation, then switched to English. "You deserve spanked!"

Igor's eyes widened and his cheeks turned a bright shade of red that I'd never seen before. He did pick up his leg and his eyes fell to the floor. "Sorry, Yuri. It is hard to keep my leg up. I miss walking!"

"Listen. It is not hard. Listen to doctor. Listen to therapist. Listen to surgeon!" The growl that escaped me was born completely of frustration.

I felt bad for yelling at him, but at the same time I didn't. The relief at finally getting my frustration out outweighed the guilt at yelling at him. "You will not walk for longer if you keep trying to walk on it! Follow the rules, you will get to walk sooner!"

"Yes, Yuri." He pivoted on his good leg. "I am going to the bathroom."

CHAPTER 3

IGOR

The bathroom door clicked shut behind me and I immediately turned on the water in the sink. "*What are you doing?*" I looked down at my dick that had become hard as a fucking rock in my shorts as Yuri had yelled at me for overdoing it again.

It wasn't that I'd intentionally driven Yuri insane. It seemed to be something I had a knack for without trying. What I had noticed was each time he got mad at me, my insides did a funny swoopy thing that I didn't fully understand.

The feelings I'd first started having in the hospital hadn't made any sense to me. Once I'd gotten over the shock of Yuri standing in the bathroom arguing with me about peeing and being safe, the feeling like I was on a roller coaster had hit me square in the stomach. Then every single time we'd argued since then, my stomach had gotten the same excited butterflies in it.

I'd accepted that I was finding it fun to poke the Russian bear whenever the opportunity presented itself, but it had been just that. Fun. Nothing more complicated. So why was I standing in the bathroom scolding my erection?

Not that Yuri would have believed me, but I hadn't intended to drive him insane by putting my foot down in the living room. It was natural to stand up on both legs, just second nature. It wasn't like there was a cast holding my leg above the ground, so I was reliant solely on my brain to remember not to walk on my leg. The truth was it hurt like a bitch to put even slight weight on my leg, so I'd already been lifting it back up when Yuri had caught me.

Then he'd started to yell. I wasn't sure that *yell* was quite the right word, but he'd ranted in his native tongue while his hands flew wildly about. But then in broken but clear English, he'd told me that I deserved to be spanked. The stupid, giddy feeling I got while arguing with Yuri took a nosedive from my stomach straight to my dick.

Before he'd finished his rant, my dick had been swelling in my shorts and I'd been trying to figure out how to make a hasty retreat. In an attempt to get Yuri to stop yelling, I'd tried apologizing, a sincere one in which I'd tried to deescalate everything. Humility had never been one of my strong points, so apologizing should have killed any and all of my arousal.

Except it hadn't. No. It had done nothing but make my dick thicken more rapidly than before. In the brief second between my apology and Yuri's continued rant, his eyes had filled with something very different than frustration. I didn't want to read too much into it, but it had looked a lot like heat to me. As quickly as the look appeared in his eyes, it had been replaced with a hard determination and he'd begun to scold me again. I'd been helpless to do anything but stand rooted to the spot while I listened, all too aware that my dick was quickly becoming uncomfortably hard.

Then he did this growl thing that he'd done a number of times this week, but that time it had felt like it was connected to every nerve ending in my body. "You will not walk for longer if you keep trying to walk on it! Follow the rules, you will get to walk sooner!"

I'd known that if I didn't get out of there quickly, he would find out just what his words were doing to me and my dick. Trying to sound properly contrite, I'd sucked in a breath and attempted to make eye contact with him while not stuttering or combusting from a combination of arousal and embarrassment. "Yes, Yuri." Then I'd figured out an exit strategy and quickly pivoted on my good leg and called over my shoulder, "I am going to the bathroom."

Which was where I still was, staring at my dick that was stubbornly refusing to stand down. I couldn't even pee with it as hard as it was. I glanced back down at my shorts. "I know you have a mind of your own, but this is taking it too far!" All I could do was hope that Yuri wasn't outside the door listening while I hissed at my stubborn cock. "Yuri is our friend. Friend! It has been too long since we had action if being yelled at is making you horny. Stop being an idiot!"

At least I wasn't tenting my shorts like I had been a few seconds earlier, but there was still a noticeable bulge where there shouldn't have been. Noticeable enough that I knew Yuri would see it if I walked out like this.

Deciding to hurry the process along so my bathroom break didn't seem too suspicious and so I could get back out there as quickly as possible, I went to the sink, turned the water to full cold, and ran my hand under it for nearly twenty seconds. When my hand was properly chilly, I stuck it down my shorts and had to bite my lip to not yell out at the contact, but it had the desired effect. My dick softened and I was finally free to sag against my crutches, the relief at being soft well worth the discomfort it had taken getting there.

I peed, washed my hands—in warm water—and dried them quickly on the towel hanging by the door, then hurried back to the living room in time to see Yuri studying the bathroom door like he'd never seen it before. "Are you okay?"

There was possibly one thing worse than Yuri pissed off... Yuri worried. I caught myself as I began to shake my head no and nodded. It wasn't that I'd been trying to answer the question with a head shake; I'd simply been trying to shake off the ridiculous thoughts that had suddenly taken root in my brain. "Fine. Sorry I took so long." Feeling exceptionally nervous, I chuckled uncomfortably. "Damn crutches make everything take longer. But I did not put my foot down."

At least that last part had been one hundred percent truthful.

"Good." Yuri gave me a smile that I swore radiated pride, then a firm, singular nod before he gestured toward the game. "Still want to play? I got waters and you still have twenty-five minutes before you can have medicine."

I could make it twenty-five minutes around Yuri with my cock behaving. I'd done it for over four years without ever having a problem and if it had been going to misbehave again, I was pretty sure it would have when he'd directed that smile toward me when I'd told him I hadn't used my leg. So my erection had been a fluke. A totally random thing that wasn't worth fretting over.

Instead of standing there and making things more awkward, I hobbled over to the chair I'd been sitting in and lowered myself into it. With the remote in my hand, I glanced over at Yuri to find him watching me carefully. Those prickles at the base of my skull were obviously a by-product of being watched.

I didn't have to tell myself that for long. As soon as we got sucked into the game, the discomfort was forgotten in exchange for the familiar banter between us as we tried to work through the next phase of the adventure. Yuri's laugh was contagious and it was easy to enjoy the slow-paced and extremely forgiving game. At least until his phone buzzed again.

"Up and move. Time for medicine."

Yuri thrived on plans and schedules, but the constant need to move was exhausting. This recovery was definitely worse than the last hip surgery I'd had, and I had to believe that it was because I was older and my body more worn down. Having the Russian drill sergeant barking at me to follow the doctor's orders every time I turned around was more exhausting than anything else. At least I could escape for a bit with a nap. He swore it was because the meds were making me tired, but it was more that he was making me tired. Sometimes I needed a break.

He moved toward the kitchen and I heard a cabinet door open just before his phone rang. "Danil!" The words that followed were all in Russian and so fast I couldn't make any of it out, but by the laughter I had to assume whatever Yuri's brother had called about was nothing major, or more likely he'd called just to talk. They were much closer than I was with my family, and Yuri's booming voice and giant smiles when he got to talk to them always made me happy for their close relationship.

Lost in my thoughts, I didn't notice Yuri return to the living room until he was standing in front of me. "Hold on, Danil. Stubborn ass must take his medicine." After a short pause, Yuri threw his head back and laughed. "Nyet! Nyet!

Not yet. Still alive, yes, touch and go sometimes. He pushes luck much."

Downing my pills with a mouthful of water, I couldn't decide if I appreciated Yuri's use of English for my benefit or not. I could tell he was joking, but it had been that constant joy in driving him insane that had caused the situation thirty minutes earlier. I didn't want a repeat of that and I worried that by knowing I was driving Yuri nuts, that exact thing might happen again.

There was no way I was going to hang around to find out. Instead, I hurried toward the room Yuri had designated as mine as I called back over my shoulder. "I am going to nap. Tell Danil hi for me." I shut the door before Yuri could say anything in response and looked down at my dick, expecting it to be hard as a rock again.

To my relief, it hadn't taken the slightest bit of interest in the interaction with Yuri. I sagged against the door, trying to keep my head from bouncing off it loudly enough to catch Yuri's attention. The two of us had obviously been cramped up in the house together too long, but unfortunately there wasn't an end in sight. I could call Seth and Maz or Trevor and Brax to see if they wanted to hang out, but I was pretty sure they had all mentioned taking a trip after the season ended.

Mentally paging through the team's roster, I couldn't come up with someone other than Yuri that I wanted to spend time with, especially when I hurt this badly. Once I started feeling better and was able to walk again, I would enjoy spending time with the other guys, but for now most of us were nursing injuries that had lingered throughout the season and weren't fit for company anyway, especially company that reminded us all of our own hockey mortality.

Thirty-five was a damn good age to have made it to playing hockey. There were only a few other players older than me on the team, so it wasn't like I was sad about my retirement.

I made my way to the bed, careful to keep my leg up until finally lowering myself onto the mattress and setting my crutches to the side. It took a bit of work to gingerly move my leg onto the bed and get myself into a position that I wasn't going to injure myself in but was also comfortable enough to hopefully get some sleep. Whether I wanted to admit it or not, I needed the rest.

My phone buzzed in my pocket, and I pulled it out to see a text from Tapio Hämäläinen, a third-line defenseman for the Grizzlies. He'd been traded just before the deadline in March and he and I had been friendly, though I didn't know if we were close enough to be considered friends yet.

Taps: *How's the hip?*

I smiled. This was the distraction I needed.

Me: *Hurts like a motherfucker, but I'm managing.*

Taps: *Kill Yuri yet?*

I laughed loudly, then watched the door for a few seconds to make sure Yuri didn't poke his head in.

***Me**: Not yet. Touch and go by the minute. He's very bossy and likes things done a certain way.*

Tapio sent a string of laughing emojis that had me smiling.

***Taps**: Really? Yuri, bossy? Never!*

My smile hurt my cheeks. Tapio was sarcastic and I could almost hear him in my head.

***Taps**: Up for company soon?*

God, yes. Please. Come get me out of this house! Though I knew I couldn't say that. I also knew that showering every two to three days and the rumpled pajamas that had become my go-to clothing choice were not suitable for company.

***Me**: Another week or so. I see the doctor on Thursday, then Indy at the end of next week. Hopefully I will be able to start moving more then.*

We talked for a few more minutes until my eyes began to drift closed without my trying. Tapio had told me to make sure to let him know if I needed anything and he'd be happy to drop a meal off if Yuri needed a break from cooking.

It was a kind gesture and I knew he'd meant the offer sincerely. I fell asleep thinking that maybe my relationship with Tapio had gone from friendly to friendship. It was getting hard to deny that I needed a few more close friends because, while Yuri was my best friend, I was starting to see that spending so much time with him might not be the best for my sanity.

How else did I explain the erection from earlier in the day?

The last thing I remembered was a smile playing on my lips as I thought about how insane I'd driven Yuri that day. It was easy to get a rise out of him and it was fun. One erection did not mean anything, but getting Yuri riled up had been more fun than I'd had since Schmidt plowed into me. I was stupid for even thinking about it, but I wanted to know what else would drive Yuri insane.

CHAPTER 4

YURI

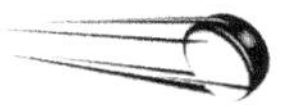

I didn't know what was worse: Igor loopy on pain meds and grouchy from pain, or Igor not in pain and grouchy from not being able to do everything he wanted to do. The man pushed limits no matter what, but when he wasn't in as much pain, he wanted to do more. For the last two days, he'd been fine with an over-the-counter pain med, and without the heavier prescription drugs, he'd become a pain in the ass with more energy than sense.

Or maybe it was more that I'd become hyperaware of both his presence and every time he tried to push one of my buttons, and I was hornier than I'd ever been. Once I'd put voice to the thought that Igor deserved a spanking, it had been as though he was trying to see just how insane he could make me.

That reason alone had to have been why I'd found him

in my kitchen before seven two mornings in a row clanking around as he tried to make breakfast. Which was also why I was standing in the kitchen before seven when I'd much rather be sleeping in order to make him breakfast. Whether he admitted it or not, the last thing he needed was to be on crutches longer because he was too fucking stubborn to admit that he was doing things he shouldn't be doing.

I loved a brat as much as the next guy, but not like this. Brats were fun, pushing buttons because they wanted a punishment. Igor kept pushing buttons because he was impatient and stubborn, and I couldn't put him over my lap and turn his ass red as a consequence.

Nope, needed to shut that train of thought down real fast. Nothing good was going to come of thinking about putting Igor over my lap. Nothing but heartbreak when I remembered that my best friend was not only straight but definitely not the bratty sub I was looking for.

He might not have been the bratty sub I wanted, but I was still the guy who loved to serve and please people, which was why I was trying to make us breakfast while keeping one ear on the room I'd given him.

Cooking while using the counter to hobble from one side of the kitchen to the other was high on the list of things he shouldn't be doing after hip surgery. I didn't do full breakfasts usually. A double espresso and a bagel was fine for me, but Igor had taken to heart that breakfast was the most important meal of the day. He'd always been like that, but finding him trying to make sausage, eggs, and potatoes at quarter to seven had made his love of breakfast feel a bit over the top.

That hadn't stopped me from standing in front of the stove making bacon, eggs, and pancakes as I sipped my double shot and nibbled at my everything bagel with cream cheese and thin-sliced salmon.

At six fifty-three, just as I pulled the last of the pans from the stove, Boris's head shot up from where he'd been lying by the counter. "Is idiot up?"

Boris turned his head from one side to the other and then stood with a speed and grace that always amazed me from a dog as large as he was and took off toward the bedroom I'd given Igor. Shaking my head, I followed the dog. "Right, idiot is awake."

Danil and I had talked for most of the time Igor had slept earlier in the week. My main complaint was that Igor refused to do what he was supposed to in order to not hurt himself. I had thought giving him a room on the main floor would keep him from injuring himself scooting up and down the steps at his house. Well, he hadn't hurt himself on the steps, but the asshole had managed to find more ways to push his limits than I could count and was testing my patience at every turn.

His inability to follow instructions was why I was following Boris to Igor's room. If I didn't, I knew he would try to get up and put too much weight on his leg while insisting he wasn't overdoing anything. I rubbed absently at my temples. *Surely he was giving me gray hairs by now... or worse.* In a panic, I felt my forehead and blew out a relieved breath when my hairline was still in the same place it had been before he moved in.

I hadn't made it fully around the corner of his doorway and I could already see Igor sitting on the side of his bed, his crutches a good five feet away from him, getting ready to push himself up. "Kozyol!" My jaw clenched so hard I worried I'd break a molar. The man was going to be the death of me and likely himself while he was at it.

Igor jumped at my outburst and swung around to face me. "Trying to kill me, Yuri?"

Before I called him something worse than a goat who did stupid things, I forced a smile onto my face and a cloyingly sweet tone to my voice. "Good morning, solnishko. You try to kill self. No crutches, Igor! How many times must you be told? No weight on leg!"

Igor rolled his eyes, his annoyed expression thankfully keeping me from focusing on his shirtless torso and the fact that his lower half was only covered in a pair of ridiculously small briefs. Thank fuck the man had petulant down to an art and it was distracting enough that I couldn't focus on his lap and the fullness in his light blue underwear. "I am not out of bed. No reason for crutches when I am not standing. Even doctor would say it is ridiculous to have crutches while sitting!"

A strangled, frustrated noise came from my throat that left me narrowing my eyes at my best friend. I walked over to where he'd left his crutches the night before. "Did surgery give you super-stretch arms? Would have been helpful in net for you to use them in games!"

Igor threw his head back and laughed at me as he reached for the crutches I was holding out for him. "Dammit, why did I not think of that before? Could have won the Vezina trophy more than once!"

In spite of everything, I found myself laughing at his antics. "You are asshole."

"Ah yes, but I am *your* asshole."

The words had barely left his mouth and Igor clamped his lips shut. I watched as pink filled his cheeks and he turned to look anywhere but at me. He held both crutches in one hand and scratched nervously at the back of his neck. "I did not mean that the way it came out."

I rolled my eyes. "Do not be stupid. I know what you meant." Though it had been harder than I would ever admit to not think about him being mine. And that was a very dangerous path that I needed to shut down before it took hold.

Igor stood—with the help of his crutches—and turned to face me. "Hip feels better. Like new hip." He winced when he moved his leg and I couldn't help my smirk, especially as he narrowed his eyes at me.

"Yes, new like old man. You hobble, curse, and yell when you move. My babushka complains less than you! Move. Breakfast almost ready. Go to bathroom. Make self look less like monster."

He grumbled and cursed under his breath but took himself, on his crutches with no weight on his leg, to the bathroom. Boris followed him as he went and I could hear Igor talking to my dog, mostly complaining that I was a pain in the ass. Despite wanting to tell him that I could show him a real pain in the ass, I bit my tongue and smiled at the two of them, satisfied and pleased that Igor had listened to me without more of a fight. The last few mornings it had been hell getting him to actually use the damned crutches as he'd made breakfast. Even as he'd winced, cursed, and bitched about pain, he had tried repeatedly to support himself on his leg.

I hadn't noticed that I'd been staring at him until Igor turned around and caught my eye. Color stained his pale cheeks. "See, I'm going and I am not using leg. Happy now? I am following the rules."

I knew I couldn't tell him just how happy I was that he had listened to me and was following directions so well. Anything that might have come out of my mouth would have sounded highly inappropriate and probably made Igor uncomfortable. I liked being listened to, way more than Igor needed to know. Way more than I would ever tell him.

Igor had never hinted that he might share any of the desire to be in control like I did, nor had he given any indication that he might like to *be* controlled. The idea of Igor being on the receiving end of control was funny enough that I had to stop myself from laughing out loud. Igor would drive a Dom or Domme insane before a scene was over.

He had talked about women—a lot. He had talked about sex—both good and bad. But through all those conversations, he had never once given me the impression he had a kinky bone in his body. And I wasn't planning on sharing that side of myself with him. Especially not at seven in the morning when I hadn't finished my coffee.

That didn't change that something about how Igor had asked if I was happy he was following the rules had lit up every nerve in my body. My dick had definitely missed the memo about not mixing sex and friendship. It took a bit too much pleasure in the snippy way Igor had spat the words at me, then had given me that slightly shy blush when he'd noticed me watching him.

Getting caught staring at him hadn't been enough to throw that proverbial bucket of ice on my libido. Not by a long shot. It left me with little option but to give an awkward gesture toward the door, unsure what to say now that I'd been thinking about our interaction in a very inappropriate way. "In kitchen when done."

Leaving quickly, I played my words back and tried to figure out if they made sense. English was a stupid language—so many words for the same thing, so many sayings, so many of the same words that meant different things. If I took the time to stop and think about my words before they came out, I was nearly fluent. My brain just didn't like to stop long enough to think before I spoke.

In the safety of the kitchen, I sucked in a lungful of air and slowly let it out. It had been too long since I'd been with someone if I was having thoughts like that about Igor, thoughts that included punishments and sexy things like spanking his ass and hearing him beg for me to stop before finally apologizing... and fuck, I was getting harder, not softer.

I'd never once had a thought about Igor like *that.* And Igor wanting to please me... I actually scoffed at the idea. Igor did not like to please *anyone,* as evidenced by his love of driving everyone insane with his questionable restaurants that had a tendency to make him sick. Igor did not like the same things I did, and I needed to remember that before I got myself in trouble or lost my best friend.

"Igor is straight," I said into the quiet kitchen. "Igor does not like men. Igor is pain in ass, not brat." Maybe if I repeated that enough, I'd get my dick to believe it. Damn my best friend and his annoying presence in my house, fucking up everything I'd thought would never be an issue for us.

Not for the first time that morning, I found myself staring into space, lost in my thoughts. Hopefully, he would be well enough to go home soon.

CHAPTER 5

YURI

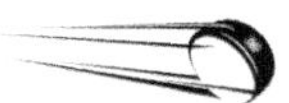

I had no idea how long I stared at my expensive espresso machine, lost in thoughts about Igor and his *not* being a sub, or a brat, or in any way inclined to be in a relationship with a man. When I finally shook my head out of the fog, the water had turned off in Igor's bathroom and I knew I was quickly running out of time to get his dry cappuccino ready before he was out for breakfast.

With milk in hand, I was ready to start the drink when my phone trilled in my pocket with an incoming text. At this early hour, I couldn't imagine who would be texting me. Checking the text pulled me away from making coffee and when I read it, I forgot all about Igor's drink.

Blaise: Sorry for the early text. I need a head count for the parade. It's in two weeks. As a sponsor of Nashville Pride, the team and families are invited to walk in the parade. Details attached. Please let me know if you will be coming and what sized T-shirts you want. Thanks!

My phone began to explode with texts from the rest of the team and members of the front office as they responded with various questions and answers. Only Seth's and Maz's names didn't appear, but I knew our alternate captain and his boyfriend—one of the Grizzlies most powerful defensemen—were not willingly morning people.

Thankfully, Nashville's Pride and the flood of texts to my phone had been all I'd needed to get my mind off Igor. Pride was always fun and the last three years the team had been a sponsor. Being part of a professional hockey team that was not only inclusive but true allies had made Pride more special.

In Russia, homosexuality was still a crime. There was no way I could be myself and still live in my mother country. I'd never taken the ability to celebrate my sexuality for granted and had participated in various Pride events every year I'd been in the US.

Nashville had been where I'd found the most acceptance and the ability to be myself. With so many queer teammates and with a number of them already out to the world, it made being bisexual easy. I never had to hide who I was going out with or change the pronouns of a boyfriend. Inside the locker room and on the ice, I was blessed with a team that accepted me exactly how I was. Outside of the Grizzlies home ice, I didn't much care what anyone said about me. There was nothing they could say that I hadn't heard growing up in Russia and during my time in the KHL. Russia's hockey league was brutal and any hint—proven or not—that a player might not be straight basically made them a target for verbal and physical aggression... thus how I became known as the goalie missing a tooth.

Nashville was special, though. I'd lived in Nashville longer than anywhere besides Russia. I'd made friends not only with the hockey team but from around the area as well. Most of my friends outside of hockey fell into one of two groups: LGBTQ+ or kink. Oftentimes the groups overlapped. But without a doubt, almost every one of my friends from all over Nashville would be at the parade.

I hadn't yet begun tapping a response to Blaise, the Grizzlies Assistant Director of Hockey Operations and all-around master of everything team related, when I heard the steady *click-click* of Igor's crutches as he made his way into the kitchen.

"I have not put weight on my leg," he said in greeting, not bothering to meet my eyes before he spoke. "Now I need pills and coffee. My leg hurts like a bitch, my head hurts just as much, and I have not had a drink since before surgery!"

He clanked over to where I was still standing and staring at my phone as I tried to figure out what to say to Blaise while also trying to keep up with the group text that had grown by the second. "You okay? You are staring at your phone like it will bite and no coffee is in the cups."

I shook both my phone and my head, then started to tap out an answer, trying to remember all the rules of English so that my text made sense. "Blaise. He needs count for Pride parade. Two weekends from now."

Igor groaned. "A parade when I can barely walk? I will barely be off crutches. Hell, I might not be off crutches. That sounds miserable." He pouted, then looked at the empty espresso machine. "Almost as miserable as an empty cup of fancy coffee."

He had a point about the parade and my brain chose to focus on that instead of the barb about the lack of coffee. "You can go on..." I knew there was a word for the decorated seating areas that were in parades, but for the life of me I couldn't come up with it. "That thing. You know what I mean... it's the big thing. It's the big thing that swims... Like boat."

Igor stared dumbly at me. So it wasn't a boat and I hadn't been clear enough that Igor understood me. Fumbling through my list of English words and phrases, I tried to come up with another way to describe what I was talking about. "Wood thing. Remember? Last year banjo fell off in parade and Coach tripped on it, cursed the rest of the parade."

Finally, something I'd said made sense because Igor's eyes widened at the memory and then he let out a loud laugh that bounced off the walls. "Float. The word is *float.*"

"Stupid word." I would never have come up with float. Float was something you did on water, not rode on in a parade. *Stupid word, stupid language.* "But yes, that. You can ride on that!"

Igor narrowed his eyes. "There is not going to *be* a float. The Zambonis are getting wrapped with Pride flags."

I narrowed my eyes. Now that he mentioned it, I vaguely remembered something about that.

Me: Igor cannot walk far. Can he sit on Zamboni?

"What did you just send to who?"

"Blaise. He asked for head count for parade. I told him you cannot walk long distance and asked if you can sit on Zamboni."

That time Igor narrowed his eyes. "I am not sitting on the Zamboni! It's bad enough to not be able to walk, but to have to sit for hours will not be fun."

My phone buzzed, and I glanced down to read the incoming text.

Blaise: I don't see a problem with that. Does that mean I can mark the two of you as yes?

Me: Yes. We are in.

I sent the text and glanced up at Igor, who had crossed his arms in protest. "I'm not going. I don't want to roast in the sun for hours and not walk. Gah! I will lose my mind if I must sit for so long. Besides, I must move every half hour. Remember?"

He had a point, but that time constraint was limited, and he could walk some too. In two weeks, he'd probably only need his crutches to help support his weight but would be able to walk a bit when he got tired or bored of sitting. Best of both worlds.

I shrugged. "Too late. I already told Blaise we go."

"Yuurrriii."

I shot him a grin as I started to make his drink. "Yes, is my name." Well, it wasn't *quite* my name, but no one called me Nikoli. Nikoli was my father, and he was an asshole. I'd become known as Yuri—a shortened version of my last name, Yurievich—when I was playing junior hockey in Russia. Yuri had stuck and I preferred it to my given name. Even Babushka called me Yuri.

At Igor's frustrated huff, I smiled at him. "Sleep well?" I had learned early on that a change of topic was often best with Igor.

"Fine. I miss my bed."

"You can see your house from window. Hello, house." I waved at his house out my kitchen window. "You sleep in your bed when you can climb stairs on your own. Without killing yourself on steps."

Igor grabbed a mug from one of the pegs along the wall and handed it to me to slip under the spout. I'd been told I was obsessive over my coffee habit, but I liked to call it precise. That was why I'd needed the expensive, professional machine and why I used scales to measure everything from the beans to the weight of the cup. People teased me about the process but never the result.

I pushed the button to start the espresso machine, then glanced up at Igor, keeping an eye on both the scale the cup was on and the timer on my machine to check extraction weight and time. "Parade. Da?"

"I do not want to sit for so long, Yuri. I like moving. I will go insane sitting all parade."

The machine stopped and made me pull my gaze from Igor back to the process of making his drink. The milk was more time sensitive. Steaming and frothing took only a handful of seconds and overheating the milk would make the drink too sweet. If I looked away, I ran the risk of making more steamed milk than froth, which would totally ruin the purpose of a dry cappuccino.

Satisfied with the temperature and the consistency, I turned off the steamer and gave the little pitcher a few taps to make everything settle. I was way too aware of Igor's gaze on me as I poured a little bit of the remaining steamed milk in the espresso before spooning the froth on top of Igor's drink and handing it over to him.

He took a sip and hummed his approval, then turned to take it to the counter where we normally ate breakfast.

Igor was always on the move, even moving his legs as he sat and watched me make my own cappuccino. His need to move had made him a good goalie. He had no problems moving side to side repeatedly while watching the puck glide all over the ice and moving his body in micro-corrections to follow it.

He was excited and alert all the time. That was why I knew surgery was always difficult for him, and surgery that made him have to rest and not be able to move frequently was even worse.

I finished my coffee and went to stand by Igor, turning our attention back to the conversation we'd been having before I started making our drinks. "Da. Move, move, move. That is Igor. You must rest leg to move, move, move again. Parade, though, you always go. Will not be same without you. Please?"

I wasn't above begging. Besides, if he didn't go, what would he do? Sit at home bored and not be able to move? Actually, he'd get bored and do something he wasn't supposed to do, like move without his crutches. At least if he was at the parade, the entire team could watch him.

"Pouting is not fair."

I grinned. All was fair in our friendship. *All but getting turned on by his listening to me.* I shook my head before I could let that thought develop more. There was no way I was going to go down that hole again. My dick had finally started to behave itself.

"Fine, I will go. Just know I am not happy about it."

With a solemn nod, I pointed to the plate. "Understood. Now eat. You have doctor's appointment in one hour."

That time Igor's groan could be not mistaken for

anything but frustration. He hated having to go to the doctor, though this one was just a post-surgery follow-up and then his care would be released to the team doctor. I knew Igor well enough to know he would fight Indy until Coach or the team captain, Trevor, put their foot down and demanded he go or get benched for the next game.

I scooped breakfast onto his plate as I absently wondered what Coach, Trevor, and Indy would do now that Igor was no longer playing. He was a coach. I guessed they could get Blaise or the general manager involved and keep him from practices and games until he listened, but I hoped it wouldn't come to that.

"No point. It's a stupid appointment anyway. Doctor will look at me, go *hmm* and *huh* and then tell me one more week before therapy can start and I can walk again."

I wasn't going to be the one to point out that walking was going to require support for weeks, and then it was going to take longer still in physical therapy. The doctor had been clear about that while he'd been in the hospital. PT wasn't going to be a walk in the park either, but at least it would be with the team's physical therapists. They knew how to deal with his grouchy ass.

When I turned around with my plate in hand, Igor wasn't looking at me but at a piece of paper in his hand. His eyebrows were pulled together in concentration as he studied the paper. "Find something interesting?"

Igor blinked up at me. "This is the recipe for your grandma's cake thing."

He'd found the recipe, which was written in my grandma's meticulous writing, that Danil had sent over. "Korolevskiy."

"Cor-a-yev-ski?" Igor repeated slowly, the butchering of the word making me chuckle.

"Korolevskiy. Kare'l—" I paused, waiting for Igor to repeat what I'd said.

"Karel? Like the name?"

Smiling at his confusion, I nodded. "Close, but not quite. You kind of need to overpronounce *e'l*."

He said it again, coming closer to the right pronunciation, and I felt my smile turn into an all-out grin. "Yes! Kare'l-ef-ski."

Igor stared at me. "Say it again slowly."

"Kare'l-ef-ski. Korolevskiy."

He blinked, then repeated the word even slower than I had spoken it. "Karel-ev-ski?"

"Close enough." I winked at him. His pronunciation was close enough that any Russian would know what he was talking about, but they would also know that he was not a native speaker. He'd be able to pronounce it later in the day, though. He usually had to practice words a few times before he could pronounce them. I suspected he was struggling that morning because he'd never actually seen it written out before. "It means royal. It is Russian Royal Cake. Many layers. Very complicated. Very fancy, for special occasion."

Igor gave me a pensive stare before speaking. "Like when NHL goalie goes home?"

I laughed. "Da! Babushka treats me like royalty. Only finest cake for my return."

Igor laughed when he threw a napkin at me. "You have big, big head." He sobered quickly. "It would be awesome to meet her."

No. No. Igor and Babushka together would be trouble. My tiny grandmother was enough of a handful on her own. She had almost been arrested for throwing a dinner roll at the mayor of our city. She'd only gotten away with it because my uncle was an officer and swore she'd never attend another parade. Of course, that was hard to enforce when the official parade route passed her house. It had fallen on Danil's and my shoulders to keep Babushka inside during political parades after that. So of course, she started drawing pictures of dinner rolls and taping them to her windows.

Igor and Babushka would be dangerous together. I didn't know which one would teach the other more.

We fell into silence as we ate our breakfast. I was already done and putting my plate in the sink when Igor spoke up. "If I have to go to doctor's appointment today, you must take me to lunch."

"Only if I get to choose restaurant."

He huffed. "No sense of adventure. None. But fine. You choose."

I felt a weight lift off my shoulders now that he'd

finally agreed to go to the doctor's appointment, even if it meant going out to eat afterward. "Date then."

The exaggerated eyebrow waggle Igor gave me told me I'd said something funny to him, but it wasn't until he responded that I knew what. "That's so sweet, but you're not really my type."

Undeniable heat filled my cheeks and I stammered. "I—You—Mudak! Not like that!" Clearing my throat, I pulled myself together and forced my voice to sound more casual. "Besides, you are not *my* type. You are too..."

What was he too much of? I couldn't say male because I was totally attracted to men. I couldn't say petulant because there was something about a bratty man that drove me wild. I couldn't even say too tall or short or skinny or fat. Body type had never mattered to me. It was the personality—a strong-willed confidence that was so beautiful when it surrendered—that drove me absolutely insane. After too long, I finally settled on the thing that should have been the most obvious. "You are too straight for me."

He just laughed as he slid off the chair and balanced himself gracefully on his crutches. "Ah, yes. Curse of heterosexual beauty. I understand."

Flipping Igor off, I headed to my room to get a shower and *not* think of the gorgeous *heterosexual* man in my kitchen who suddenly hadn't felt like just my friend. Being up so early to make sure that Igor didn't get into things he shouldn't was starting to fuck with my head. Maybe I could ask the doctor for sleeping pills while we were there. It would help me get the sleep my brain desperately needed to remember that Igor was off-limits.

I looked down to see my dick jutting out in front of me, quickly on its way to fully erect. Now if only I could get my erection to remember that Igor was not an option.

And I'd probably have the same conversation with my hand when I was out of the shower... after I released the built-up tension in my dick. I poured conditioner into my palm and wrapped my hand around my cock, telling myself that it was not Igor's red lips I was imagining wrapped around me and those were not his light eyes blinking up at me as I stroked myself fully hard and on the edge way too quickly. It absolutely wasn't Igor's name that tumbled from my lips as I sprayed the shower wall, and it absolutely wasn't his light brown hair I imagined as I leaned my head against the tiles to catch my breath.

It hadn't been Igor in my imagination, and I'd keep telling myself that as long as I had to until I believed it. While it might not have been Igor sucking me off, I was easily able to admit that I was well and truly fucked up for even thinking about him like that.

How long until Igor got to go home again?

CHAPTER 6

IGOR

"I can do it!" The words hadn't fully left my mouth and I already felt guilty about yelling at Yuri the way I had.

He gave me a look that nearly made me give in. "Let me help," Yuri said, sounding more annoyed than the first two times he'd said the same thing.

"I have it." I really didn't. The few steps from the side of the car to the car seat were looming in front of me like a giant chasm I was going to have to cross.

Yuri growled, actually growled, and the sound vibrated in his chest and echoed in the arena's parking garage. I'd probably pushed more than a few buttons that morning, from my stubborn attempt to insist that I didn't need crutches as we left the house to refusing his help as I struggled through getting ready after therapy, and now not allowing him to help me into the car. We were both stubborn, but there was something about Yuri that took my stubborn streak to a different level.

But that was before he had growled at me. The rumbling noise in his chest was nothing short of feral, like he was ready to throw me over his shoulder and place me in the car. I wanted to growl back and tell him to back the fuck off, but my words died in my throat as an unexpected wave of heat hit me low in the gut and I felt my dick shift in my briefs. It was the same wave that had overtaken me in Yuri's kitchen over a week earlier.

I knew the feeling well, not that it was one I'd had since then. Between pain and the painkillers, my dick hadn't found much of anything interesting. So why was it taking an interest now? Why was it the frustrated growl that Yuri let out that had me trying to resist the urge to squirm where I stood?

Then it dawned on me that I couldn't remember the last time I'd jacked off. It was just a random reaction, an inconveniently timed moment of arousal. It had nothing to do with Yuri or his growl and everything to do with the fact that pain had tamped down my arousal for over a week. It was just my body finally waking up. But that still meant that I needed to get in the car quickly, which was what Yuri had been *trying* to do since we'd walked from the building.

I'd been stubbornly denying that my first therapy appointment had left me in pain. I could only hope the Advil Indy had given me before I'd left would kick in before we got home so that I could collapse into bed and sleep for the next week. Or until the next morning, because she'd informed me that she'd see me then for the next round of torture.

Indy was the best doctor I'd ever worked with. Blaise, the heart and soul of the behind-the-scenes operations of the team as well as Indy's twin brother, had suggested the position to her when she'd been in med school. She'd joined the team during her residency in sports medicine and the head office hadn't hesitated to hire her when she'd graduated.

While her normal position as the team's doctor had her creating therapy plans and overseeing the team's physical therapists, it was summer and she'd decided to take on my PT herself. The truth was, she—as well as the rest of the team—probably knew no one else could keep me in line.

Indy had definitely earned her spot with the Grizzlies, not receiving any favors because she was Blaise's sister. She knew her shit and had repeatedly proved she could not only get players back on the ice but back on the ice and in the best shape possible. Pushing us in and out of the therapy room took a spine of steel and Indy had it in spades. She was only about five six but held herself like she was eye level with the tallest player on the team. That also meant she refused to budge and when she gave orders, she expected them to be followed.

Yuri leveled me with a cold stare that for some reason

was not tempering the arousal flaring to life inside of me. "You need help, Igor! You are in pain. Your face says so! Let me help." Out of patience, he crowded my space. "Hold onto door." He pointed stubbornly to the door and waited for me to place my hands on it before he took the crutches from me. The last thing I wanted to think about was putting all my weight on my leg to get into the car.

Both the surgeon and Indy had warned me to take it slow. I was just at the point that I could put any weight on my leg at all. Indy had dashed any hopes of leaving the crutches behind when she'd pointedly told me that it was going to take me another three to four weeks to be able to put enough weight on it to support my entire weight while walking.

As much as I hated to admit it, it had been nice to use the crutches to support some of my weight. But now that I was faced with getting into the SUV, I was not doing so well, though I was refusing to admit it.

I'd clearly pushed Yuri too far because he'd taken control without my asking. The back door was already open for him to toss the crutches into the back seat. He slammed the door shut as soon as they hit the pristine leather, causing me to wince at the sound. When he turned his attention back to me, Yuri was all business, putting a hand on my waist before tapping my left arm. "This hand on seat, that hand stays." Something of my disbelief must have crossed my face because his voice softened slightly. "Trust me."

Faced with the climb into the large SUV, I finally understood how our pint-sized team captain felt every time he climbed into one of our tall vehicles. Without the ability to plant my weight on my leg as I climbed in, the normally effortless step up was proving difficult.

Yuri squared his legs with the car to help me. "'Take SUV,' you say. 'Big car, I can do it. Do not take reasonable car. Big car better.'" Yuri was muttering the words mostly in English but he'd added something as an afterthought in Russian. Between the muttering and quiet cursing, I had no chance to make it out, but I suspected he was cursing me out.

My skin was hot where his hands rested on my sides, the weird flutters in my stomach only intensifying as he steadied me. My damned libido had chosen the worst time in history to make itself known and if I didn't get into the car quickly, I knew Yuri was going to see exactly what was going on beneath my gym shorts.

Fucking meds, fucking injury, fucking surgery, fucking Schmidt.

Yuri's voice drew me from my thoughts that were beginning to border on panicked, his tone soothing and confident. "I have you. Lift." It was an assurance I hadn't known I'd needed until he'd said the words. His hand around my waist and eye to eye with me, Yuri displayed a steely focus I didn't normally see outside of the net. His dark eyes were as confident as his grip and I knew immediately that I trusted him implicitly. He wasn't going to let me get hurt.

The touch that had burned a moment earlier had my thoughts settling, like I didn't need to worry about the pain my hip was currently in or the nagging fear that my leg was simply too worn out from the day to really support my weight as I climbed into the car.

With Yuri steadying me, I was able to slide into the seat with little trouble. Begrudgingly, I let myself admit that it had simply been a lack of trust in my own body that had made me freeze outside of the car. Now that I was in and pulling the seat belt around me, I let out a breath. I was safe, my dick hadn't gotten harder, and now we could focus on getting back to Yuri's house.

Then he smiled at me. It wasn't a normal smile. It was unlike any smile he'd ever given me before. "Good job." The words shouldn't have fried my thoughts or made me forget how to speak, yet they had. They left me unable to say anything. Maybe it was because the praise had sent all the blood in my brain south and had made my dick go from interested to aroused and beginning to harden at an alarming rate.

Squeezing my legs together hurt just enough to snap the fog from my thoughts and I found myself nodding. "Thanks for the help."

Somehow, the smile on Yuri's face only grew wider. "You are welcome, solnishko."

"What does that mean? You called me that before."

Yuri winked as he stepped back. "Russian nickname."

Before I could ask what it was, he shut the door. When I adjusted in my seat, ready to insist that Yuri tell me exactly what it meant, the movement reminded me that I was hard and the awkwardness of that made me forget all about what he'd called me. I wanted to get home and take care of the problem in my shorts, and then I could fall asleep for the next few hours, wake up, and everything would be back to normal. I shook my head at myself just as Yuri climbed into the car.

"You okay?" His eyebrows had formed a straight line as he studied my face. "You look..."

I braced myself for any number of ridiculous things to come out of Yuri's mouth. He had a habit of butchering English words and American sayings. Half the time, he confused people so much with what he said that someone had to help them figure out what he actually meant.

His hand hovered over the gearshift, the car still in park, as he studied me closely before finishing his sentence. "Scared."

My blink was not just in surprise that he hadn't destroyed a random saying, but that he'd been studying me closely enough to realize I was off. I had to force myself to nod. "Fine, fine. Yes. Just..." I couldn't tell him that my dick was pinched between my legs at an uncomfortable angle, nor could I tell him that his presence had made me inexplicably hard. I tried to look casual when I nodded my head. "I am just tired. Indy pushed hard today."

I uncapped my water and began to take a long chug.

Thankfully, Yuri laughed. "Indy is screw leader. She push, push, push. But will make you better."

The last half of his statement was nearly lost on me as I struggled to not spray the water all over his dashboard and windshield. It had been a while since I'd heard him destroy a saying to that magnitude. Even I couldn't come up with what the hell he meant by screw leader. "She's a what?"

Yuri put the SUV in reverse and began to back out of the spot. "You know. Person who yells a lot. *Go! Go! Go! Harder!*"

"Drill sergeant?" It was the only thing coming to mind, but even at that, I wasn't convinced that I had the right meaning. *Screw leader.* Shit, my brain definitely hadn't gone to drill sergeant at first. I'd been thinking of many other things, but not a drill sergeant.

Yuri narrowed his eyes. "In military, no?"

All I could do was nod and try not to laugh as I imagined someone leading a screw... of either the sexual or hardware variety.

"Then yes, drill sergeant. Indy is drill sergeant. Gives directions, expects results."

I shook my head and let out a little laugh.

"She takes work seriously. You will be better than ever soon."

And back to my house.

Shit, I couldn't go home yet. I still couldn't tackle more than a few steps and my bedroom was up an entire flight of stairs. I didn't even have a guest room on the main level like Yuri did. It was going to be awkward as hell to jack off in his guest bathroom while I showered, but it was going to be a lot worse if I didn't release this building need that was sucking my brain cells from my head and giving me insane thoughts.

The sooner we got back to his house, the better. But not too soon. My dick needed time to chill out.

Yuri poked my side. "I promised you lunch for PT. Hungry?"

By the way he was staring at me, I had a feeling he'd asked the question more than once. "I could eat something small. As long as I don't have to get out."

I'd clearly said what he'd wanted to hear because his eyes lit up and he nearly bounced in his seat. "Want to eat weenie?"

And I nearly choked to death in the passenger side of Yuri's SUV on nothing but air. "What? N-no! Do not want!" Why would he even say something like that?

Yuri deflated. "I have craving for I Dream of Weenie. Best hot dogs in all Tennessee."

Digging the heels of my hands into my eyes, I groaned. "Hot dogs?"

"Yes. Hot dogs. What else?" A moment later he started to laugh. "Not dick. Get your mind out of drain. Hot dog!"

My embarrassment kept me from correcting him. "Fine, we can have *hot dogs.*"

I was having regrets as we sat in his car and ate our lunches. I'd never seen a man happier than Yuri about eating a hot dog. The lewd noises he was making as he moaned and groaned around each bite, the little comments he made about how plump and juicy they were, and the quips about his jaw being sore after the first one he ate were doing nothing to quell my arousal. With every bite he took and word he spoke, he was driving me more insane while confusing my brain even more.

After listening to him eat three hot dogs, I finally crumpled my last wrapper and angled myself in the seat. "Seriously, do you always sound like this while eating a weenie?"

Yuri's eyebrows waggled in a purely suggestive manner. "I enjoy weenies of all kinds."

Nope, wasn't touching that. I swallowed hard and tried to focus on my food.

There had been a minute where I'd almost had to tell him to shut up or I was going to come in my pants just from the noises he was making. Of course, my brain hadn't stopped replaying the interaction on a loop.

It was official. I needed to get laid.

The thought was still playing on repeat when we got back to the house. Yuri's noises at lunch had not helped matters. Actually, they had only compounded the problem because I hadn't gone completely soft since he'd taken the first bite of his first hot dog. Then my stupid question about if that was the way he always sounded while eating hot dogs… Nope, not going there.

At least getting out of the car hadn't required any more help from Yuri besides handing me my crutches from the back seat. He was halfway up the front walk before I had the car door shut, and he was working on opening the door before I'd made it halfway up the walk.

"I take Boris out." Yuri left the door open for me while I made my way up the two steps and into the house. After resting for half an hour, my leg was feeling strong enough to move again with very little effort and I was relieved that the steps were easier than they had been that morning. Easier, not easy. I was nowhere near being able to climb an entire flight of them, meaning I still wasn't near getting home.

"Sounds good. I'm going to shower." I just hoped like hell that Yuri didn't turn around before I made it into the bathroom. My pants had shifted between the car and the walk to the house, so my erection was painfully noticeable and reaching down to adjust myself would be a screaming indication that I was hornier than I'd been in weeks if not longer.

I made a beeline, or at least as much of a beeline as my crutches would allow, toward the bathroom, finally taking a breath when the door locked behind me. There was no point in wasting time. The only thing I wanted was my hand around my dick so that I could come, and I was undressed in a flash, thankful for the loose shorts that I was able to drop to the floor then step out of on my way to the shower.

Indy had warned me that I couldn't put my full weight on my leg, but at least I could finally use it to support myself as I showered. It was a small blessing compared to the chair I had been using.

The water warmed quickly and I stepped under, the rain showerhead leaving my skin tingling as it soaked me from head to foot, the water rushing from my chin to my chest and abs and finally over my hard dick. I pumped a generous handful of conditioner into my palm, impatient to have my hand wrapped around my erection.

I hissed as my fingers encircled the base and I slowly worked my way up to the tip where I twisted my hand around the head. Losing the battle to keep a moan inside, I stuffed my free fist in my mouth, leaned my forehead against the cool tiles, and let the muffled groan free. The first handful of strokes were frantic as I chased my release, but as I found a rhythm, some of the need and the desire to scream out how good it felt finally lessened to the point that I dropped my hand from my mouth and let it graze over my nipples. My thoughts wandered from the hand wrapped around my cock and the water pelting my shoulders and back to one of my favorite fantasies.

The thought of a gorgeous woman on her knees in front of me, her mouth stretched wide as she sucked me down, never failed to bring me to the edge. There were tears in her eyes after choking herself on my length while she reached around to my ass and dug her fingers into the flesh.

"Mmm, baby." I hadn't been able to help the whisper as I tweaked my nipple hard enough to send zaps of pleasure through me.

I could easily imagine her looking up at me, her brown hair already soaked from the shower spray. It had been too long because my orgasm was building before I pictured her looking up at me with piercing brown eyes. Brown eyes that were shockingly familiar and on a face that did not belong wrapped around my dick. The sounds she was making turned deep, and murmurs about my cock being *plump* and *juicy* escaped from where I was filling his mouth

Putting it all together at the last second, I heard Yuri's moan of pleasure, identical to the one he'd had in the car while eating his hot dog, just as I came with a startled shout of his name. "Yuri!" It was my cum hitting the tiles in front of me instead of being swallowed by the man my imagination had conjured up without invitation that finally pulled me back from the brink.

"Fuck." I had not meant to be thinking of Yuri when I came. It was awkward enough to come in his shower, but coming to the image of him sucking me off in that shower was too much. I'd never be able to look at him again.

"Damn hot dogs. *Asshole,*" I said under my breath, as though Yuri was there. "Putting images in my brain." That was it, that was what it had to be. I'd gotten so caught up in the noises he'd been making, because they *had* been hot, and then I hadn't watched porn in two weeks, so my brain had gone to the most recent sexy thing it had experienced. The most recent thing had been Yuri, in the car, moaning around his hot dogs.

"Bastard."

I stepped back into the water and made sure to wash the rest of my cum off the shower wall and down the drain, right where I was going to need the thoughts of the last two or so minutes to stay.

CHAPTER 7

YURI

I had no idea what had changed after Igor's physical therapy appointment the day before, but he'd been acting strange ever since. It had started when we'd gotten in the car. He'd been struggling to find things to say to me when I'd climbed in. Then there had been a minute there that I'd thought I was going to have to do CPR on him when I suggested going to I Dream of Weenie.

My obsession with the shop had been indirectly caused by Igor himself. He'd been trying to go to a greasy spoon next door, but I'd been quick to shut that down when I'd seen the notice from the health inspector that hadn't been taken down and was dated only a few days prior. I didn't care if Igor had some twisted obsession with getting food poisoning, but I did not.

I Dream of Weenie had been the best find of the season. It had quickly become my favorite place to eat. It was relatively cheap and by far the best hot dogs I'd ever had. They put the chicken-based hot dogs in Russia to shame. Babushka couldn't prepare a sosiski as good as the bright yellow and white VW bus could make a French toast weenie, a Flamin' Frank, or my personal favorite, the Thanksgiving weenie. My stomach always rumbled at the thought of the plump, juicy weenie covered in cornbread, gravy, and cranberry sauce. I already couldn't wait for Thanksgiving to roll around and it was only June.

Then during lunch he'd managed to go white as a ghost and I'd noticed him squirming uncomfortably. I'd initially thought he wasn't feeling well, but after he'd mentioned wanting a shower, I'd had to assume he'd just been uncomfortable after moving so much that day. Indy had definitely put him through the wringer with his stretching and I'd seen how much he'd been struggling by the end. It had been more than he'd moved since his surgery.

I'd thought he'd be better after his shower, but he'd lain low and had gone to bed early, not talking much to me as I'd built the giant LEGO set I'd bought. That was last night, and now it was before seven and clanking from downstairs had woken me from a dead sleep. It was the first morning I hadn't had to get up to either take Igor to a doctor's appointment or make sure that he didn't use his leg when he wasn't supposed to. Which also meant that until three minutes earlier, I'd been looking forward to sleeping in.

With my dream of sleep thwarted, I made my way down the steps in a pair of athletic shorts that I'd found in my drawer, trying to figure out what was making the noise. I followed the sound to the kitchen and stopped dead in my tracks as I desperately tried to process what I was seeing. Except no matter how hard I tried, my brain only had two words dancing through it: kokova chordata?

What the devil?

Repeated blinking did not make the situation in front of me make sense or disappear. If anything, it made it worse. Igor was making breakfast, or at least something that I assumed was breakfast since it was still early in the morning. His using my kitchen to cook didn't bother me; it was the fact that every drawer and cabinet he'd touched had been left open.

I was already up earlier than I'd wanted to be. My feet reacted before my brain could stop them and I stalked toward the kitchen to begin shutting the cabinets. "Ozols!" His name came out as more of a spat. "Shut! Shut! Shut! Shut!" I punctuated each word by shutting a cabinet or drawer, thankful the designer had talked me into the soft close hinges that kept me from slamming each one. "Not hard, Ozols! Open." I opened a cabinet. "Shut." I shut the door and looked at him, expecting my friend to apologize to me.

Instead of an apology, Igor raised an eyebrow as he hobbled to the sink to wash the knife he'd been using to cut peppers. "I shut them... when I am done. Might need something again." His dismissive shrug left me to growl in frustration.

It was way too early to be dealing with this level of insanity. Boris still needed to be let out and a headache was already blooming behind my eyes. I rubbed my temples as I headed to the door with Boris, only to trip on a slipper that had definitely not been there when I'd let him out before going to bed the night before.

My stuttered step made Igor give an uncomfortable laugh. "Oops. Sorry. I went outside to sit last night. Needed to stretch my leg and I wanted to sit by the pool."

This definitely called for more than one shot of espresso. There was no way I was going to respond to him without it because I'd end up calling him a brat or telling him that maybe a good spanking would help him remember to clean up after himself.

Shit. Once again, too early in the morning. Yeah, I needed to focus on organizing my thoughts before I said something that would send him running from the house screaming.

He definitely wasn't up to running yet. Indy would kill me if he got hurt again. The goal was to have Igor take over Coach Harrington's position as the goalie coach. His experience in net, numerous awards to his name, and respect in the league, paired with his planned retirement, had made him a shoo-in for the position when Harrington was recruited for a spot with the Canadian women's league.

Pacing on the back deck, I started thinking about the contacts on my phone. If my first reaction to being frustrated was to want to take my best friend over my knee, that had to say it had been too long since I'd played with someone. Someone who wanted to push the limits for the reward of my hand spanking their ass, heating their backside, and making them writhe in all the best ways.

There had to be someone I could call or text who might want to meet up with me for a scene, maybe a good fuck while we were at it. I needed to get this out of my system, the sooner the better. I couldn't risk fucking up my relationship with my best friend.

I absently flicked through the contacts on my phone, the names of the people I'd played with in the past scrolling rapidly by. My few regular hookups weren't doing it for me. None of them sent my pulse racing or my thoughts to anything more than the mundane. Each name that passed by was just that, a name with nothing more than a blurry memory as it scrolled off my screen. Every one of their memories had been tainted by Igor.

Ivan stretched out on the bed after a hard spanking became an image of Igor in the same position. Navayah pouting as I warned her that she was pushing for punishment faded until I was looking at Igor. I couldn't even get Misha, my longest play partner, to stay solid in my mind. Misha's hot red ass draped over my legs stayed put, but when they looked up at me, Misha's face had suddenly become Igor's, staring up at me with a silent challenge.

Growling, I pocketed my phone and raked my fingers through my already messy hair. Igor and whatever had been happening between us lately had gotten into my head and I needed to figure out how to get my thoughts back in order before Boris was done with his business and I had to face Igor again.

My feet led me to the deck railing and I leaned heavily against it, my weight resting on my elbows. Igor was a friend. My best friend, who was also painfully straight. I smiled at the grass in our backyards that still showed signs of where the rink we'd taken down in March had been from late November. The gardener we used was still bitching at us about the damage we did to our lawns every year.

Then my eyes found Igor's house, a modern home with white stucco siding and a black roof. Clean lines decorated each side, and the inside was just the same. It was the complete opposite of my own warm brick-and-rock-sided home with a light gray roof and dark gutters.

Our houses were a metaphor for us—side by side yet opposites in every way. We were night and day, yet our worlds combined into a friendship that had withstood living next door to one another, fights with the homeowners association, and working with one another.

But what kept our friendship strong was that we were careful to never mix friendship and relationships. I never dated his exes, he stayed far away from mine, and I'd never once thought about him as more than a friend. It had never been a problem before, so why was it so hard now?

Lost in my thoughts, I never heard the door open or Igor's crutches approaching until a plate of scrambled eggs, sausage, and toast appeared in front of me. "I'm sorry. I did not mean to upset you."

Turning, I could see that Igor was nervous and I hated that I'd made him feel that way. "Thank you. It is okay." Boris came running toward us and I had to lift the plate off the railing and over my head before he ate my breakfast. "Boris, down!"

My dog whimpered as he sat, giving me eyes sadder than Igor's had been as he'd handed me the plate.

"Boris, come. I made you breakfast too." Igor inclined his head toward the door as he began to walk and I watched as my dog left me.

"I see how it is. Food is way to your heart. Bastard." Neither my dog nor Igor looked back at me and I found myself following in their footsteps with a shake of my head. I wasn't but a few steps behind them, but when I joined the two in the kitchen, Boris not only had his own plate of scrambled eggs and sausage, but there was also a serving of his dog food in the bowl by the plate he was eating off of. If I wasn't careful, my dog was going to leave when Igor did.

Igor was standing next to the espresso machine looking sheepish. "I do not know how to work this machine. It's very complicated. Too many buttons and nozzles. I cannot make you coffee. Sorry."

And fuck if my cock didn't try to react again to Igor's sincere apology. My mouth went inexplicably dry when I finally tried to find a way to respond. "D-da." My voice cracked in my struggle to get words out of my parched throat. "I can make for both of us." Looking over at the plate of breakfast Igor had prepared, I found myself smiling. "Breakfast, bal'shoye spasibo. It is very nice."

Turning to grab the bag of coffee beans, I caught a glimpse of Igor pursing his lips in thought. "Bless you?"

I poured a serving of beans into the grinder and turned it on as I tried to work through how to respond. "Did not sneeze," I finally said as I turned to face Igor. "Bal'shoye spasibo, big thank you. Thank you for breakfast and clean kitchen."

Now that we were actually talking instead of me stewing, my libido was finally calming down and words were becoming easier as my dick stood down.

Igor's laugh filled my kitchen. "Oh, then, bal'shoye... welcome?"

My laughter tamped down the remainder of my arousal and I was able to set to work making coffee for the two of us. We weren't going to have nearly enough time for my liking before we had to leave for Igor's therapy appointment with Indy, but from the little I'd seen that morning, he was moving better than he had been after we'd left the appointment the day before. He was even putting some weight on his leg, though he continued to let his crutches do most of the work.

With any luck, he'd be back home in under a week and I could go back to not having inappropriate thoughts about my best friend.

"One more, Igor. You can do it." Indy was crouched in front of Igor as he worked through a few stretches. Twenty minutes into the appointment he'd lost his shirt, so I was being cursed to work on the exercise bike while my eyes continued to find his bare back and watch as sweat formed on his skin, gradually covered each of the countless tattoos on his back, and then began trailing down his shoulders and spine.

"Stare any harder at him and he's going to catch fire."

The voice beside me made me nearly fall off the bike I was pedaling, though I somehow managed to keep the yelp of surprise to a startled gasp that didn't interrupt Igor or Indy. Then I had to blink to make sure my eyes weren't deceiving me.

"Blaise?" He was normally shy and quiet. I was pretty sure that had been the first time he'd ever spoken to me without stumbling over his words.

He grinned at my reaction, though I was almost relieved to see the blush I was so accustomed to appear in his cheeks. "Guilty as charged." He picked at his nails but not as furiously as he usually did.

"What are you doing here?" I winced at how accusatory I sounded, as though Blaise had no business being in the training room. To my surprise he only shrugged. "I'm supposed to go to lunch with Indy. Thought she'd be done by now."

"That is right. You two are... what is English word?"

"Twins." He gave me a smile that reached his eyes. "Somehow we haven't killed each other over the years."

My feet continued to work the pedals as though I could use them to put space between Igor and me.

"Want to talk about it?"

I looked over at him, pursing my lips for a moment while trying to figure out if I had missed something. "Talk about what?"

"You seem stressed about something. Is Igor still living at your house?" He shrugged a shoulder casually like it didn't matter, but the fact that he'd asked at all told me I must have looked bad. Blaise didn't go out of his way to make small talk. He usually went out of his way to avoid it.

"Da." I nodded for emphasis. "Still lives with me. He does not know how to sleep in, makes me very tired. Even my dog is tired."

Blaise chuckled at my words. He managed to keep it quiet enough that Igor didn't lose focus, though Indy did look over to see who had laughed, then gave her brother a smile.

"Is exhaustion making you zone out while staring at his very nice back?" Color stained Blaise's cheeks again and he held up a hand. "I'm sorry, I shouldn't have said that. It's just a little distracting."

Blaise had done a great job of keeping quiet, and until that sentence came out of his mouth, so had I. Once he mentioned Igor's *very nice* back, though, I wasn't able to hold in my laughter, making both Igor and Indy stare at me.

"Unexpected coming from you, Blaise. I like it!" Though poor Blaise looked like he might actually turn into a blaze from embarrassment. I leaned close to him, trying to keep my voice low enough that Igor wouldn't hear me, especially now that we'd drawn his attention. "He has very nice backside. Sadly, he is hopelessly straight."

Blaise feigned a dramatic sigh. "Truly unfortunate."

"Yes. Unfortunate. Da." I sighed, especially as Igor grabbed the hand towel he'd been using and draped it over his shoulders and around his neck, making his lean shoulder muscles ripple hypnotically.

Igor had barely left for the shower when Indy stalked over, waggling a finger at the two of us. "You two, you are awful! The least you can do is tell me what you are looking so guilty over now that you broke his focus."

Her scolding only made me laugh harder; however, Blaise looked truly apologetic. "Sorry, Indy. My fault."

My head bobbed eagerly. "Igor has very nice back."

Indy sighed. "You are not wrong! He's got a very, very

nice back." She looked toward the locker room like the thought would make him reappear. When he didn't come back, she turned to us. "Do I need to institute a shirt policy in the training room so that the two of you don't interrupt us?"

"No!" I yelped at the same time that Blaise answered, "Yes!"

"Traitor." I pointed at Blaise. "You drain all fun with bath water."

Blaise turned his head from side to side, studying me like I was an alien creature. "Um... that isn't how that saying goes."

I blew a raspberry. "You understood enough."

"I guess. He *is* very distracting, though."

Indy waggled a finger in Blaise's direction. "No more distracting than you are when you show up in the training room. You hate this place."

Blaise shrugged, but I noticed he started to pick at his thumb again and he cleared his throat a few times. "Only sometimes. Not all the time. It depends on who's in here."

Indy rolled her eyes. "You're ridiculous. You need to get over your crush on—"

"Indigo Emory, if you finish that sentence, I will... I will..." Blaise struggled to find an appropriate threat and I was left hoping he wouldn't find one. I really wanted to know who Blaise was crushing on. "Feed Elzebub to the eagle!"

Indy gasped, putting a hand over her heart. "You wouldn't!"

"I would."

"Who is Elz-a-bub?" I asked, breaking the name down slowly to try to repeat it.

"My goose."

I was glad Blaise had come up with a good enough threat to keep his sister quiet because now I needed to know who this goose was and why Blaise would give it to the eagle. There was a story there.

CHAPTER 8

IGOR

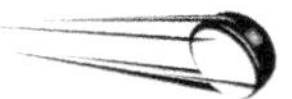

My hip pulled and strained with every stretch Indy put me through. The exercises were a special form of hell, the discomfort second only to the way my dick had responded to Yuri yelling at me that week.

It had taken me five minutes to talk my dick into behaving itself and a lot longer than that to sort out what was happening. At least Indy's strict orders kept me focused on my stretches and not on the thoughts that were beginning to plague my every waking moment.

The first time had been easy to ignore or at least brush off as a fluke. Hell, I'd hardly been horny since the surgery and my dick hadn't understood what it was reacting to. But then it had happened over and over again and always when Yuri got frustrated at me. I hadn't put it all together until the night before and had decided to see if I could get a rise out of him and see what would happen.

I'd hit my head on so many damned cabinet doors by the time he'd woken up that I'd been worried I'd give myself a concussion before he got his ass downstairs. That one would have been really hard to explain. But he'd headed down the steps and immediately started cursing at me. And that was all it had taken. Every cabinet door or drawer he shut while chastising me had made my dick harder.

So what did that mean?

"Igor!"

The snap of my name on Indy's tongue pulled me out of my thoughts. Shit, the stretches weren't even enough to keep my thoughts away from Yuri.

"Sorry, screw leader Indigo. I will pay attention now."

Indy blinked. "What?"

I started to laugh and had to hold my hand up as I composed myself. "Sorry. Yuri messed up drill sergeant and came up with screw leader instead. It just popped out of my mouth."

Far from offended, Indy just chuckled. "Sounds like Yuri." She smiled and looked over my shoulder. My eyes fell on Yuri. He had his shirt draped over the seat of the stationary bike beside him as he pedaled like he was trying to escape his shadow. My dick shifted in my shorts and I had to peel my eyes away.

"Yes." The word was clipped, but I feigned a little

wince as I stretched my hip and it brought Indy right back to what we were doing.

"Not too much. Don't push this recovery. The slower you take this, the better you're going to feel in a few weeks."

I didn't like the idea of taking it easy. Calm really wasn't in my vocabulary, but I also knew that Yuri and Indy would take turns strangling me if I didn't listen to the recovery orders. We made it a few more minutes before I finally had to take my shirt off. Simple stretches shouldn't have been making me sweat like I was halfway through a game, but they were.

At least the level of effort that I was putting into doing the stretches exactly like Indy was telling me to had my attention completely off of Yuri for the first time since the day of my surgery. I probably pushed harder than I should have, but after a while, the stretches actually started to feel better. I was no longer wanting to curse in pain but was able to focus on each muscle group and localizing the stretches so they were doing exactly what they were supposed to.

My focus remained until my attention was drawn to Yuri and another voice behind us. "Is exhaustion making you zone out while staring at his very nice back?"

I had no idea who'd said that, but I was instantly intrigued. The voice continued, trying to stay quiet, but the room was almost silent and the whisper carried our way. "I'm sorry, I shouldn't have said that. It's just a little distracting."

The voice belonged to Blaise. I knew that immediately by the way he had apologized so quickly.

The laughter that bubbled out from Yuri echoed through the room and I forgot all about the exercises I was supposed to be focusing on. I didn't feel too bad about it since Indy's attention also drifted to Blaise and Yuri.

When I turned, Yuri was grinning broadly. "Unexpected coming from you, Blaise. I like it!"

In true Blaise fashion, he turned as red as the carpet in the hallway outside our locker rooms. Yuri either didn't notice or didn't care. "He has very nice backside. Sadly, he is hopelessly straight."

Blaise sighed and shook his head. "Truly unfortunate."

"Yes. Unfortunate. Da." Yuri gave a frustrated sigh that matched Blaise's.

My body felt warmer than it had before, and I was unsure why I suddenly felt the need to fan my face. I'd been the focus of appreciation before, but this was different and I didn't know why. Placing my mouth near Indy's ear, I tried to whisper more quietly than Blaise and Yuri had managed. "Are they talking about me?"

Indy's answer was a push to my shoulder and a sly smile. "I think we're done for the day. I don't think we're getting anything else done with those two here."

My stomach went on a private roller coaster that left me reaching awkwardly for my towel to clean some of the sweat off my face. I hoped like hell that everyone thought the flush of my skin was due to exertion and not the looks I was getting from Yuri and Blaise.

Fuck. I was right back to where I'd been earlier in the day.

The faster I got out of the weight room and into the showers, the better. All I could do was hope I'd be able to wash the thoughts out of my head with a very cold shower. Indy headed over to her brother and Yuri and I grabbed my crutches from the weight bench and hurried toward the locker room for that much-needed shower.

Ten minutes later, ice-cold water dripping down my back, I was ready to admit that a shower wasn't going to get rid of the thoughts. I just didn't know what was. "Dammit, Yuri!" I didn't bother hiding my curse, but I made sure to keep it as quiet as possible, not sure where Yuri was and not wanting him to hear me.

I turned the shower off with more force than was required, but my frustration had grown tenfold as my thoughts hadn't worked themselves out. If anything, they'd gotten more complicated as my brain tried to replay every single interaction we'd had over the last two and a half weeks.

My feelings had moved well past the desire to drive Yuri crazy. Besides, I'd managed to do that over and over again, trying or not. That morning had been a test of what my body did when I pushed him just a little too far. I couldn't ignore that my body liked it.

I was getting some sort of sick pleasure out of driving my best friend up a wall. Every time I knew I'd pushed just a little too far, my dick liked the way he got frustrated. Then the way he thanked me when I corrected whatever it was would make it hard to concentrate for a few seconds. *That* was what was truly bugging me. It wasn't the fact that my body liked pushing Yuri's buttons; it was how much it craved soothing his frustrations.

"Ryyyy," a deep, gravelly voice said from the hallway. The tone was shockingly similar to the one Yuri had used on me a number of times. It spoke of frustration and I knew whoever Ry was, he was pushing buttons.

I expected a kid's voice to respond, but the whine that answered was far from juvenile. "But you said we'd go home to watch a movie!"

The first person blew out a long breath. "And we will. But Irvine asked if I could swing by to talk about the parade. If you can behave yourself, then we can get a treat on the way home." Their footsteps were coming closer as they spoke and I was too distracted by their conversation to pretend to not be eavesdropping.

There was a short pause, and then the second voice sounded skeptical as he responded. "Milkshake?"

Two heads popped around the corner and into the locker room. The older man groaned. "Shay's gonna have our heads."

"Yay!" The younger one bounced and kissed the other

man's cheek. "Thank you, D—" He noticed me standing there and flushed before finishing his sentence. "Mal."

It finally dawned on me who I was looking at: Malcolm Ward and his husband, Ryder, the offensive coach and the wide receiver for Nashville's NFL team. Not that I would have known them if it hadn't been for the fact that the teams had a good relationship. Off the field and out of football pads, Ryder looked a lot smaller than when he was playing.

Their appearance had my brain confused. What about their conversation had piqued my interest so much? Why did I care? There had been something about their interaction that had made my heart soar and my pulse rate speed up, but now I couldn't remember what.

Defeated by my own brain, I sagged against my bench. My ass hit the seat in front of my locker harder than I'd intended and I hissed through my teeth as a jolt of pain radiated up my back and down my leg.

"You okay?" Ryder turned to face me, the playful expression wiped clean off his face. "You look a little green." Then his eyes fell on the crutches by my bench. "Ah, PT. Yeah, that sucks. Mal was an asshole when he was going through PT after his injury."

I gave a curt nod. "Sat too fast. Hip does not approve."

Ryder grinned. "You need a milkshake too!"

I wanted to tell him milkshakes weren't going to fix the pain in my hip, but his smile was so earnest I couldn't find the words. Besides, I'd bet if I asked nicely enough, Yuri would stop on the way home.

What the fuck was wrong with my brain?

Thinking about ways to get what I wanted from Yuri should not have been on my radar, yet I found myself nodding. "Maybe."

Ryder looked me over, his eyes falling on my feet, and then his head turned toward my locker. "Do you need help getting your shoes on?" He leaned backward and grabbed my tennis shoes from the locker.

I took them and shook my head. "No, already tied, just need to slide them on." It was a trick I'd picked up early on in the recovery process. I hated tying shoes in the first place but when I couldn't bend myself in half, there wasn't much choice but to tie them just loose enough that I could slide them on but tight enough that they wouldn't fall off.

"Mal gets frustrated with me when I do that. He tells me I'm going to ruin my tennis shoes and they aren't going to be tight enough and I'm going to fall." He let out a little laugh before leaning in conspiratorially. "But what he doesn't know won't hurt him."

"But it might just hurt you, brat."

We both jumped in surprise as Malcolm and Coach Cunningham walked through the locker room. Ryder didn't look at all offended by Malcolm's comment. If anything, he smiled wider. He definitely winked. "Punishment or reward?"

I nearly choked on air at Ryder's question. I was fluent

in English, had been for most of my life, but sometimes humor went over my head. I was wondering if this was one of those moments because all I could come up with was that Ryder and Malcolm were definitely talking about sex. And I'd swear Malcolm had just threatened to give Ryder a spanking.

So why did Ryder look more excited than worried?

Cunningham shook his head. "I'm really glad to see that I'm not the only one who has his hands full with a team."

Our locker room had seen a lot of interesting conversations over the years, and I was pretty sure Coach had just confirmed my suspicions. Really, from some of the things we'd talked about in here, that exchange was pretty tame, but it was doing something to my insides that I didn't understand or have the ability to process with others around.

Malcolm's laugh echoed in the mostly empty locker room. "Not even close. I bet that one alone could give you a run for your money."

Cunningham looked between Ryder and me, then grinned. "Which one are you talking about?"

"Hey!" I tried to protest more but Cunningham just raised an eyebrow in my direction.

"Don't even argue that one, Ozols. I have a list of games you've missed because of food poisoning in my office. And do I need to remind you of the Puck Bunny Incident?"

Ryder forgot all about looking innocent as he swung his attention to me. "What is this Puck Bunny Incident? I feel like there's a story here and I want to know! Scratch that, I *need* to know."

Yuri interrupted my story before I could start it, causing me to jump. I'd had no idea when he'd come into the locker room, but he was there and now speaking directly to Ryder, a smirk on his lips. "The only story is Igor is pain in the ass." He turned toward me and his face softened. "However, Indy says you work hard today. Earn reward."

And now I was thinking about things that were way different than milkshakes or fast food. The last ninety seconds had fucked with my brain and all my thoughts.

Movement from my side pulled my attention away before I could respond to Yuri. Ryder was getting comfortable against the back of the empty stall beside me and fishing a handheld game system out of his pocket.

"Oh! I have that system. What are you playing?"

Ryder laughed. "Actually, I'm basically just doing a color by number right now. I usually play *Minecraft* or *Fortnite*, but no one was on last night, so I found this coloring thing and I want to finish the one I was working on. Then I'll probably get back to something else."

I craned my neck to see what he was coloring. From the angle I was at, I was pretty sure it was a complex rainforest with a giant bird in the center. "Cool. What's your gamertag? I can add you later. I play those games sometimes if I'm not building LEGO or playing one of the LEGO games with Yuri."

Ryder's eyes lit up. "Really? That would be cool! Most of the guys play *Call of Duty* and stuff like that, but I haven't really gotten into it." He waited for me to pull out my phone to take down his name. When I was done, he turned to Yuri. "We've got the Titanic at home that we just started working on!"

Yuri's grin turned devilish. "See, asshole." He wagged a finger in my direction. "Big ship. Huge ship! I opened box recently."

Sighing, I stood and grabbed my crutches. If I let Yuri start talking about LEGO, we'd be there all afternoon and I was pretty sure the reward he'd talked about had been fast food. I was sure I could get a milkshake out of it too if I asked nicely.

"Let's go get food." I made it a few steps, putting minimal weight on my leg, then turned to wink at Ryder. "And maybe a milkshake."

Ryder let out a laugh that sounded a lot more like a giggle. "Oh, have you been to Legendairy?" He patted his flat stomach. "It's worth all the extra minutes in the gym!"

I blinked over at Yuri. "To Legendairy! I think Burger Republic is by there too. Burgers and a shake. I've earned them. You said!"

Yuri shook his head and I chose to take that as a win. "Brat."

My face flushed at the word, much like Ryder's had

when his husband had said the same thing to him. But instead of a quip about what it might mean, I was left to let my blush slowly fade.

Yuri shook his head and turned to leave the room. I followed dutifully as we made our way down the hallway toward the parking garage under the rink. We were near the door when I finally noticed my eyes had been glued to Yuri's ass and the way the light gray shorts he was wearing hugged his ass and thighs as he moved.

If I'd been alone, I'd have yelled at myself and dug my hands into my eyes in an attempt to shake the thoughts from my head, but I wasn't alone. All I could do was force my eyes upward and chastise myself.

I needed to get my head out of the gutter, at least until we got back to Yuri's house and I could begin to start analyzing my thoughts. I was getting the distinct impression that something was shifting inside me. Something that was likely going to change my life as I knew it.

The real question was how long I could hide from it. As Yuri stopped to open the door leading to the garage, I knew it wasn't going to be much longer.

CHAPTER 9

IGOR

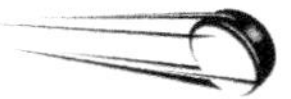

"Can't I have twenty?" Ryder's question made me jump in surprise. We'd been playing *Minecraft* together while talking to one another over the phone. Everything for the last hour had been about zombies, mobs, and spiders, and then there was a question about twenty, and for a few seconds, I didn't understand what he wanted twenty of.

Then I heard his husband sigh. "Ry, baby, bedtime is ten thirty. You know that."

He huffed. "Fine." Then he turned his attention to me. "Ten more minutes and I've got to call it a night."

Because his bedtime was ten thirty. I had questions, but I knew ten minutes wasn't going to be long enough to have them answered. "Okay. Then we should probably start finding our way back to the house."

We'd made it halfway out of the cave we'd been exploring, still keeping an eye out for any ore that might help us craft weapons or armor while chatting about when we'd both have a free night next, when Yuri rapped on my doorframe. I glanced away from the screen, ready to tell him to give me five minutes and we could talk, to find him standing in my doorway in just a pair of black boxer briefs. His hair was wet from a shower and he was holding a glass of water and some Advil that I was still taking at night to help me sleep.

I'd done a damn good job pretending I hadn't been staring at Yuri's ass and thighs while we'd left the arena earlier, but without anything but underwear covering him, my brain completely short-circuited for a moment. Thankfully, Ryder's voice in my ear asking me what the hell I was doing brought me back to the present in time to keep from falling off a cliff.

"Oops. Thanks." I got myself back on the path. "Yuri walked in to give me pills." *And a show.* Yeah, there went the ability to avoid thinking about the way Yuri was making me feel.

I'd just figured out that driving him absolutely insane was fun and was still conflicted as to why that was, and now I was having a hard time focusing on anything but the way his dick was filling out the front of his underwear as he walked over to me. My brain was right back to hurting and I was beginning to feel like I was going through puberty all over again.

My throat felt unnaturally dry as I held my hand out for the pills while trying not to let on that anything was up. "H-hold on." I cleared my throat and tried again. "Hold up, Ryder." At least I didn't run the risk of falling to my death and losing the treasure I'd found in the cave we'd been exploring when I stopped trying to play and focused on Yuri.

Then again, that probably wasn't any better because now I had nothing to keep my attention from him or my eyes away from his crotch. Holding my hand out for the water, I could only pray that Yuri didn't notice how hard it was for me to keep my eyes on his face and not the rest of his body. A very well-defined body with pale skin and a light covering of chest hair, not dark or thick enough to cover his caramel nipples or the light definition in his abs yet dark enough that the trail leading from his belly and disappearing in his underwear was plenty distracting.

I gulped the water he handed me like a man who'd been stranded in the desert, barely remembering to stop long enough to pop my pills in my mouth before draining the glass. "Th-thanks."

Yuri gave me a weird glance that told me I wasn't acting any calmer than I was feeling. "You good?"

I swallowed hard then wheezed around water I'd somehow managed to get lodged in my throat. "F-fine."

He looked far from convinced but headed back toward the door. "I will be in living room for a bit. Do not die, okay?"

I gave him a thumbs-up, not fully relaxing back in my bed until I could no longer see his perfect ass in the hallway. The noise that escaped my throat was a half wheeze, half sigh. I didn't have time to gather my thoughts before Ryder's laughter in my ear drew my attention.

"If that wasn't the most awkward exchange I've ever heard."

"Shut up. We need to get back to house. We have four minutes before you must go to bed."

If I'd spat the words a little more forcefully than I'd intended, Ryder didn't mention it as his character started up the winding cave wall. "Does Yuri know you're crushing on him?"

"Crushing?" Had my voice cracked?

Ryder sobered quickly. "Do *you* know you're crushing on him?"

My groan was probably answer enough, but I did manage to find words. "I am straight... or have always been."

An understanding hum filled my ear. "Ah yes, I remember that feeling. Kind of a mindfuck, isn't it?"

"Language, Ry." I could hear Malcolm in the background.

"Sorry." There was a smile in Ryder's voice and I could imagine the mischievous grin he was giving his husband.

A mindfuck was a great description of my feelings at the current time. I had no idea how to work through my thoughts. "Yes. That's it." After a long pause, I deflated slightly. "Fuck. I do not know what I feel. Is this just because we are stuck together? I have always teased Yuri. Always make him nuts. But now it is..."

"Different?" Ryder opened the door of the house we'd built that evening, both of us safely out of the mine and entering the house just before dark.

"Yes." I shut the door and we exited out of the game. "Different."

We sat in silence for a few long seconds. "I know what you mean, but I don't have any words of advice. I'm here if you need to talk, though."

"Thank you." The two words were all I had to offer, and it was a good thing since Malcolm chose then to remind Ryder of the time.

"Bedtime."

Ryder gave a warm chuckle. "He's very impatient. I've gotta go. But I'm here and conveniently I'm only doing training camps right now."

"Ry..."

"Coming! Talk later."

"Bye." The line went dead and I found myself staring at a dark game and phone screen, unsure what to do with the remainder of the evening. It was only ten thirty. I wasn't tired, but I didn't want to go out to the living room, especially with Yuri taking up the couch in only his underwear.

Damn sexy underwear that did not cover nearly enough to keep my brain off of highly inappropriate thoughts. Hell, just the thought of Yuri in that underwear was enough to have my cock twitching to life.

It had been over twenty-four hours since I'd last jacked off. Going from living alone with ample time to hook up with a woman or take matters into my own hands to living with Yuri and lacking complete privacy had been a big change. It had definitely put a damper on my sex life.

There was no doubt that I was beginning to question my sexuality, but there was also a lingering question about just how much this was an attraction to Yuri and how much this was way too much pent-up sexual tension.

Maybe a few orgasms would make everything go back to normal.

There was a pesky voice in the back of my head that was telling me I was fooling myself, but I was willing to humor myself for a bit longer. Anything to keep from facing the very big, very real elephant of sexuality in the room. Besides, an orgasm or two was easy. A lot easier than confronting my thoughts about Yuri.

A pending *sex*istential crisis was not enough to make my dick go down. If anything, it had only gotten harder as I'd contemplated why I was getting aroused for Yuri. My laptop was sitting on the nightstand and it was time to at least give my dick some relief.

Clicking over to my favorite porn site, my cursor hovered over a video I'd always loved. The woman with ample curves and breasts that bounced every time her partner slammed into her was enough eye candy to bring me to orgasm in just a few minutes, and that wasn't taking into account how vocal she was about her partner fucking her hard and fast.

Except my finger didn't press the play button. My eyes kept drifting to the sidebar where a thumbnail of two men taunted me. The one guy was in skimpy briefs that reminded me of the pair Yuri had been wearing when he'd come into my room. He was kneeling on a bed between the legs of a very naked guy whose cock was resting against his stomach.

I hadn't been aware that I'd made a decision, yet my finger clicked on the thumbnail of the men and I was left watching a scene unlike any I'd ever seen before.

The video opened with the guy in underwear walking toward the bed, asking the second guy if he'd gotten his chores done that day. My eyes watered from staring at the second guy's cock for so long. As soon as he'd been asked the question, his cock pulsed and a bead of precum dribbled down his erection and got caught in the patch of well-trimmed pubes.

A whimper escaped the guy on the bed before he managed a nod of his head.

"I need words, Cody."

The stern words made my cock pulse harder than Cody's had.

"Y-yes." The stammered word sounded like it had

taken all the energy Cody had to get it out, but it hadn't been enough for the guy beside him.

"Yes, what?"

"Y-yes, Tanner, sir." Cody's chest heaved as Tanner's hand hovered over his erection. "I did my chores."

By how my body reacted to the way Tanner wrapped his hand around Cody's cock and stroked him, he might as well have done it to me. A breathy gasp escaped both our mouths and I shot a look at the door to see if it was shut. To my relief, Yuri had closed it as he'd left.

Tanner hummed in pleasure as he climbed onto the bed. When he spoke to Cody, his words dripped with a combination of pleasure and desire that had both of us anticipating his next move. Tanner settled between Cody's legs, resting his ass on his feet, and the camera angle changed to the side, allowing me to watch everything he was doing to Cody.

"Such a good boy. You made the house look very nice while I was gone today. You had dinner ready when I got home and even managed to mow the grass. I didn't even ask you to do that."

Cody's mouth opened as though he was going to say something, but his words died on a moan when Tanner leaned forward and licked up Cody's dick, wrapping his lips around the head and sucking for a brief second before releasing it with a slurp.

My hand found the front of my shorts and I languidly stroked my erection through the material, absently wishing Tanner's lips were wrapped around my cock but mostly glued to the scene playing out in front of me. It was fucking hot. Way hotter than the video I'd always gravitated toward.

Tanner placed his index finger into his mouth and Cody moaned as though it was his cock Tanner was sucking. A few seconds later, Tanner pulled his finger free and pressed at Cody's pucker. Cody's back bowed off the bed and he let out a keening noise that had me pressing the volume key rapidly in hopes of getting it quiet enough to not draw Yuri's attention to my room.

When Cody found words, they tumbled from his mouth as Tanner barely breached his entrance. "Please. Please, Tanner. Fuck me. Need... need you."

"That's right, Cody, open up. Let me in." A click could be heard off-screen and Tanner's left hand appeared, sliding a finger into Cody's ass with ease. Cody's groan could barely be heard over my own as I lifted awkwardly and shoved my pants down, letting my good leg fall completely to the side and adjusting my bad leg so that it was at least lying straight, leaving my dick fully exposed and my hole partially unobstructed by my cheeks.

I didn't have lube like Cody and Tanner, but I could at least spit into my palm to ease some friction. My ass was virgin territory, a place I'd never been curious to discover before Cody started begging for anything and everything Tanner was willing to give him. Now I was curious, desperate to figure out if it was as good as Cody made it out to be but knowing enough to be aware that I needed lube—lube that I didn't have. Spit would at least let me touch myself without the calluses of my fingertips abrading the skin around my hole.

At the first contact of my finger with my pucker, my eyes rolled back in my head and a needy noise unlike any I'd made before escaped me. On the screen, Tanner had worked three fingers into Cody's ass, and Cody was busy begging for his cock.

I couldn't imagine taking a cock inside me when I was barely managing to get my fingertip past the muscle, but by the way Cody was begging, I was left to assume it felt good. Forcing myself to focus on more than Cody's ass stretched around Tanner's fingers, I saw that Tanner had lost his underwear at some point and his dick was jutting proudly from his body.

"Oh, yes, please." Since Cody was in the midst of a long hum as Tanner removed his fingers, I knew the words had come from me. More surprising than that, I'd meant them. I didn't know if I wanted a dick in me, but I knew I wanted to see that dick being swallowed by Cody's tight ass.

Thankfully, I didn't have to wait very long. Tanner's fingers and hand had still been covered in lube when he'd pulled them from Cody's body, but he didn't hesitate to pour more on his palm before wrapping his hand around his dick and coating it as well.

"Fuck, yes." I pushed my fingertip in my ass and

wrapped my other hand around my cock as Tanner lifted Cody's legs onto his shoulders and lined up with Cody's hole to start entering him. A string of encouraging words fell from Tanner's lips as Cody's body accepted all of him. Far from aggressive or rushed, the moment was punctuated with sweet, soothing words and a gentle rub against Cody's lower stomach when he tensed before Tanner was all the way in him. The praise picked back up as soon as Tanner finished sliding in. When his heavy balls landed against Cody's ass, I couldn't figure out which one of us was more wrung out.

Cody's eyes were blown wide, but my breathing had picked up and I swore my orgasm was building at an alarming rate with just a fingertip in my ass and my hand wrapped around the base of my cock. Then Cody rocked his hips, a smile playing across his lips at the hiss Tanner let out.

"I was good. I deserve a reward. You said so."

"Reward, yes," I said to the computer screen. "Please, give us that reward."

Tanner slapped the side of Cody's hip and I felt my body shake, the sound lighting up nerve endings I hadn't known existed before that moment, and my balls tightened further. "Fuck." It took everything in me to keep focused on the scene, desperate to come with Cody.

Something electric passed between the men on screen and Tanner began rocking his hips into Cody's ass, Cody letting out unintelligible babbles as his body rocked from the force. "That's it, baby. Take my cock. Do you want my cum in your ass tonight?"

I worked my cock in time to Tanner's thrusts, my body hovering between desperation and euphoria. This was gearing up to be the most intense orgasm of my life, and I'd reached the point it didn't matter that I was watching two men fucking or if Yuri heard me. All I cared about was Cody and me finding relief.

"Ye-yes. All your cum. All in me. Ta-Tanner. Need to come. Need. Need."

Jesus, yes, we needed to come. My orgasm was building rapidly and I didn't know if I was going to be able to hold off much longer. My balls and the base of my spine tingled and my world had gone black at the edges, everything focused on the men on my computer and my building orgasm.

"That's it, baby. Come for me. Paint that gorgeous stomach with your cum. I want to see it, feel it."

"Thank fuck." My cock pulsed with Cody's first spurt from his dick. Cum painted his chest and stomach while Tanner praised him for being good before speeding up and pounding repeatedly into Cody's ass until he eventually stilled and grunted as he filled Cody as promised.

My dick hurt from overstimulation, my chest ached from breathing so fast, and my heart was at risk of beating from my chest, but my body was sated in a way I'd never experienced before.

Tanner reached over and clicked the camera off,

leaving me alone in the darkness of my room to finally analyze my thoughts. The thoughts that had become crystal clear over the last fifteen minutes.

I, Igor Emil Ozols, was absolutely not straight.

But what did that make me?

CHAPTER 10

YURI

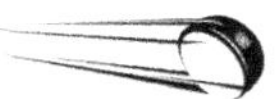

Boris and I made it down the steps at ten to seven to find the house quiet and Igor's door shut. After three and a half weeks, I was finally used to waking up before seven to Igor's clanking in my kitchen as he attempted to make breakfast while bitching about my complicated coffee machine.

He'd come a long way in physical therapy over the last week, but when he'd tried doing stairs on Friday, he'd only made it up four before cursing and hobbling back down. It was two steps farther than he'd made it on Thursday and four steps closer to leaving my house.

I should have been excited by that. A quiet house, the ability to sleep in past seven, no messy kitchen, and no more driving him to and from the rink four days a week. So why did the thought leave me rubbing absently at a void in my chest?

It wasn't like one of us had gotten traded and I'd never see him again. Hell, it wasn't like he lived on the other side of Nashville. I could literally see his house from nearly half the windows in mine. Our backyards connected, and we routinely drove the HOA insane. I glanced toward the backyard where we'd replaced forty feet of fencing with removable panels that only went in the ground far enough that they stayed upright throughout the spring, summer, and early fall. That had nearly gotten us both sued three years earlier.

The look on the neighbor kids' faces when they got to come over to skate throughout the winter months made any battle with the crazies with an overinflated sense of importance totally worth it. Igor and I had agreed to fight if they'd sued us, but we'd also found loopholes in the bylaws that we knew were ironclad. Even though they'd since closed the loopholes, our rink had been grandfathered in.

I smiled at the memory, a warm emotion filling the space that had felt empty at the thought of Igor leaving soon. "Pee break," I said to Boris as we moved through the eerily dark downstairs.

Boris barely waited for the door to be open far enough for him to squeeze out before he was gone, his need to pee clearly greater than he'd let on upstairs. At least with Igor still asleep, I could make coffee in peace. It would be a nice surprise to have it made for him when he finally woke up. Then again he was only going to be able to sleep thirty more minutes. We had to leave for the arena with enough time to get there and park before the roads in downtown shut down.

It was going to be a long day and I knew Igor wasn't happy that he was still on crutches. Actually, he'd been off them for the better part of the week. He still found enough ways to bug the hell out of me on a regular basis, though, and I'd uttered some variation of "*Teebya nada nakazat?*" more times than I could count. He'd actually nailed the accent on the way home from therapy the day before, so it was only a matter of time before he figured out that I was asking him if he needed a punishment. That was going to be an awkward one to explain when he finally looked it up.

Despite the fact that he was still trying to make me go gray before my time, I had caught Igor staring off into space more times than I was comfortable with. A few times a day, he would stop talking and when I'd look over at him, his eyes were a million miles from Nashville. Maybe in Latvia? He'd always said that he didn't miss his home country, but I couldn't figure out why he was so distant either. I would need to figure it out sooner rather than later as the last thing I wanted was for him to go back to his house and be sad or lonely.

Shaking my head, I pressed the start button on the grinder to begin my morning coffee routine. I could make an espresso faster than the barista at the coffee house next to the arena, and after three weeks, I had Igor's dry cappuccino mastered as well. With both coffees made, I cleaned the espresso counter and went to let my dog back in. It was weird that he wasn't scratching at the door, but that thought didn't occur to me until I was at the door and he wasn't there.

I stepped onto the patio to see what he'd gotten into, only to find him on one of the pool loungers draped across Igor's lap. Boris was sleeping and Igor had his hand resting on Boris's massive head while he stared at the blue water of my pool, once again lost in thought. Boris was no lapdog. At over a hundred and twenty-five pounds, he was approaching large for a Rottweiler, though he couldn't be convinced that he didn't belong on laps.

Watching the two from the porch made my heart pinch in a way I'd never experienced before. Boris and Igor fit together in my life but also on that chair. It was like it had been specifically designed just for the two of them. They hadn't noticed me, so I went back to the kitchen and grabbed our coffees and headed back out to the pool.

Igor hadn't stopped staring at the still water by the time I took the seat in the lounger next to him and held out his cup. "Good morning, solnishko." Igor didn't startle at my quiet greeting, only held out his hand for the mug, barely taking his eyes off the water.

"Thank you. You might spend a stupid amount of money on beans and an absurd machine, but it does make good coffee."

The compliment settled inside me and made me smile.

"I am glad you approve. I like making it because you enjoy it." Igor's cheeks immediately tinted with pink, causing me to play the sentence back in my head. Nothing I'd said should have caused him to be embarrassed, yet he wasn't meeting my eyes.

"Thank you." The words came out small and breathy, almost flirtatious, but I had to remind myself that this was Igor, not a potential hookup.

We sat in awkward silence, sipping our coffees while watching little ripples in the pool surface as the wind blew. It was going to be hot that day, but Pride always was. It was late June in Nashville, after all.

A bug jumped into the pool and caused a ripple that finally broke the quietness between us. "Are you okay? You are quiet this week."

Igor chuckled, though it lacked any humor. "Fine. A lot on my mind."

I had always been the guy that tackled problems head-on, so trying to tiptoe around the situation was not natural to me. When Seth and Maz were figuring their shit out, I confronted Seth. When Trevor and Brax were tiptoeing around dating, I bet Igor they were together—and won a hundred dollars. Things were different with Igor, though. This wasn't a relationship between my friends. This was something going on with my best friend, and part of me couldn't help but worry that there was something going on between us, like he'd figured out that he was driving me up a wall. Not up a wall mentally, but sexually.

If I pushed, was I going to find that I'd made him uncomfortable and he didn't want to be around me?

Being a good friend meant I needed to be an open ear for Igor, even if he told me something I didn't want to hear. "I am here if you need to talk." The words had been far harder to casually say to him than I thought they should have been, but I was going to take his small smile as a win for now.

"Thank you. I know you are. I just need to... figure stuff out."

All I could do was accept his answer and change the subject to something safer. "We must leave for parade soon."

Igor's smile finally reached his eyes. "You're not going to let me get out of this one, are you?"

His more relaxed posture had my insides uncoiling and I finally felt like I could breathe again. "Not a chance."

"Fine. But you're going to have to convince Boris to move first."

That was easy. I had a rainbow bandana with the Grizzlies logo on it in the house for Boris. He had come to every Pride parade with me since I'd gotten him and this year was going to be no different. "Boris, come. Hot dog."

He didn't move at his name, but as soon as I said hot dog, his head popped off Igor's lap and he lumbered to the door as quickly as his massive body would allow. I was shutting the door behind me when I heard Igor chuckle quietly. "Damn dog likes hot dogs as much as you."

Boris really did. He even had a preferred brand that was decidedly not chicken. He liked the ones I bought fresh from the butcher's shop on the outskirts of town. I went to the fridge and grabbed a hot dog and some eggs to scramble for all of us—dog included.

Igor had followed us into the house, though he was substantially slower, and was already in his room getting ready. His gait was no longer as lopsided as it had been when he'd started PT. The exercises Indy gave him every day and the time he was putting in at home was paying off quickly. He was still relying on his crutches and would be for a number of weeks to come, but he definitely wasn't as stiff and hadn't taken anything for the pain in a few days.

Thinking about that, I grabbed the bottle of anti-inflammatories from the cabinet and threw them in the bag I was taking with us. The odds were someone was going to need them by the end of the day. I knew Igor well enough to know that he'd push himself too hard and regret it, so I was going to be ready.

Boris ate his kibble while I made eggs and he was waiting at my hip for his extra breakfast by the time I was plating them. "Pain in ass," I said to the dog as I set a plate beside the counter and handed over a bagel and eggs to Igor.

We ate quickly, then hurried to get ready and head to the arena. We had pushed it close on timing but made it with twenty minutes to spare before the roads around the parade route closed for the day. Broadway was already decked out in rainbows, the banners on the outside of the arena had been changed to the various sexuality Pride flags, and our TVs were showing slideshows of LGBTQIA+ members of our team and staff as well as the building.

The outpouring of support for Pride had only grown over the years as more of our team and the football team had come out. Each summer more of downtown turned rainbow, the attendance was larger, and the vocal support louder.

And Boris ate up the attention paid to him.

Igor was quieter than normal on our drive to the arena, though I couldn't figure out how to make him more like his normal self. His reserved, almost sullen mood ended abruptly before I'd had the SUV fully parked in the garage. He flung the door open and called across the parking deck to someone just stepping out of their car. "Ryder!"

Igor and Boris left me sitting in the car, my hand still on the gearshift, staring at them heading across to a large black SUV. Trevor appeared by my window, grinning widely. He was already wearing the T-shirt that Blaise had ordered for us a few weeks prior, a pair of cargo shorts, and a rainbow ball cap with a helicopter-looking thing on top of it. "I think your dog found a new friend."

I could only shake my head. "I am happy Igor smiles now. He has been... not sad, but quiet."

Trevor looked to where Igor was chatting excitedly with the football player. "Could have fooled me. Do you know Ryder and his husband, Malcolm?"

I waved my hand to indicate just a bit. I'd seen the two around rather than being formally introduced or personally knowing them. Malcolm was a coach for the football team and was Ryder's husband and friends with Coach Cunningham. I was pretty sure I had heard Igor mention Ryder a few times this week.

Watching them, I felt a growl of frustration growing. A very real part of me wanted to go over and demand to know why Igor was greeting Ryder the way he used to greet me. When my molars ground together and Trevor gave me a worried look, I tried to mask my frustration better.

"You okay, Yuri? You said that Igor was off, but I'm pretty sure you just about broke a tooth."

"Fine." The look Trevor gave me said he bought it about as well as I did, but I wasn't sure why I was suddenly mad at Igor and a married man I didn't know.

Since Igor knew Ryder so well, I decided to go over and introduce myself to him and his husband, and excused myself from Trevor. He stepped aside, though I could feel his eyes on my back. Trevor was a protector on and off the ice, his tiny frame belying the lengths he'd go to to stand up for any one of us. I knew he was contemplating following me, so I quickened my pace and hoped like hell

Trevor would get sidetracked by someone else before he did.

I was watching the way Igor and Ryder interacted. When Ryder threw his arms around Igor and hugged him tight, only to have Igor return the hug, inexplicable white-hot rage burned in my chest. My knuckles cracking alerted me that my hands were balling into fists at my sides and I tried to relax and figure out why I was so angry.

It took a few deep breaths and Ryder unwrapping himself from Igor to grab his husband's hand and beam over at him with undeniable love in his eyes for the anger to fully subside. Only when the rage had passed was I able to see that I hadn't been angry—I'd been irrationally jealous of a married man hugging my straight best friend.

Instead of going to introduce myself, I turned away and headed toward the building where I knew brunch was being served—brunch that I hoped like hell included something strong to drink.

The champagne mimosas were nowhere near strong enough to take the edge off my feelings, but at least the tiny bubbles tingling in my mouth and down my throat were a good distraction from the fact that Igor still hadn't found me, Boris was ignoring me thanks to all the people around, and I was still pissed.

When we finally made our way out of the building and to the parade route, the oppressive Nashville heat and humidity had never been so welcome. "Yuri!" Igor's voice coming from behind me couldn't be ignored. When I turned, I saw him hurrying as fast as his crutches would allow, Boris beside him and Ryder and Malcolm directly behind him. He caught up with me only a few seconds after I stopped and was grinning like I was used to seeing him. "Ryder said you all have not formally met. We've been playing video games together the last week or so. I thought you should meet him and his husband, Malcolm. Guys, this is Yuri."

As he talked, he pointed to each of us in an awkward introduction that only raised my agitation. Igor had been holing himself up in his room the past week for hours at a time. Now I knew it was because of Ryder and it wasn't helping the jealousy from earlier fade.

"Hello." I didn't mean to spit the word out, but it was clipped and I could hear the coldness in my tone.

Malcolm didn't look bothered, only stepping forward and extending a hand. "Nice to meet you. Igor's been keeping Ry busy while I've been doing some unavoidable work stuff."

Behind us I heard Ryder mock gag before stage-whispering to Igor. "He has to do boring coach stuff."

Malcolm looked behind us and gave his husband an indulgent grin. "Yes, I have to do preseason coach stuff. I am so sorry you have to keep yourself entertained sometimes."

There was something just different enough about their interaction that it snapped me out of my funk. More of my attention became focused on the two men behind me as we walked, and I attempted to feel out their relationship while I tried to make polite conversation with Malcolm. The longer I listened to Ryder and Igor talk, the more convinced I became that Ryder and his husband were in a nonconventional relationship. It was little things Ryder slipped into the conversation about being happy to eat junk food that day and that Malcolm was already worrying that they were going to be out late.

Nothing about the conversation was overt, but reading between the lines and watching the way Malcolm continued to look back at them, I got the distinct impression there was a uniqueness to them that I could appreciate and understand. What I didn't know was if Igor had any clue. He seemed happy just to talk about games with Ryder as we walked.

As we rounded the corner to the parade's starting point, I was finally feeling more relaxed than I had since we'd arrived at the arena that morning. It was hotter than hell and sweat was already pouring down my back and face, but relief had finally washed away the last of my jealousy. Ryder wasn't anyone to be jealous of. He was more like a bouncy puppy with extra love to give, and it looked like Igor had been chosen to give extra attention to him. That was okay by me, and I was more confident that things would go back to normal.

Turning to ask Igor if he was still doing okay after the hike up the hill with his crutches, I came face-to-face with a man in blue sequin underwear, blue platform boots, and body glitter from head to toe. The only thing more surprising than the amount of glitter covering his body was the face attached to the glitter.

"Marco!" I'd met Marco at an event shortly after I'd moved to Nashville and we'd been friends since. He was bubbly and loud and over the top—as witnessed by his attire for the day—but was also one of the sweetest people I knew.

He gasped, his sparkly blue gloved hands covering his mouth. He flung them into the air and squealed my name before leaning forward and pressing his lips to mine in a searing kiss just as over the top as Marco. By the time he pulled back, I knew I'd have glitter all over me and my lips were probably as blue as his, but I was smiling.

We caught up for a few seconds, asking about how the other was doing, and he told me that he couldn't wait to introduce me to his boyfriend. I didn't have a boyfriend to introduce him to, but I thought Igor would like to meet him. I looked past the balloons that made a peacock fan around Marco's body to beckon Igor over, only to find the space he'd been standing in empty. Ryder was still there holding Boris's leash and looking uncomfortable.

"Where is Igor?" I asked, looking around the crowd.

Ryder lifted a shoulder. "He handed me the leash and left." After a long pause, he added more. "He was fine until you started playing tonsil hockey with Glitter Smurf over there. He hightailed it after that."

What the hell?

CHAPTER 11

IGOR

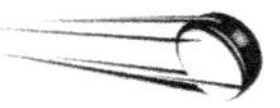

Ryder's exuberance for everything was contagious. He was always bubbly and happy and the way he so casually discussed his marriage had become a balm to my confused soul. He wasn't conflicted about his relationship or his feelings toward his husband and spoke openly about some of the ups and downs, but what I'd related to the most was how his feelings for Malcolm had taken him totally by surprise.

Of course, he'd been eighteen, not thirty-five, and had told me about an immediate spark of attraction between them, not being best friends for five years before being slammed upside the head with an unexpected crush. I still hadn't figured out how the hell that had happened, but it had and I was still working through what it all meant for me.

I'd almost broken down when Yuri had sat next to me

that morning. I'd been a breath away from telling him that I didn't think I was as straight as I'd always thought I was when he'd decided it was time for breakfast and gotten up. I'd lost my nerve by the time I'd gotten into the house. Of course, his lack of shirt and his low-slung sweats hadn't helped me get my thoughts in order. They'd gone from coming clean to anything but clean as I'd watched him make breakfast while speaking to Boris in Russian.

I'd only made out him saying something about solnishko, and the only reason it had rung a bell was because he kept calling me that. I still had no idea what it meant despite figuring out how to pronounce it well enough that I could have looked it up. There was something telling me that I didn't want to know and it had kept me from typing the word into a translator to figure it out.

Seeing Ryder climb out of his vehicle when we'd arrived at the arena had been a breath of fresh air, an escape from my thoughts that I'd desperately needed at the time. Of course, the reprieve had only lasted a few minutes. Ryder had taken one look at Yuri and had grinned knowingly at me before pulling me into a hug.

"He's the one you like?"

"I'm going to regret telling you that, aren't I?"

Ryder had shaken his head earnestly then looked around for his husband, who was still on the other side of the car talking to a giant of a man who must have been part of the football team. "Nope, I am not going to give you a hard time. The heart knows what it wants. Besides, he's cute. Very brooding, though."

My instinct had been to refute that statement, but when I'd looked over, my breath had caught in my throat at the intense stare Yuri was giving us over Trevor's head.

"I love Pride!" Ryder had bounced a little. "It's going to be even more fun now that I know you better. It's always been weird that our teams walk the parade route together but we never really talk." He'd thrown his arms around me in a hug that had felt right. It had settled nerves that had been frazzled for most of the day. Something about knowing I was going to be walking in the Pride parade while coming to terms with no longer identifying as straight was fraying my nerve endings. Today had been looming large for many reasons, but the biggest reason had come as a surprise to me. The day was feeling special in a way that I hadn't experienced before. I had really wanted to tell Yuri, yet hadn't been able to find the right words.

Ryder's hug had been grounding, his solid weight nearly pulling me down and putting my nerves back in place. The deep breath I'd managed to pull in had been long overdue and I'd wrapped my arms around him in return, not wanting the comforting contact to be over so quickly.

When we'd finally parted, Yuri had been gone and hadn't turned up again until we'd been on our way to the parade starting line. Of course, it was an uphill walk with crutches, which wasn't the most fun thing ever. Ryder kept my thoughts off the grueling pace and the padding that continued to dig into my arms with constant chatter about anything and everything. From football to his husband's daily nap times for him, nothing was off-limits, though I found myself smiling more than anything else.

Though my smiles might have had something to do with the view of Yuri's backside the entire way up the hill. I knew I was responding to Ryder, yet I wouldn't have been able to repeat a thing we talked about. I just kept watching Yuri's ass move beneath his snug tan shorts as he walked with Malcolm.

Seth Johnson strutting by wearing a pair of light blue short-shorts and sparkly rainbow platform tennis shoes wasn't enough to draw my attention from Yuri's ass for more than a brief glance. If his painted nails, makeup, and strut couldn't keep my eyes off Yuri, nothing could.

It made the walk feel less grueling, though when we stopped I had to admit I was relieved that the parade itself would be slower paced and mostly downhill from our current location. Boris continued to tug at his leash in my hand as he went from person to person looking for attention, treats, or food that had been dropped.

Malcolm walked over and talked to Ryder for a second, whispering something in his ear that had Ryder blushing. I wondered what Malcolm was telling him but my eyes caught on a flash of blue.

Blue sequin underwear with high-heeled boots that

matched. Blue balloons fanning across the man's naked back from a frame that looked like a giant fan. He was wearing more glitter on his skin than a glitter factory made in a year. There was glitter everywhere from his hair to his boots, and his hands were in the air while he screamed Yuri's name.

That had my attention in a hurry and I didn't miss how he dropped his hands directly to Yuri's face and pulled him in for a kiss in the middle of the sidewalk. Bile rose in my throat when their lips met. Who was the blue glitter monster and why had I never heard of him before?

My stomach lurched again, an unsettling combination of anger, regret, and jealousy swirling like a hurricane inside of me. I looked around us for any excuse to leave. At the front of our group, Blaise was standing with Coach Bouchard, the team's assistant coach, handing out waters. It was the perfect exit before Yuri and Blue Glitter stopped sucking face.

I shoved Boris's leash into Ryder's hand. "I go now." I was halfway to Blaise before I thought about what I'd said as I left Ryder. I'd sounded shockingly like Yuri, my Latvian accent and speech patterns coming back in a hurry when stressed, and I most certainly was stressed.

Coming to a stop next to Blaise, I held out my hand. "Water, please?"

He handed over a water and I uncapped it in time to see Indy crowd my space. "Are you okay? Igor, you look like you're about to pass out. Did you overdo it? Are you in pain?"

Holding up a hand, I downed half the bottle in one breath, then capped it and looked back at her while trying to come up with a response. I didn't know what to tell her because I was not okay, but it didn't have anything to do with my hip. Yuri was nowhere in sight and I couldn't decide if that made it better or worse. He wouldn't be coming after me. We were just friends, and friends didn't get upset when one friend kissed someone else.

"Fine. Got hot. Feel better now."

Blaise lifted a questioning eyebrow, clearly not buying my clipped words of assurance. "Want to hang out with us for a bit?" He looked over my shoulder like he was looking for someone himself, then shook his head. "Indy has just informed me that we're going to be at the front of our line." He didn't look very happy at that, but his twin sister was beaming.

Indy had left nothing at home. From her rainbow wig to her rainbow glitter platform tennis shoes, she had embraced the spirit of the event and so had her kids. Her twins were wearing rainbow overalls and rainbow sneakers, their hair tucked under hats that matched hers, and her third was still in a stroller that had been decorated with every Pride flag I'd ever seen and a few I hadn't.

Indy elbowed her twin brother playfully and a rare, genuine smile graced Blaise's lips. Then she looked around the crowd. "Where's your shadow?"

Until she looked right at me, I wasn't expecting the question to be directed at me and found myself fumbling for an answer before waving vaguely behind us. "He got distracted kissing Blue Glitter Man."

Unaware of my inner turmoil, our assistant coach spoke up. "Oh, the guy wearing the blue balloons and pretty much nothing else?"

At my nod, Bouchard continued. "I saw him. He's with a bunch of other people wearing basically the same. They make up the colors of the rainbow."

Not helping, Bouchard. Maybe Blaise knew more because he elbowed his sister and shot her a look that was not playful. Indy took one look at her brother's face and turned to grab Bouchard's elbow. "Hey, can you help me with the kids? They get into everything and since Jonathan is at the hospital today, I'm here alone." Despite his protests that he knew nothing about kids, she guided him toward where her twins were digging through a cooler of drinks.

Blaise gave me a small smile. "Sorry, he's dense. I'm pretty sure he couldn't read the room if it had a teleprompter. You okay?"

Not sure how much to say, I gave a curt nod, though without Indy and Bouchard, some of the tightness in my muscles was finally easing. Blaise had a calming way about him that made it hard to be tense around him. Maybe it was more that Blaise usually had enough anxiety for all of us.

"You want to go punch Blue Glitter Man?"

The question was delivered with such sincerity that I started to laugh. "Yeah, I kind of do."

Blaise guided me to a van the arena had supplied to hold water and Pride swag and let me sit on the side to give my leg a rest. His sister would be proud of the way he was making sure I took care of myself. "You and Yuri... are you guys..."

When Blaise's words trailed off, I knew what he was struggling to ask and shook my head. "We are not."

"Seriously?"

Now I was confused. "Seriously. We are not, have never been, a thing."

Blaise sank down beside me and studied my face for an unnervingly long time. "But you want something?"

Looking over at him, I had no idea how to answer. This was Blaise, the most anxious man I'd ever met. He was normally so keyed up he shook. I'd watched him bobble everything from a pen to a water bottle to his laptop on more than one occasion, yet he was finding the courage to ask me about my relationship with Yuri without fumbling over the words or his thoughts. I really must have looked bad.

"No? Yes? Fuck, Blaise, I do not know." On a sigh, I rested my head against the seat behind me. "I am... I was... I thought I was at least... straight. But—"

A slobbery black-and-brown face landed on my lap and big brown eyes looked up into mine.

"You feel things for Yuri." Ryder finished the sentence for me and sat down on the other side of Blaise. "Ryder Ward." He stuck his hand out to Blaise. "I play for the Pride." He pointed to the giant lion logo on his shirt.

Blaise couldn't seem to make heads or tails of the new arrival and gawked awkwardly for a second before shaking his hand. "Uh, hi. Blaise Emory, Assistant Director of Hockey Operations."

A giant smile lit up Ryder's face. "Nice to meet you." Then he turned back to me. "Yuri's looking all over for you. It won't be long till he finds you. I just found you faster because I asked Hulk here to find you."

"Hulk?" Blaise and I asked together.

"I don't know his name. You just dropped him with me and ran."

"Boris. Though I kind of like Hulk more." I fished a water out of a cooler behind us and uncapped it. I didn't have Boris's bowl with me, so I just started pouring it near his mouth and watched in awe as he did an impressive job lapping up nearly every drop. The rest of it he managed to spray on the three of us. Judging by the laughs beside me, I didn't think the two minded too much.

Ryder waited to speak until Boris had stopped drinking, stuck his head under the trickle of water, and then shaken it off on us. "Think Da—Malcolm would believe that I've had a bath already today?"

Blaise snort-laughed but my jaw hung open as little bits of confusing conversations over the last week began making a lot more sense. I'd known there was something unique about the relationship Ryder had with Malcolm since Malcolm was never far away and Ryder had cut a number of conversations short due to bedtime, but until that moment, the pieces hadn't all fallen into place.

A few of the guys on the team were in rather unique relationships. Our team captain had accidentally called his boyfriend Daddy a few too many times for it to be a joke. And when Maz growled Seth's name, Seth became putty in his hands. There was no mistaking that someone liked to push his boyfriend's buttons.

That was the piece I'd been missing, the information I'd been trying to put my finger on for the last three weeks. I liked to push Yuri's buttons because I liked to hear him growl. I liked when he got frustrated with me, but I always pulled back and apologized before I actually made him mad. And damn did I like the way he smiled at me when I apologized.

Lost in my thoughts, I almost missed the way Ryder's cheeks turned pink with embarrassment and how Blaise ended up being the one who sat a little taller and spoke with more confidence. "Good luck with that. I don't think it's going to work."

Ryder blew a raspberry, his color quickly returning to normal, then sighed dramatically. "He's so picky."

"How the fuck is it that I have made so many kinky friends and no one speaks of it? Maybe I would know before now that I like Yuri and I like to make him nuts because it makes my dick hard as a rock and very horny. Does not matter he is a man. He makes me crazy!"

Ryder and Blaise looked at me like I'd become an alien. Blaise turned a frightening shade of red, but Ryder started to laugh. "TMI, dude. TMI. But I'm glad you figured it out. Now what are you going to do about it?"

I threw my hands in the air and pushed myself to standing. I could no longer sit in the van; my body needed to move. "Fuck if I know. How do you tell your best friend that you do not know what you are anymore but know you are not straight?"

CHAPTER 12

YURI

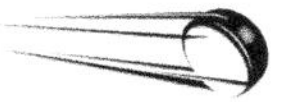

Ryder turned on his heel and left, still holding Boris's leash. I figured he was going to find Igor, but I still hadn't processed what he was trying to tell me.

Fucking English speakers talked too damn fast and used too many sayings.

What was tonsil hockey and who was Glitter Smurf?

I turned to Marco. "Did you understand what he said?"

Marco had his bottom lip between his teeth, worrying it uncomfortably. "Uh, yeah. I think he just told me that I made a mess for you."

"Marco!" He had not answered my question and was instead talking around the problem. "What does he mean? Who is Glitter Smurf? And what is tonsil hockey?"

Opening his mouth, Marco pointed toward the back of

his throat. "Tonsils. You know those things in the back of your throat? A lot of kids have them removed when they are young." He stopped and shook his head in clear frustration. "Wait, *what* tonsils are is not important. What *is* important is that it's an analogy for kissing when tongues are involved."

"There was no tongue." *Why did Americans have to use such ridiculous sayings?*

Marco placed his hands on my shoulders and shook me. "Yuri, listen to me. Focus on the meaning, not the words."

Easy to say when you did not have to think about almost every word said because it was not your native language.

"He called me a Smurf. A little blue cartoon from way back when. Kinda funny, honestly, but again, not the point. What is important, once again, is that he told you Igor got upset when he saw us kissing."

"That is ridiculous. Igor does not have reason to be upset. Igor likes women. Many women. Big women, small women, tall women, short women, blond women, ginger women. Igor likes *all* women."

Marco pinched the bridge of his nose and let a nasally growl escape before using his hands to gesture in front of him and accentuate the point he was trying to make. "Maybe so, but I am pretty sure you were just told that there is a tall brown-haired, brown-eyed Russian goalie he has feelings for."

My mouth parted to tell Marco that the words he said still didn't make sense, but I knew that wasn't true. His words did make sense. I just couldn't make them make sense with what I'd always known about Igor.

"Me?" I pointed to myself, my eyebrows and voice rising in shock.

"Ding, ding, ding! We have a winner!"

"Fuck you." My voice lacked bite, my head too confused to really care about Marco's sarcasm.

He waggled his finger in front of my face. "Ah, ah, ah, not anymore. I have a boyfriend, and *you* have an admirer." His hands landed on his hips, and he popped the left one out and leveled me with a stare. There was the sassy man I knew so well, and at least he had his attitude back as well. "Now, what are you going to do about it?"

My mind went completely blank. I had no idea what I was going to do.

Marco let out a sigh. "You are going to go find him. You have"—he pulled a cell phone out and all I could think was that I really didn't want to know where he'd been keeping that thing—"an hour before the parade starts. Go find your secret admirer." His hands landed on my shoulders, but instead of shaking, he turned me around and pushed me in the direction Ryder had gone. "Go, my dense little Russian matryoskha. Find him!"

What the hell did matryoskhas have in common with me? I didn't have time to ask. I might not have had a clue what I was doing, but I knew that Marco was right about one thing: I needed to find Igor. If there was any truth to what Ryder had insinuated and Marco had translated for me, the two of us had a lot to talk about and not much time to do so before the parade started.

After asking five or six people if they'd seen Igor, I finally thought to call for my dog. He was well trained and I knew he'd respond to my voice. "Boris!"

His name was barely out of my mouth when he barked and I turned to where I'd heard him. "Boris!" Another bark, that time dead in front of me, so I picked up the pace and jogged toward where I'd heard him. I found Boris, Igor, Ryder, and Blaise by a van at the front of the group.

Ryder was still holding Boris's leash and he and Blaise were standing on either side of Igor.

Ryder looked around me. "Where's Glitter Smurf?"

Igor stifled a laugh but Blaise didn't bother hiding his. He snorted, then shook his head. "I really need to see Blue Glitter Smurf Man."

"Well, he left some of his Smurfiness on his lips for proof of his existence." Ryder pointed to my face as he spoke.

Igor flinched like he'd been slapped and I made to quickly wipe my lips. The back of my hand came away blue and glittered. *Fuck.*

Ryder leaned toward Igor's ear. "You can walk with Mal and me if you want."

Igor's mouth parted and I knew I couldn't wait for him to respond. "Can we talk? Please?"

Igor's mouth shut and he stared at me for a long time, then looked between Ryder and Blaise and eventually back to me. The indecision on his face worried me and the amount of time he took before finally nodding had my stomach tied in knots.

When he took a few steps toward me, I thought I was going to throw up from relief that he was at least willing to talk to me.

Ryder stepped over to Igor and handed him Boris's leash. "You have your phone, right?" Igor nodded. "Great. Call us if you need us. We'll be close. I'm going to go try to find Glitter Smurf for Blaise to see." He patted Boris's head. "Okay, Hulk, I'm leaving you here. Don't let Yuri hurt Igor."

Boris barked like he totally understood what Ryder had said and I was left to try to make sense of everything that had happened in the last ten minutes. It was like people had been body snatched since we'd arrived at the arena. Marco telling me Igor liked me, talk about Smurfs and kiss hockey and matryoskha dolls, and now my dog got called Hulk. Sometimes I missed Russia, if only because I understood the language and the meanings of things better.

At least Igor was smiling when Ryder and Blaise left. While the smile didn't reach his eyes, it was better than the conflicted expression he'd had a minute earlier. We found an alley that hadn't been taken over by the parade or parade goers and ducked in for privacy.

"You have talked with Ryder much lately."

Igor nodded, though he offered no words to me.

Fuck, the two of us had always had easy conversation. He was the person I didn't have to worry what I said to. If Marco was right, though, the last ten minutes had changed everything. And now here we were in an alleyway in downtown Nashville and things were still changing.

My brain was as blank as it had been when Marco had tried to tell me that Igor liked me as more than a friend.

"What do you want, Yuri?" Igor crossed his arms over his chest and waited for a response.

This was when I was supposed to talk things out, but my mind had turned into a muddled grumble of English and Russian words I was having trouble sorting out. "You act weird lately. What is weird?"

Igor looked anywhere but at me, his eyes finally coming to rest on the brick wall behind my head. "Things have changed."

Despite having Marco's words still fresh in my head, my brain refused to believe he was right. Igor was straight. He always had been and had given no indication otherwise. "Did I do something to upset you?"

He scoffed. "That is complicated."

We were getting nowhere. Time was ticking down to the start of the parade, and we were eventually going to be missed. Boris wasn't going to stand being in an alley for long while there were countless people a short distance away that could give him attention. "Enlighten me."

Igor's eyes widened and for a moment I thought I had fucked up another saying, but then he gave a light hum of surprise. "You did not fuck that saying up." His face fell as quickly as it had risen. "My brain is so confused. So many thoughts and feelings. You are my friend."

Nodding slowly, I tried to figure out where to go with that statement. He wasn't giving me much to go on. "I am. You are my friend. I am worried because you are quiet. Usually, you talk and talk and do stupid things that make me crazy."

His cheeks flushed at my words and I had to blink a few times before I believed I was really seeing bashfulness on Igor's face. "You are fun to tease."

"I am glad you find it fun. I get gray hair telling you, 'No, no, no.' You make me feel old. Could have been in Russia. Could eat Babushka's fancy cake. Instead I get a roommate who runs away from me and friend who drives me insane."

Igor stretched his neck from side to side. "I am not trying to ignore you. I might try to drive you insane, though. You make it easy."

"Tebe nuzhno nakazat." He was just proving how insane he drove me by telling me he'd been *trying* to drive me nuts.

"What does that mean?"

"It means you need punished. You deserve punishment for trying to drive me crazy."

Igor's eyes dilating and him sucking in a sharp breath

had not been the response I'd expected. I was becoming more certain that someone was playing a joke on me. A confusing and cruel joke but a joke nonetheless.

"I'm sorry for pushing. I know I get under your skin." His eyes strayed back to the brick wall above my head and he dragged a hand down his face, scratching at his light beard. In the tiny alley, the noise was amplified, the rough sound of his beard against his blunt nails sending goose bumps down my spine. "I hope you are not upset with me."

"Not upset." *Not even a little.* Shit, the last thing I was feeling was anger. At least not at him. There might have been some anger directed at myself, my dick in particular. This was not the time for it to go hard. Despite my brain telling it to behave, between what Marco had said, how Blaise and Ryder were acting, and Igor's words, it had decided that Igor was flirting with me.

Igor visibly relaxed. His shoulders dropped and he let out a sigh of relief. "Good."

"Do you ignore me because you like to drive me crazy?"

He actually laughed at my question. "Damn, that would make things easier. I have *avoided* you, not ignored. And I have done so because I am confused. I do not know what to make of my thoughts."

This conversation was going in circles and I needed to bring it around to the point quickly. "And earlier when you left suddenly?"

"You were kissing Blue Glitter Man!" Igor forced the words out with such venom I had to stop myself from stepping backward.

"Marco is friend."

"You kiss friends now?" His eyebrow went up and light reflected in his eyes, turning them the color of freshly cut ice.

"Some, yes."

His fists clenched the handles of his crutches tightly enough his knuckles turned white. "You do not kiss me!"

Frustration grew inside me and my hands flew around as I tried to gather my thoughts. "Would you want me to kiss you? Kiss you like that?" I threw my hand behind me, trying to indicate that I was talking about the way I'd kissed Marco and smacking the brick wall in the process. There would be blood on my knuckles and it was going to hurt like a bitch later, but for now it only served to increase my anger at everything.

The kiss Marco and I had shared was nothing more than a kiss between friends, two gay friends, with a long history of encounters both sexual and platonic. The kiss, heightened by the mood of our surroundings, had meant nothing to either of us but it was not a kiss I would give a straight friend. A light peck on the cheek was out of character for me, so I would definitely not allow tongues to get involved if I happened to brush my lips against a straight man's.

"Yes!" Igor spat the word so fast we were both taken

aback. He shook his head then spoke again, his voice coming out quiet and unsure. "Maybe. I think. My brain, it hurts. It's confused. It wants things that it's not wanted in the past."

Maybe Marco had been right after all. The problem was I had no idea how to gently ask if Igor was discovering he wasn't so straight. "Things with men?"

"Yes and no." Igor looked completely away from me, focusing his attention on my dog instead.

My brain knew I should tread lightly. It wasn't hard to see that Igor was a mess of emotions, especially since he was struggling to keep his eyes on me. He was normally loud and confident, so watching him dodge my eyes should have sent warning bells through my body to be gentle with him. My heart was thudding so hard, though, that it drowned out my brain's cautionary advice and I dived in, desperate for answers.

"What does that mean? Were you jealous? Is that why you left?" I worried that my tone had been harsh, but since I'd barely heard myself, I didn't think it was possible for the whisper to have sounded anything but awestruck, maybe a little hopeful.

Color rose in Igor's face, a red I'd never seen on him filling the apples of his cheeks and spreading downward to his neck and under his collar. "Maybe. A bit. Probably. Yes." He waved a hand in front of his face like he could brush away the thoughts.

Unfortunately for him, his discomfort wasn't enough to stop my brain from working in overdrive and demanding answers that were not appropriate for the current space or time. "Maybe? Yes? Igor, what does that mean? I need clear. My brain does not understand."

He let out a sigh that told me he did not want to be having this conversation, but he was the one who'd walked away, so we were going to have it.

"Funny, because I do not understand it either! Until a few weeks ago, I was straight. No thoughts of driving any man crazy. No thoughts of wanting to make any man happy. No thoughts about when you kiss other men. Now my brain doesn't understand it. It's not as clear. I'm not able to just ignore *things*."

It felt like the air had been sucked out of the alley we were standing in. Taking a breath was harder than it should have been. Igor had chosen words I didn't have to decipher. I understood the meaning of them perfectly well, but now my brain was refusing to believe that I'd heard him right.

I knew just a few feet away thousands of people were standing, laughing, walking, getting ready for one of my favorite days of the year, but they might as well have been on the other side of the state for all I was aware of them or the noise they were making.

"You are bi?"

Igor lifted a shoulder. "I don't know. Maybe?"

Biting my lip, I debated asking a question I hadn't dared think thirty minutes prior, but it now felt like a boulder pressing on my chest that would only be removed when the question was out. "You." The word cracked as it came out and I needed to clear my throat before I could continue. "You like me?"

Igor's face turned redder than it was after a shoot-out and his shoulders lifted so high they nearly touched his ears. "I think."

The admission should have sent a wave of relief through me. I should have been able to breathe more easily, except I couldn't. I had no idea how to tell Igor that, while I was attracted to men, I wasn't attracted to just any man. It was one thing to tell someone in the lifestyle what I was looking for, it was something very different to tell someone who wasn't. It was why I normally avoided anything more than casual sex with someone outside of the BDSM scene. Talking about kinks was awkward and my limited English made in depth discussions difficult.

Add to that, Igor's knowledge of himself was turning on its head, and he'd admitted that he had feelings for me, so I had to approach the situation with care. Simply telling him that he'd made me hornier than a teenager the last three weeks wouldn't help anything and would likely give him the wrong impression.

Yes, Igor was hot. Yes, he pushed my buttons more than any play partner I'd ever had before, but those things did not mean that Igor and I were compatible. I needed a submissive. I needed someone who liked punishments and pushing limits. Igor liked pushing limits, but that didn't mean he was into punishments or wanted to be my submissive.

Fuck my life.

"You drive me crazy, Igor Ozols." I said the words with a smile, hoping that they would be enough to help him calm down. His coloring was still a long way from what could be considered normal. Softening my voice, I said the first thing that came to mind. "Thank you for telling me. I am happy you trust me to tell. It was really brave of you."

I needed to be careful what I said because I was skirting the line of words I'd use to praise a nervous sub.

He scoffed, though it sounded a lot more amused than hurt. I was going to take that as a win. "I do not know how brave it was when I ran away instead of hitting Blue Glitter Man."

I laughed. "Marco. His name is Marco."

Igor's eyes fell from mine and he glanced toward the entrance of the alley. Ryder, Malcolm, and Blaise were standing there, Ryder holding tightly to his husband's hand and doing his best to stare menacingly at me. We'd been at the Super Bowl game in February and I'd seen Ryder face down guys twice his size without blinking, but gripping his husband's hand and wearing a bright yellow T-shirt with a rainbow lion on it, he didn't look very dangerous.

We'd officially run out of time, though I needed to

make sure I said something before we left our little private bubble. "There is much to talk about later. I feel things for you too, but it's just not that simple." I really wished it were that simple.

CHAPTER 13

IGOR

The last thing Yuri said to me before we left the alley had stayed with me the entire way through the parade. I hadn't known how much I'd needed to hear those words from him until he'd said them. Simply knowing that I was not alone in how I felt had me feeling like a balloon ready to float away. The one thing keeping me from doing just that was the weight of his parting words. *It's not that simple.*

No relationship was easy. Seth and Maz, Trevor and Brax, they had all had their share of struggles, especially in the beginning, but they'd made it work. I had a feeling that his worries were bigger than working together or the world of hockey. The way he'd delivered the statement with finality made me think it was bigger than friendship or a worry that whatever feelings we had would self-destruct. This was bigger than all of that, but I just didn't understand what he meant. That worry was always there to pull me down when I got too comfortable with Yuri's admission.

The distance he'd put between us when we'd left the alley and quickly found Seth, Maz, Trevor, and Brax hadn't helped my worries. While I'd wanted to be frustrated with him for avoiding me, I had quickly discovered that I'd felt more relieved than upset. I'd needed space and I suspected he did too. We'd said a lot in a short period of time and then we'd had to leave that little protected space and be engulfed by a crowd of people. I didn't think I'd have been able to act casual if Yuri had hovered around me like he had been for the last three weeks.

A single growl or stern look from him would have had my heart rate picking up and my dick taking notice and that was definitely not a family friendly event like this was supposed to be. We weren't at Leather Week; we were at Nashville Pride. We were expected to be gay or allies to the community but not in your face about it. Sporting an erection in the middle of the parade would definitely be way outside of the boundaries.

Ryder and Blaise refusing to leave my side the entire day had also been a much-needed support. Once the words were out there, I hadn't been ready to talk more about my feelings toward Yuri. Ryder had nearly skipped beside me, waving to people along the parade route and occasionally bouncing over to give someone a hug or take a picture but returning to my side immediately after.

Blaise had interacted with the crowd less and appeared happy next to me. Then again, I was pretty sure he would've happily ridden in the passenger seat of the swag van had it not been for everything that had happened between Yuri and me before the parade. Either way it was nice to have them close by, especially as our entourage crossed the finish line of the parade.

"Igor?" The unfamiliar voice calling my name had me turning to see who was there. My eyes must have given away the warring shock and anger roiling inside me because both Ryder and Blaise quickly swung around to see who had gotten my attention.

Ryder narrowed his green eyes and stared at the man who had been the catalyst of the events before the parade. "Glitter Smurf."

"Ryder Andrew Ward." Malcolm had come up behind us and surprised us all with his stern words.

Blue Glitter Man—Yuri had called him Marco—only smiled and waved Malcolm off. "It's fine. Honestly. I probably deserve it, and I think it's funny."

Ryder didn't back down or respond to either his husband or the man in blue and I wasn't exactly sure what I should say or do. Thankfully, the decision was taken out of my hands when he continued without waiting for an acknowledgement from any of us.

"I wanted to apologize for any discomfort my actions caused earlier. Yuri and I are friends from way back."

He tugged at a red balloon bouquet attached to a man

beside him. "I'd actually gone over to him to introduce him to my boyfriend, Paul."

A man dressed exactly like Marco, only in red instead of blue, gave an awkward wave. "Hi."

My eyes bounced between the two of them as I tried to make heads or tails of what he'd said, though I was going to blame being totally distracted and nearly blinded by the sun reflecting off the copious amounts of glitter and bare skin for my lack of coherent thoughts. Blaise found his voice before I got my mind back on track. "How will you ever get all that glitter off?"

Somehow, Paul's cheeks turned even redder at the question. "It's an art, really. And it involves a lot of baby oil and scrubbing."

Ryder snickered beside me. "Kinky."

His response broke the awkwardness of the situation and I found myself laughing. "Get your mind out of the gutter."

Marco gave me a weak smile. "I really just wanted to tell you I'm sorry for making things awkward for you or making you uncomfortable. I honestly had no idea something was going on between the two of you."

I kneaded the back of my neck. "There really isn't anything going on between us. At least not yet, maybe never."

Surreal was the only way I could describe the moment. I had barely accepted that I had feelings for Yuri. Three weeks in a lifetime that had spanned three and a half decades was not very long to come to terms with being attracted to men. And now I was talking about what might or might not happen between Yuri and me with a group of guys, half of whom I didn't know well.

Malcolm cleared his throat and I was pretty sure I heard a *liar* escape him.

Marco shrugged. "Okay. I just felt like I should let you know that anything between Yuri and me has been casual at best, and nothing has happened between us in over a year." Thankfully, he didn't seem to be in the mood to push the issue but had also wanted to make sure that I knew whatever had happened between the two of them was in the past. I couldn't decide how that made me feel. I shouldn't have been jealous that Yuri had a past.

I had a past; Yuri had a past. Yuri had met some of my past girlfriends. He'd actually met more of my exes than I'd ever met of his. So why was I reacting so irrationally to meeting someone that he'd had a relationship with in the past? It wasn't like I was a saint and I certainly didn't expect Yuri to be one either, but it didn't stop the tendrils of jealousy from wrapping around me.

Lacking polite words, I nodded once and hoped like hell that they would go away quickly. Marco returned my nod, though his didn't appear as curt as mine had felt. "Go easy on him." He gave me a warm smile and hooked his boyfriend by the elbow before turning. "Have a good day!" He waved at us and somehow managed to disappear into the crowd.

Malcolm gave all three of us a stern glare that had even me squirming in my spot. "Be nice." We all nodded, though Ryder was grinning at his husband as he left.

"He's so serious sometimes." Ryder gave an exaggerated huff, then turned to us. "Okay, now that the awkward stuff is over, let's go watch the drag show!" He grabbed both our hands and started pulling. After the Drag Bus incident of last fall when Seth Johnson had booked the tour bus and managed to convince his siblings to join us, there was no way a few drag queens performing on a stage would surprise me. No one had been aware that a traveling drag queen from the UK would be performing that day, and nothing had prepared us for the events of that afternoon. No matter what happened at this show, it would be tame in comparison to the bus.

Of course, I hadn't taken into account that I was a member of the queerest hockey team in the NHL. That obviously meant that the majority of the team was around the stage hooting and hollering, many of the guys with a beer in their hand as they enjoyed the show. Yuri was there too, sitting on the other side of the lawn with Brax, Tapio, and Bouchard. Seth and Trevor were dancing with Toby and Luc not too far away from them. Seth's sequin shoes reflected the sun as he moved and were nearly as blinding as Marco's and Paul's body glitter had been.

Ryder bounced in place as the next queen, Lady Orgazma D-lite, was announced. "I love her!"

Blaise nodded. "Did you go to the drag brunch she

hosted?"

Anything Ryder might have said in response got drowned out when a queen strutted onto the stage, big yellow wig bouncing with every step she took. Every eye on the lawn was drawn to her. From her huge yellow gemstone-encrusted stilettos to her high-cut yellow bodysuit with a gem-encrusted frill on the hips and around her ass, to the overdone makeup and massive fake lashes, Lady Orgazma D-lite demanded attention from the crowd.

"What's up, bitches!" She put a gloved hand over her bright pink lips and looked toward the announcer. "Oh shit. I think I heard this was supposed to be a family show. Am I allowed to say that?"

The crowd erupted in laughter as the announcer shook his head. "If that is the worst thing that comes from those lips of yours tonight, I think we're going to be fine."

She threw her head back, her yellow wig bouncing as she did so. "Oh, you aren't kidding. You don't know where this mouth has been. Mmm, but let me tell you, Peach's Surprise... oh, now that was a pleasant surprise!"

"Okay, family friendly, Orgazma." The announcer was laughing too hard to really try to rein her in and the crowd was eating her up.

The hair stood up on the back of my neck as my senses told me I was being watched. I glanced to the side and saw Yuri staring at me, doing nothing to hide that he was looking right at me. Maybe I should have behaved myself, but I'd never been known to be quiet or meek, no matter the circumstances, and knowing I had an audience only egged me on.

I cupped my hands around my mouth and let out a loud call. "Tell us more!"

People around us clapped and agreed and Lady Orgazma looked my way and winked. "Wouldn't you enjoy that, honey?" She took a few steps in my direction and pointed to my crutches. "Poor baby. You look like you're in pain."

Ryder elbowed me. "He might need some of your D-lite to help him feel better."

She laughed, then waggled a finger in my direction. "Unfortunately, I'm being told to keep this PG, or at least PG-13, and what I'd like to do with Cutie Pie there is nothing short of NC-17."

My laughter died off when I glanced toward Yuri to find him all-out scowling at me. If it was okay for him to kiss a man he wasn't involved with, then it was fine for me to flirt with a drag queen I hadn't seen before she was announced.

Maybe I shouldn't be pushing Yuri to get annoyed with me, but it was too much fun to poke at him. It was what I'd been doing for three weeks, and I didn't see why it would hurt doing it now. It was time to admit that I might have been relieved he'd given me space when we'd first left the alley, but with hours between then and now, I was more than a little hurt that he had been avoiding me completely. If Lady Orgazma D-lite was going to be the person that got under his skin enough that he stopped ignoring me, then bring on the flirting.

Music started to play and she gasped, turning around and jumping so that her skirt swayed and caught the light. "Oh! It's my song!"

As she bounced around on the stage, it was easy to see that she was in her element and it was just as easy to get swept up in the show. Even Blaise shed his anxiety and danced with Ryder as she performed. I did as much dancing as I could, but the crutches made anything more than swaying almost impossible. It was refreshing to let myself go and enjoy the moment, though.

As her part of the show wound down, Lady O bent forward and blew me a kiss, then pointed between Blaise and Ryder. "Take care of that sweet boy!"

My cheeks heated at being called a sweet boy, though I didn't fully understand why it made me embarrassed. She waved to the rest of the crowd and disappeared while muttering something about going to get another taste of Peach's Surprise.

We stayed through three more performers, the last being Peach Surprise herself. Dressed in head-to-toe peach, she lived up to her name. More surprising to me, Peach spotted me in the crowd immediately, then raised her voice like the pounding speakers didn't announce everything to the surrounding area. "Orgazma, your boy is just fine! Right where you left him."

She then turned her head in my direction and stage-whispered to me. "But you might not be okay if you stay there much longer. I might need to come and sweep you off your feet. Damn, Lady O was right. You're a cutie!"

Ryder giggled. "You have all the queens fawning over you! You're going to end up being spoiled rotten if you stay here after the show."

"He will not be spoiled by drag queens." Yuri had come up behind us without me seeing him moving our way. "Igor comes home with me to sleep in his bed."

Ryder gave a shake of his head that said Yuri didn't get it. "Yes, all alone in *his* bed. He could go home with Lady O or Peach's Surprise and get all sorts of wonderful care and be snuggled all night."

Not that I wanted to be snuggled by any of the queens we'd seen perform that night, but the idea of being snuggled instead of being the snuggler was appealing. Though in my daydream, the arms wrapped around me didn't belong to any of the queens we'd watched that afternoon. They were pale, slender, covered in tattoos, and deceptively strong.

Turning to face him wasn't easy, not because I didn't want to but because as soon as I put weight on my leg, I knew I'd overdone it today.

Pain radiated from my hip up my back and down my leg and made me hiss between my teeth so I didn't actually yell. All at once everything hurt, my armpits included after walking on the crutches for so long. Fuck, this was not the place to figure out I hurt like hell.

"What is wrong?" Yuri moved quickly to stand in front of me. All the frustration he'd been showing a moment earlier had been replaced with concern.

Stubborn as I was, I knew this wasn't the time to act the hero, and the truth slipped from my lips easily. "I hurt. My leg, my arms, my back. I hadn't realized until I started to move."

Yuri reached into his pocket, pulled out three Advil, and placed them in my hand. "Take these." Then he looked between Blaise and Ryder. "You two stay with Igor. I will be back." He took off before anyone could respond, quickly disappearing into the crowd.

Ryder chewed on his bottom lip. "What can we do to help?"

I downed the pills with the last of my water bottle while trying to figure out if there was anything they could do to help. The thought of sitting on one of the hard folding chairs was enough to make my stomach turn. If I managed to get down, there was no way I'd be gracefully getting up again and I really didn't want to make a scene. Admitting that I was in pain was bad enough—the last thing I wanted was to draw attention to it.

Blaise looked up from his phone. "Problem solved."

Ryder opened his mouth, probably to ask what he meant since I was wondering the same thing, only to have the question cut off by a golf cart pulling off the sidewalk. Indy's rainbow wig bouncing was the first thing I saw, followed by the concerned scowl of Yuri.

Never had I been so happy to see that grumpy face and I fought to contain my smile as the golf cart stopped in front of us. "I hear you pushed too hard today, Ozols."

My cheeks warmed in embarrassment but I hoped that between the heat of the day and the pain, no one would think anything of it. "Maybe a bit. Did not try. Turned and pain. Everywhere." When my brain was focused on more than the sentences coming out of my mouth, my words became more broken and my English less crisp. Usually I corrected myself quickly, but with the way my hip was protesting, I was more worried about having done damage to it after it had been feeling so much better than worrying about how my words sounded.

Indy gave me a soft smile, one that I'd seen her give one of her twins when she'd fallen during the parade. "We'll get you back to fighting form. I'm guessing you just need some rest. I didn't see you doing anything dangerous today. The walking at the parade was probably good for you, but I bet standing here, you locked up pretty tight."

She led me over to the back seat of the golf cart. I was thankful I didn't have to maneuver myself into the front seat since the back allowed me to ungracefully collapse into the seat in a half-slouched stance that didn't hurt my leg too much.

I really hoped that Indy was right and all I needed was some rest because this was a bitch.

Yuri reached around and grabbed my crutches while Indy got back behind the wheel. "Hold on tight!" We didn't get any more warning before Indy put her foot on the pedal and started the bouncy trip back to the sidewalk, where it was at least a little smoother.

Indy spouted off care directions to Yuri as she drove through the crowds of people, periodically pressing the small horn or yelling at someone who didn't move fast enough. "Sorry. Gotta get back. Willow just bit Brett. Irvine has no idea what to do with the kids, Toby and Luc are trying to keep them entertained, and Nora's hungry. We've got to break Willow of this biting thing."

I had a hard time keeping everyone straight. Imagining Coach Cunningham trying to take care of Indy's three kids had me laughing in spite of my pain. At least I could see Toby and Jean-Luc trying to help out. As two of the younger members of the Grizzlies, they were balls of endless energy, especially Toby.

She stopped by Yuri's SUV and let us get out of the cart before pulling forward in a wide U-turn. "Remember, anti-inflammatories, alternate heat and ice, gentle stretches, and rest, rest, rest. He's still got some of the painkillers from after surgery, right?"

Yuri barely had the *Y* of "yes" formed and Indy had pulled away, waving to us as she sped off toward the exit. "Awesome. Use those if needed. Later, guys! Call me if you need something!"

"—es." Yuri finished as she turned the corner that would take her back to street level. "We do not call Indy."

At least Yuri and I agreed on that.

CHAPTER 14

YURI

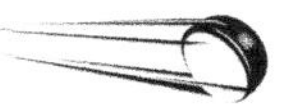

Igor actually let me help him into the car. While his cooperation pleased me, the fact that he didn't argue told me he was in a lot of pain. Just his agreement to let Indy drive us here was enough to let me know that.

We didn't say much as I wove through the various police roadblocks that had been set up after we'd arrived. I had to explain to more than one police officer that we were leaving unexpectedly due to an injury, and the going was slow until we reached the highway.

I made it to highway speeds and Igor finally chuckled, though I could hear the strain in his voice. "First day the highway's easier to navigate than the city."

"True words." People who weren't familiar with Nashville never believed me when I said the highways were a nightmare most days.

With the engine finally moving, the interior cooled quickly and Igor gave a light sigh before drifting off to sleep. Yeah, he definitely was not feeling well, though I had to assume that the Advil I'd given him must have just kicked in if he was able to drift off in the car. He slept so hard I debated whether I should wake him up when we pulled into my driveway. The garage was climate controlled, so he would stay cool if I parked inside, but I worried that he'd cramp up even more if he stayed.

Thankfully, I didn't have to make a decision because Igor woke up when I put the car in park. He rubbed his eyes and stretched, then winced when he pushed himself upright.

"I come get you." I got out of the car before he could object and ran to his side. To my surprise, he had only unbuckled his seat belt by the time I got around to him. He watched me pull his crutches from the back seat, then open his car door, and all he did was sigh as he moved his body around.

After three weeks, he was able to get in and out of the car without thought. His good leg was easily able to support him and after the first grueling day of PT, he'd been able to use his bad leg to help with his balance. The first bit of hope I'd had since I saw him wince on the lawn back at the Pride festival was when he still used his leg to steady himself without showing pain.

Then he reached for the crutches and looked as though

he wanted to crawl in a hole and die. "Two steps. Bed is not far."

He muttered a few curses under his breath and made his way slowly up the two steps leading to the kitchen, then with slow and deliberate movements, made his way to the bedroom. Igor looked longingly toward the bathroom as he peeled his shirt over his head, hissing as he moved.

"A shower sounds good, but I hurt so damn much."

His strip was slow and unintentionally sensual. I had to glance away from his rippling back and the tattoo on his shoulder of his old dog's paw prints. The feelings I'd had before that day were complicated enough. Learning that Igor was discovering an attraction to men—and me specifically—had those crazy feelings and inappropriate thoughts multiplying like naughty rabbits in my brain.

When I finally convinced myself to turn around, Igor had stripped down to his boxer briefs and was standing by the bed, his bad leg slightly bent but bearing weight just fine, while he pulled his wallet and phone from his pockets.

"What are you doing?" It was impossible to hide the way my voice rose in surprise at the way he'd casually dropped his pants in front of me, and I knew I was openly gawking at him. Dammit, the last thing I needed was more food for the bunnies. *Why hadn't he taken the stuff out of his pockets before taking his pants off?*

Igor didn't know what I was looking for in a man, so it

was wrong of me to let him see I was interested in him yet. It was definitely wrong to lick my lips at the bulge in the front of his underwear when he turned around, yet there I stood like an idiot, wetting my lips and wishing I could wrap them around his cock. Yeah, I'd turned into a perv, and it was all his fault. Or maybe Marco's fault. I was going to blame Marco for this one, and there was nothing he could do to stop me.

"Debating how much it would hurt to get a shower right now."

Talking about him in pain at least had my brain kicking back into gear and away from sucking him off. "You said you hurt, but you put weight on your leg. Are you okay?"

"Oh. Yeah. Once the Advil kicked in, my leg felt fine. I honestly think I'd been standing too long, moved too fast, and it locked up for a few minutes. What's really hurting right now are my arms. Which makes showering hard."

Focusing on Igor's arms was a lot safer than focusing on him naked in the shower. "Why arms?"

He started to shrug, but his face contorted in pain. "Fuck. I was being careful with my leg. The crutches dug into my armpits and holding onto the handles so long..." He didn't finish the sentence but held his hands up to show me how they were shaking.

"Oof, that sucks."

"Yes. Sucks to be me. It's like arm day gone wrong."

I snorted a laugh, but only because we'd all been there

before, unintentionally going too hard on a muscle group only to feel it for days after. And no matter how badly it hurt on day one and two, day three was always the worst. My problem was leg day the first day of summer training. For days, I would walk around the house like I'd ridden a horse for hours, when in reality I'd just neglected doing any training over the summer break and my muscles were pissed at me.

It shouldn't have come as a surprise to either of us that Igor hurt. Since he'd had surgery, we hadn't been many places. We'd gone to the store a few times and to PT and home, and that was about it. Those trips were nothing compared to walking from the arena to Eighth Street, then down to First Street, then over to the river to the field by the Lion's stadium for the performances. That was hours of walking and miles traveled when he'd only been accustomed to walking the length of a store.

"Warm water in shower might help?"

"That was what I wanted to do. And I have been sweating all day and have sunscreen on me and just feel gross."

"Then you should shower." *Why was the stubborn man stalling?* The warm water on his stiff muscles, cleaning the sweat and grime off his body—all of it would make him feel better.

He shook out his shorts and dropped them in the basket at the foot of his bed. "Mmm. Would be nice. But my arms."

My eyebrows drew together in silent question and Igor just shook his head and chuckled at me. "How will I wash my hair and my body? My arms hurt so much I'm trying to decide how to get to the bathroom. The shower is a whole different beast."

Understanding dawned on me. "Oh. Right." I fell silent as I thought, then said the words I knew I'd regret before I'd finished the sentence. "I can wash hair and body for you."

Igor nearly fell over in surprise, thankfully toward the bed and not onto the floor, and he caught himself just before actually falling. "You can *what*?"

There was a chance that I could backtrack my offer, pretend that I'd said something else entirely, but I knew how miserable it was to be hot and feel dirty and not shower before climbing into bed. Since he was in pain and unable to do it himself, the most logical thing was for me to help. We were friends, no matter what our current messy feelings were telling us. Friends helped friends.

"I can wash your hair and body." *Just not the parts between your legs*. I was going to avoid that like a twelve-year-old avoided cooties. Absolutely, positively no touching Igor's junk with my hands.

I looked down at my cock. *Absolutely none.*

Igor's light eyes studied me closely, looking for the trap, trying to figure out how to get out of the current predicament. I saw the moment he finally gave up and his shoulders sagged in defeat. "Are you serious?"

"As heart attack. I am hot too. I planned to go upstairs and shower when you were comfortable. It is not fair to make you not shower if you want to." He really did deserve a shower, and many rewards.

If he were my sub, I'd have him bathed and stretched out on the bed while I—Shit, no, I needed to wipe that thought from my mind. He was not my sub; he was not my boyfriend. While we had talked about it, I knew we hadn't reached any sort of agreement on a relationship and I shouldn't even allow the thought to take root. Yet it had, and Igor stretched out on my bed writhing beneath me while I took my time nipping at his skin and sucking little bruises on his chest and shoulders would be an amazing sight.

Now that I'd allowed the thought to take root, I couldn't let it go. That was going to get me in as much trouble as allowing myself to touch his dick in the shower would.

Where could I find a supplier of brain bleach? There was a possibility that it was the only way I'd get my wits about me and make it through the shower I'd offered.

Igor made to squeeze the bridge of his nose but stopped with his arm bent at a ninety degree angle, then cursed under his breath before he finally nodded. "Yes. Shower. Thank you. I feel disgusting, but..."

"Your arms, I know." For added reassurance, though maybe boundary was a better word for it, I clarified. "But they do not hurt down. You can clean"—like the awkward boy afraid of cooties that I was proving to be, I gestured toward his crotch—"down there. I will do rest for you."

At least my awkwardness made Igor laugh and finally relent. "Okay, as long as I wash *down there*." He gestured with his hand at his underwear, clearly poking fun at me. I couldn't even dare to hope yet that there'd be a day in the future that I'd punish him for getting smart with me, so I kept the thought to myself, walked over to his bad side, and wrapped his arm around my waist.

"Use me as crutch. I can hold you. It is only a few feet and your arms will not strain as much."

Igor actually sagged against me, relief clear in every one of his muscles despite his overused arms still shaking against my waist. "Thanks, Yuri."

His words made a dopey grin spread on my face that I tried hard to hide. I didn't do dopey, I didn't do giddy, yet for Igor I was beginning to think I might. "You are welcome."

We moved slowly into the bathroom and I let him work his underwear down while I stripped. We'd been naked together countless times, but even without the earlier conversation, this moment would have felt different. This was way more intimate than being in a locker room after a grueling game while sweating your ass off in fifty pounds of gear. This was entering the same shower space to help the man who had been keeping my dick hard for weeks shower.

There was no way this wasn't going to be awkward. I

wasn't foolish enough to try to convince myself otherwise, especially as I continued to sneak looks at him as he slowly removed his underwear.

Blyad.

Things were only going to get more uncomfortable as my dick swelled in my underwear before I'd even managed to get my pants down. I was already second-guessing my resolve to help Igor shower, but I'd given my word and I planned to keep it, even though it very well might kill me in the process.

Igor was more focused on getting the water temp right and hobbling into the shower than watching me strip down. I wasn't sure if it made me feel better or worse. Did I really want him focusing on me like I was on him? That would only make things more awkward, but being ignored was a blow to my ego that shouldn't factor into the current situation at all.

Damn irrational thoughts.

I finished undressing. My dick was still hard but there was nothing I could do about it. The thing really did have a mind of its own that had nothing to do with what I wanted. Standing there buck naked dwelling on it wasn't making it go down and was only making the entire situation more awkward.

This was shaping up to be the least sexy shower I'd ever shared. That was saying a lot since I'd been showering with hockey players since I was fifteen, and house league showers were about the least sexy place to be. At least the gross shower rooms and strong stench that was completely unique to hockey had always been enough to keep even my teenage libido in check.

An oversized shower with dual shower heads, a glass door directly across from a giant mirror, and a pristine marble-tiled stall was most certainly not a smelly locker room, and Igor was most certainly not a pimply-faced asshole whom I tolerated on ice. He was a gorgeous man who, until nine that morning, I'd thought I'd known inside and out. He was funny and kind and pushed everyone's limits with a smile on his face that made it nearly impossible to be mad at him, even if he was leaning over a toilet bowl puking his guts out after eating bad fast food.

Igor was tall with lean muscles, a brilliant smile, and contagious laughter. He was kindness and caring wrapped up in a package of milky white skin and light eyes that took in everything. Including the erection that was sticking out in front of me like a beacon guiding the way... to him.

Awkward, party of two.

I swallowed and stepped inside the shower, swiping the soap from the ledge as I went. *I can do this.* The spray Igor was under hit my body and I yelped at the heat and jumped backward. "Fuck! Do you have skin left?"

Igor chuckled as he stretched his neck and rotated his shoulders under the water. "Loosens muscles."

"Ice baths help too."

"Always hated ice baths." At least he reached forward

and turned the dial cooler. Cooler, not cool. It was still hotter than I preferred, but at least I wasn't worried about second-degree burns any longer. And yet my dick had not gone down.

Igor continued to roll his shoulders and try to stretch out his sore muscles while I lathered my hands. I'd forgotten a washcloth, and now that I was soaked, I wasn't going to traipse across the bathroom to dig one out of the closet. My hands were going to have to suffice, even though they'd be in direct contact with Igor's body.

When my hands were properly lathered, I ran them across his back and shoulders. Igor let out an immediate hum and his head lolled backward slightly. It would have been so easy to let him lean against me while I focused on his chest, abs, and arms. His crease wrapping around my dick was nowhere in my thoughts. Neither was how amazing it would feel as he wiggled and writhed if I plucked his nipples.

Fuck. There I'd gone again.

Igor's long sigh finally pulled me out of my head and my focus turned toward my hands, which had begun to knead at hard balls of muscle in Igor's shoulders. "You are very tense."

"Your hands feel like magic right now. Jesus, I didn't know my upper body could get so sore from crutches!" I continued to dig at his shoulders until I felt the muscles give and Igor grunt in surprise. To my dick, it was way too close to a sound he'd make during sex, and it warned me that I needed to move this shower along. A massage was not the same thing as helping in the shower.

I pulled away to lather my hands again and returned to my task of washing Igor. His biceps and forearms were just as tight as his back, and I made a mental note to send Indy a text to ask about having one of the massage therapists work his muscles loose. For now, it was going to be on me but hopefully not while we were in the shower.

When his arms were clean, I focused on his chest and stomach, making sure to stay well above the belly button. It wasn't until I'd knelt down to wash his legs that I realized I'd made a grave mistake. Igor's dick was just as hard as mine, sticking out from his body with a slight curve toward his right hip. His balls were shaved smooth and only a small trimmed patch of pubic hair was above his cock. His dick was inches from my mouth and tempting me to lean into it. It wouldn't take more than a small adjustment on either of our parts to bring his dick in contact with my lips.

"It doesn't understand that you are being nice. Sorry." His words said one thing, but his voice said something else entirely. That was when I knew I needed to move quickly. If I stayed that close to Igor or his dick any longer, I would act on impulse and regret it later.

Standing, I headed over to the second shower head and stepped under, my cock pulsating as the water ran over it. "You can clean rest."

Igor grunted, but I had my focus completely on my

own shower, and my eyes avoided Igor. Of course, they settled on the bathroom mirror, barely visible through the fog that the shower had caused but visible enough that I could see Igor grip his balls as he began to clean himself. The dark shadows suggested enough for my brain to fill in what the fog blocked out. If I touched myself, even to wash, there was a better than zero percent chance I'd come on the spot.

In the grand scheme of things, it didn't much matter since I'd have to wash up after I came anyway. In my room. Far away from Igor.

CHAPTER 15

IGOR

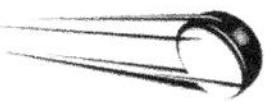

Yuri had bounced out of the shower like his ass had been lit on fire, and he'd dried in record time. Actually he hadn't been dry at all by the time I'd managed to turn off the water and hobble toward the shower door where my towel hung.

That had been the most erotic shower I'd ever had, and Yuri hadn't done anything sexual to me. His hands on my body were enough to light my nerve endings on fire and make me aware of sensitive spots I'd never known existed. Like why did his hand grazing over my nipple make me want to gasp and arch into his touch? And why did my abs try to quiver when he ran his hands over them? Hell, my dick had pulsated when he ran his hands over my calves and down to my feet. I had never been interested in having someone worship my feet before, but there was something about Yuri's hands on me that had turned my blood boiling.

Any questions that had been lingering—not that there had been many—about my sexual awakening had been answered in those few minutes he'd washed my body. Then the heat I loved so much had become a curse because everything had become slightly hazy through the steam as Yuri scrubbed his own body clean. When he'd stepped out of the shower, breathing way too hard for the effort exerted, the hot water pounding on me had felt cold. I'd tried to act unaffected by his rapid departure, pretending to focus completely on cleaning my dick while I watched the fogged-up mirror out the corner of my eye.

He'd left the shower without a word to me, but his complete focus on avoiding my eyes had left me plenty of time to watch his ass and low-hanging balls as he'd bent over.

Definitely not straight.

The biggest question I had was how I'd missed this part of myself for so long. It wasn't like I'd secretly watched gay porn or ever paid attention to the guys in my favorite porn before. I'd never been attracted to a teammate or another man despite spending so much time in locker rooms, nor had I looked at a guy and thought, *Damn, he's got a gorgeous dick.*

So why was I having these thoughts *now* and why had my brain chosen *Yuri* to fixate on?

Whatever the reason, there was no doubt I was

focused on him.

I'd gotten so lost between my thoughts and Yuri's backside, I'd nearly missed him turning around. The only reason I managed to blink the world back into focus was because his ass disappeared behind a towel and it broke the trance he'd had on me.

I was already reaching for the shower handle before Yuri turned around, which meant he hadn't seen me staring at him. At least my shoulders weren't hurting as badly as they had been when I'd stepped into the shower. Yuri had magic hands that had worked some huge knots out of my shoulder blades in the few minutes he'd kneaded them. If it hadn't been for the years of sports massages I'd had, the pain would have taken me to my knees, but after playing professional hockey for thirteen years and spending time in the minors before then, an aggressive sports massage had come to feel like a relaxation massage for most people.

With the shower off, I turned around to see Yuri holding a second towel open for me. "Come. Dry off, then bed."

His no-nonsense words left my dick and brain at odds with one another. My brain wanted to tell him that I didn't want to go to bed, I just wanted to take some time to relax on the couch. My dick wanted to tell him that I'd do anything he asked. Thankfully, my mouth stayed silent and I walked into the towel, surprised when he wrapped it around my body and began to dry me off.

I'd been hot and uncomfortable when we'd arrived home, so there was a chance I'd been overly dramatic about how sore my arms were. Now that I was showered and cooled off, I wasn't anywhere near as grumpy and could have easily dried off on my own. Except once Yuri started, I couldn't find the words to tell him to stop. And even if the words hadn't been hard to find due to my surprise, the overwhelming peace at being cared for would have made finding those words impossible.

In what was simultaneously the longest and shortest moment of my life, Yuri dried me and then pulled the towel around me, expertly securing it at my waist before wrapping an arm around me. "Come. Get to bed. Will make dinner while you rest."

Try as I might, no words came out of my mouth. Instead I ended up looking like a fish out of water as my mouth flapped open and closed. After a few attempts, I shut my mouth and nodded my agreement, and we slowly made our way to the bedroom.

Yuri got us to the bed in just a few seconds and let go of my waist before pointing at the bed. "Sit. Do not hurt yourself more."

There was a steely edge to his voice that I hadn't heard since I'd woken up after surgery and I was seated on the side of the bed before I ever thought to argue with him. Then he was over at the dresser that had become mine, digging through the drawer that contained my underwear. He turned with a pair of gray boxer briefs in his hand. "Shorts?"

My voice had clearly been left in the bathroom because all that came out was a squeak that I tried to approximate as a yes. Yuri didn't question the weird crack in my voice and turned back to the drawer to pull my shorts out as well. When he turned around, his face was tinted red and he was struggling to meet my eyes.

"Good?"

I'd been rendered mute, way too drawn to Yuri's bare chest and defined abs to do more than nod at his question.

Yuri set both items on the bed, avoiding my eyes. "Good." He stepped back and repeated himself, sounding awkward and uncomfortable. "Good. I go. Rest now."

He left me sitting dumbstruck in the bedroom, my underwear and shorts beside me on the bed and my thoughts a muddled mess. I knew how we'd gone from friends to roommates, but I was struggling to figure out when we'd gone from friends to this awkward point where we both had feelings for one another but didn't know how to act on them or what to do with them.

I stared at the door hoping for, maybe willing Yuri to return until the air conditioner kicked on and goose bumps rose on my skin. It was safe to say we were both chickenshits who couldn't talk about our feelings now that we knew they existed.

Cold or not, my erection hadn't flagged in the slightest, but exhaustion was beginning to take over and I needed that nap Yuri had insisted on when he left my room. It still took a few minutes to get dressed, but once I had my underwear and shorts on, I was ready to collapse into bed and sleep for the next few hours.

Hopefully by then my dick would have decided it was done being hard as a rock and maybe we could talk.

Nope, my dick was not going to behave. I was officially screwed, without *being* screwed. My mind kept ping-ponging between how fucking hot it had been to have Yuri washing my body in the shower earlier in the afternoon and the lingering uncertainty about why having feelings for one another wasn't enough to see where they could lead. Unfortunately for me, my dick had decided it was completely focused on how much I liked the shower and much less on my confusion and Yuri's coldness toward me since I'd woken up.

As for Yuri, he'd done everything in his power to interact with me as little as possible: he'd made dinner, pushed Advil at me, and disappeared into the den with his LEGO set. I'd fucked around on my phone as long as I could before I was no longer able to ignore the awkwardness between us and hobbled into the den. Yuri was hunched over the coffee table sorting through a pile of bricks.

With the way he hunched over the table, I'd never

believe he had such perfect posture in the net, though the furrow of concentration in his brow was undeniably adorable. His unbrushed hair had fallen into his face and he'd pursed his lips, his full bottom lip sticking out in a light pout as he searched. I stood in the doorway for a moment just watching Yuri work, in awe of how gorgeous he was without even trying.

His pursed lips reminded me of the porn I'd watched a few nights ago with one guy looking disapprovingly at his boyfriend. The video had opened with a man narrowing his eyes and counting to three while the other had stood petulantly just inside the frame of the video. When he'd gotten to three, he'd crooked his finger and his boyfriend had come over, a mischievous grin on his face that had made me inexplicably hard as a rock. And damn if Yuri hadn't nailed that exact stern look on the man's face before he counted to three.

I'd never been as drawn to anyone before as I was to Yuri. So much so that I'd put myself out there and told him how I felt. While he'd acknowledged the attraction was mutual, he'd also been vague. There had been a *but* in his statement, though he hadn't addressed it didn't look like he was any closer to doing so now.

The confusion about my attraction to Yuri had been replaced with annoyance that he wasn't willing to talk about what was going on, especially after he'd not only taken a shower with me but had washed me. His hands on my body had erased any lingering questions about how I felt about him. Now watching him focus so intently on the task before him, oblivious of my presence in the doorway, my heart decided to do a somersault in my chest. I rubbed idly at the spot, trying to make the odd feeling dissipate.

"Did you eat bad street food today?"

The unexpected question made me jump. I hadn't realized I was leaning against the entryway staring at him while I thought, yet that was right where I was. "No. Why?"

He gestured toward me with a long red LEGO brick. "You are rubbing your chest like you have heartburn."

"No. No heartburn." Definitely not heartburn. Heartburn didn't make my heart dance and flutter in irregular rhythms. If it didn't stop soon, I was going to need to talk to Indy at my next appointment. Though I didn't know what she could do for lust-induced arrhythmia.

Yuri raised an eyebrow like he didn't quite believe me. "If not heartburn, then what? You keep rubbing your chest. Should I call doctor?"

"I do not need a doctor, Yuri. I need to get my fucking thoughts in check." And maybe stop thinking about how good it would be to have Yuri beckoning me closer to him, all the concentration he was paying to the LEGO focused on me.

It shouldn't have made my dick twitch, but I found myself wondering what it would be like to have him looking at me the same way he was looking at the damned plastic pieces. Why was it that I'd been trying to figure out ways to make Yuri frustrated with me? And why did I continue to be drawn to his deep growls and frustrated grunts like I was?

Yuri set the brick down and stared at me. I swore he was trying to see into my soul. *Good luck with that, Yuri.* All he was going to see was a swirl of emotions ranging from excited to trepidatious.

After a moment, he dragged his hand over his face and let out a sigh. “We should talk.”

I lifted my shoulder, trying to pretend I didn’t care while taking a perverse pleasure in the frustrated growl Yuri let out. I was definitely going to ignore the way my dick shifted in my underwear, reminding me of exactly what I was trying to avoid telling him. If he hadn’t been willing to talk earlier, then he wasn’t going to want to know that he was pushing buttons I was just discovering I had.

If this continued, I was going to need to call Ryder and ask him why my dick was reacting to Yuri the way it was. After watching him with Malcolm today, I had a feeling that Ryder could shed some serious light on the situation I’d found myself in.

Yuri pinched the bridge of his nose. “Do not be brat, Igor. You are thinking about something and you know exactly what it is.”

I’d intended for my groan to sound annoyed, but it came out sounding more like the whimper the man in the porn from a few nights ago had let out when he’d been told to get over his boyfriend's lap. Of all the things I'd expected when I'd hobbled my ass into the den, getting a stern stare down from Yuri had not been it.

"Sit. Talk. Tell me what is bothering you, Igor."

I sat, mostly because I was worried that my dick was going to give away the porno running through my head. I'd reached the point that I'd begun cursing the rabbit hole I'd gone down to find that video.

"Why did you say it's not that simple?"

Yuri sagged against the couch, the sigh escaping him a lot closer to defeated than I cared to admit. "You will not accept that we work together as an answer, will you?"

There was no reason to pretend otherwise. "No. Seth and Maz, Trev and Brax. They are players. I am not playing now. Work is not the reason. I know that."

Yuri shook his head, clear resignation in the movement. "Fine. We talk. What if you do not like what you hear?"

I really just wanted to hear something. At this point in the day, after trying to figure out what he was going to say for the last ten hours, I'd be happy to have a reason from him. My brain had conjured up some crazy things during my nap and I'd dreamed of some pretty strange scenarios, none of which were logical when I'd woken up, but they had all felt real while I'd slept.

He angled his body toward me, his jaw set and his back straight. His posture and focus were exactly what I was used to when he got in net. It was a look reserved for serious situations and one I'd never had aimed at me. Our friendship was light and more often than not jovial. We spent more time laughing about stupid shit than talking about anything serious, and this was clearly serious.

"I have questions. When did you know you were attracted to me?"

When he was standing in the hospital bathroom with Yuri glowering at me and stubbornly refusing to leave. I'd felt both fragile and protected, two things I'd never felt before then.

That thought felt too big for the moment, so I settled on something easier. "Right after my surgery." And he had been so damned protective of me and growly when I'd done things I wasn't supposed to. I was stubborn, so I'd pushed back. The more I'd pushed, the more stubborn Yuri had become and every time he'd gotten frustrated with me, my dick had thought it was time to play.

Yuri was quiet for a long moment before letting his eyes drift shut as he gathered his thoughts. "Fuck. It was a lot easier when I could tell myself you were the straight boy."

Tell me about it. "It was a lot easier when I *was* the straight boy."

At least my statement drew a laugh from Yuri. "Okay, you have me there, except I'm not looking for just a gay boy to sleep with."

"But the gay part helps, right?"

A sly grin played across Yuri's lips. "That is an important part, da. I do not sleep with straight men."

"Okay, well, I'm not straight. Or at least I am as confident as I can be without actually having some sort of sexual encounter with a man."

"Do you need sex to know you are not straight?"

The question drew me up short and I stared at Yuri while my brain worked through the question. "My feelings say I am not straight." If we were going to have this conversation, I was going to be honest with Yuri. After weeks of confusion and uncertainty and questioning myself, I had finally figured out what I wanted. Hard as it was to wrap my head around, what I wanted was Yuri. "I want to kiss you. I want to feel your hand on my dick. I want to feel your dick inside me. Those things are enough to tell me I am not straight. What I do not know for certain is how I will feel once I get those things. Will reality match fantasy?"

Yuri's eyes fell shut again and I knew he was processing everything I'd said. He opened his eyes slowly, unintentionally giving me bedroom eyes that made my dick confused about what we were supposed to be talking about. "That is pretty good sign you are not straight." He blew out a breath that was resigned in a way I hadn't expected. "Thank you for telling me. It could not have been easy. Telling Babushka and Danil was the hardest conversation I have ever had."

It had been more of a relief to tell Yuri than stressful. Once I'd convinced myself that Marco was not his boyfriend, or even a friend with benefits, I had found my thoughts and emotions were clearer. Telling Yuri had been awkward as hell, but at the end of it, I was glad to have it out in the open. "If Ryder had not been by my side while I was figuring this out, you would have been the first one I talked to. I cannot think of someone else to say this to."

Yuri's smile turned even softer, though I could sense a frustration about something burning just below the surface. "Thank you, Igor. Really." He glanced up the steps. "I would like to talk more but I need some time to process. Is that okay?"

I tried to hide my surprise as I nodded. It wasn't the way I'd expected this conversation to end, but then again, showering with Yuri hadn't been how I'd expected things to begin either. It was a fucked-up, backward start to anything, and I could understand his need for space and to sort his feelings out. I needed space too.

Raking his hands through his hair, Yuri muttered something in Russian, then still talking to himself, stood and started toward the steps. "If only solnishko was submissive."

My mouth hung open in shock as I thought about that little bit of information he'd shared as he'd walked away. It was giving my brain something to latch onto.

Submission. I knew what it was, but I'd never considered it before now. Pieces and parts of the jigsaw that had recently become my life were starting to fill in the blank spaces. I'd need to take some time and figure out what the entire picture looked like before talking with Yuri again.

CHAPTER 16

IGOR

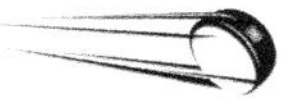

I retreated to my room in a hurry and glanced at the clock. It wasn't ten yet, so that meant it was before Ryder's bedtime.

How had I missed it? How had I missed something so major?

My finger found Ryder's contact on autopilot, and he answered without my noticing the phone ringing. "Hello?"

The thoughts whirring through my head were too fast to keep up with and my mouth started talking before I knew what was going to come out of it. "Have you always been Malcolm's submissive?"

Ryder didn't so much speak as he squeaked, the startled "What?" cracking over the phone like painful feedback.

There was no time to check on him, my brain moving

too fast to stop. I needed answers and I couldn't call Seth or Trevor. I liked them both and we'd been friends for years, but we weren't close and I was pretty sure neither of them had any clue that I had feelings for Yuri. Ryder was my only confidant as well as my only hope of figuring my shit out.

"You have a unique relationship with Malcolm. He tells you to go to bed—I checked the time before I called. Bedtime is at ten. He calls you baby. He threatens you with punishments and bribes you with rewards. You are submissive, no?"

"I-I—What was the question?"

Maybe I had been too blunt. Was there any way to soften my delivery after the fact?

Before I could figure out what to say, Ryder gathered his thoughts. "What happens between Malcolm and me is private. I don't know what you think you've figured out, but it really isn't your place to judge," he said, each word terse and clipped. Only then did I figure out that he thought I was disgusted or bothered by his relationship.

"Don't hang up!" I held my hands in front of me like he could see me idiotically trying to show him I hadn't meant any harm. "I am sorry. My brain hurts. Yuri said something tonight and I... I need someone to talk to who will understand."

"Huh?" I was starting to worry about all the emotions I was causing Ryder.

"I like driving Yuri crazy. But I like when I make him

happy too." I collapsed on my bed. "I have never felt like this before."

Ryder's warm laughter was a balm to my soul, as was the way his voice had lost the hard edge when he spoke. "Sexual *and* kinky crisis. You don't do anything by halves, Ozols."

That statement successfully broke the tension between us and I was now chuckling. "Go big or go home."

"Okay, okay, okay. Let's break this down. What happened tonight? Because we left this afternoon with him telling you it wasn't as easy as having feelings for one another. Now you're telling me that he said *something*. From the way this conversation started, I think whatever he said made your brain go boom and your dick go hard."

Laughter burst from me at the accuracy of his statement. "I would not have put it that way, but pretty much, yes."

Muffled sounds came over the line as Ryder adjusted himself on the couch and then I heard Malcolm whisper something in Ryder's ear. Whatever he'd said made Ryder happy. "Yes, please. And thank you." Then he turned his focus back to me. "Now, where were we?"

"My fucked-up world. I am thirty-five. Is it too soon to have a midlife crisis?"

The raspberry Ryder blew in my ear made me wince. "Yes, because that means that Mal will have one soon, and I don't want to deal with that. What did Yuri say that made you realize you're not only bisexual, but you're also a kinky fuck?"

"Language, Ry." From the annoyed tone of Malcolm's words, I suspected that hadn't been the first time he'd said the same thing that day.

"Sorry," Ryder said, the apology lacking any true remorse. "Now, back to you."

I stared at the spot in the ceiling above my head that the painters must have missed. It was a small patch that didn't match the rest of the ceiling color. "I might have told Yuri that I want to kiss him, feel his mouth on me, and have him fuck me." My cheeks burned with the admission. "I cannot believe I said that to him."

"You did not!"

I groaned. "I did." Ryder's strangled laughter was clear over the phone, but to his credit he did try to bite it back. "Laugh, go ahead."

The dam burst and Ryder guffawed in my ear. "I'm sorry," he said as sincerely as his laughter would allow. When his laughter died down slightly, he sucked in a deep breath. "Okay, I'm good. But I have to know, what did he say to that?"

"Well, he said that he was honored that I felt comfortable telling him, or something like that. Then he walked out of the room muttering in Russian. But just before he walked up the steps, he said something along the lines of, 'If only solnishko was submissive.' That is when everything fell into place and I called you."

Ryder whistled low. "What does sol-nis-ka mean?"

He'd butchered the pronunciation as badly as I had the first few times I'd heard Yuri call me that. By now he'd said it so frequently, I was pretty sure I could say it in my sleep. "I do not know. He says it's a Russian nickname. I have never looked it up."

"Why?"

I'd been honest about everything else, so there was no reason to avoid answering now. "I don't think I want to know what it means. It's been kind of fun to think it's something kind and not some other way to call me a pain in the ass."

"That's kind of hysterical and a lot heartbreaking. I can't believe you've been harboring all these feelings for the last few weeks. Okay, let's work through this."

That was the most welcome sentence I'd heard all day. "Yes, please." My first attempt at broaching the subject had taken us way off course, so I tried again after carefully thinking my words through. "I need to talk to someone who can explain things to me. Am I right? Are you Malcolm's submissive?"

After a pregnant pause, Ryder sighed. "I am... yes."

"You are not comfortable talking about it."

"It's not something I've ever had to talk about before. Truthfully, it happened so naturally, aside from a small number of awkward conversations, it's never been something we really talk about. It's just..." He trailed off, clearly gathering his thoughts. "It's just part of us, I guess."

I didn't know if his admission was helpful or not, but I could appreciate the honesty. "Part of, yes. That I understand. What I feel, it is natural. It is not something I must try to do." I was normally better with my English sentences, but my brain could only focus on one thing at a time and the crises at hand were consuming my entire brain, including the parts that made my English flow better.

The pause over the line didn't feel as heavy. I could sense Ryder thinking for the handful of seconds he took before speaking. "Have you always liked to drive people nuts and gotten turned on by it?"

"No! I like to drive Yuri nuts all the time. He is fun to drive nuts, but lately it is different. I want to push and push but not make him mad. I do not want him mad at me."

"Igor!" Ryder squealed my name the same way the piglet at the petting zoo had squealed when Trevor tried to cuddle it. "You're a brat!"

I found myself nodding despite Ryder not being able to see me. "Igor has said same, yes."

Something about my response struck Ryder as funny and he let out a giggle. *He giggled more than anyone I knew.* "Not in the *I'm annoyed with you* way. I mean it in the *submissive* way."

"What is the difference?" *Was there a difference?*

"Huh. You know, I never thought of it that way. There's a bratty kid or those social media people who are totally vapid and ignorant that you see and want to strangle immediately. The kids that can't take no for an answer and throw an absolute fit because they aren't getting their way. They are brats. And then the adults who think they should get their way because no one ever told them no as kids or adults and every interaction with them is soul-sucking. They are brats too.

"But there's this subsect of the BDSM community where the submissive is a brat. They push their Dom's buttons, just like I sometimes push Malcolm's buttons, on purpose. Usually looking for a reaction. The difference is, as a functioning adult, brats know not to go too far... at least most of the time. The other difference is any Dom worth his snot isn't going to punish you if they're actually mad at you. Then you have to have a conversation... which is sometimes worse from what I hear."

There was an emoji I used while texting, a little round face with smoke and flames coming out of its head. I was feeling just like that emoji. My mouth was hanging open and I was staring straight ahead hardly blinking. I couldn't believe my ears. The brat that Ryder was describing felt a lot like me and how I felt around Yuri.

"These submissive people you call brats, there are Doms that like that?"

"Absolutely!"

"How do I find out if Yuri is a Dom like that?"

"Honestly?" Ryder asked slowly and I knew I wasn't going to like his answer. "You have to ask."

"Fuck. I do not want to ask. Talking to Yuri is complicated now. I do not like complicated. I liked easier. I liked friend."

The *tsking* noise Ryder made told me he at least understood a bit. "Yes, I know. But you'll have to. Mal always tells me that communication is important. I need to tell him how I'm feeling and if I don't like something he does."

"Are you a brat?"

"Ha! Not hardly." Ryder was emphatic enough that I knew not to question him. "The only time I get kinda bratty is when I get tired, but then Daddy just puts me to bed."

I bit my cheek to keep from laughing at Ryder's statement, since I was pretty sure I felt the phone grow hot from Ryder's embarrassment at his words. "Oh my god, I cannot believe I just said that. Please just forget I said anything."

"Um, nope." Because my mind was much happier focusing on Malcolm being Ryder's Daddy than Yuri being my... what? Dom? My brain wasn't ready to go there, so instead I focused on Ryder. "I thought that Malcolm was your Daddy, now you have confirmed it. Now I can ask questions. How long? Why Daddy? What does that entail? I know Daddies. I am not that clueless. You have rules to follow?"

I would have kept going, but Ryder's drawn-out groan made me stop. "Seriously, you knew already?"

"Yup." I popped the *p* for emphasis. "I knew. Now we talk about about."

At least you knew what Daddies were. I was confused the first time Mal told me he thought I needed a Daddy."

I'D FALLEN asleep when Ryder started yawning and Malcolm put his foot down and said it was time for him to go to bed, even if it wasn't quite bedtime. So much had happened that day that sleep hadn't taken long to find me, but I'd drifted off thinking about how well the two of them fit their roles.

Now that morning had rolled around, I could no longer ignore the things I'd discovered while talking with Ryder and was focused more on myself and discovering what made me tick. What Yuri had said to me last night had been eye-opening, but I just hadn't expected the conversation I'd had with Ryder after that to make so much of my life fall into place.

I'd never been spanked, never been in—I didn't know what to call it—pretend trouble with a lover? Hell, every time a previous girlfriend had gotten mad at me, shit had exploded and the relationship ended. That was it.

Unable to remain lying down, my legs too restless to stay still, I got up and grabbed my crutches. My arms still hurt like a motherfucker and I hissed through my teeth at the first step, though the pain was a good distraction from my racing thoughts. It took longer than it should have to make it to the kitchen for the bottle of Advil, but I made it there eventually and had never been happier to see a bottle of anti-inflammatories in all my life.

I dumped three into my hand and swallowed them dry, then went in search of a drink. Damn Yuri and his fancy coffee maker I couldn't figure out how to use. I wasn't about to try to figure it out either. I had a very real fear of actually messing that thing up and wasn't about to piss Yuri off to that level.

And... that was the type of brat Ryder was talking about. I liked pushing Yuri's buttons but I knew my limits and I knew the limits he could handle. The expensive coffee maker that required a rocket scientist—or crazy Russian goalie—to operate was where I knew my line was drawn. Messing something up on that would not annoy Yuri in the way I liked to annoy him.

It was only five in the morning, but the two of us needed to talk and I wasn't getting back to sleep now that I was up. I needed caffeine, and like Ryder had said, I was going to have to talk to Yuri whether I wanted to or not. This awkward space between us had only gotten more awkward after my admission the night before and the only way it would ease was if we talked to one another. I needed to know if we wanted the same things or not. He needed to know what I was thinking as well.

If he was beating himself up like I was, it wasn't fair to either of us. If he didn't want the same things I did, I had to hope that I could find a way to move on and put my feelings for him to the side to preserve our friendship. The last thing I wanted was to lose my best friend. Then again, there was a chance I already had.

Fuck. Fuck. Fuckity fuck. This had turned way more complicated than I'd ever imagined.

Before I got ahead of myself, I needed to find a way to get Yuri up and I was pretty sure I knew just the way to do it.

CHAPTER 17

YURI

I tossed and turned the entire night. Between Igor's admission about what he'd discovered and his wants and what I knew about myself, there'd been no chance in hell I was going to sleep well. Every time I closed my eyes, I dreamed of Igor: him on his knees, my dick in his ass, *Yes, sir* slipping from his lips just before he draped himself over my lap for a spanking, and the horror on his face when I told him I wanted the last part.

Boris's large paw scratching at my door finally made me give up on sleep just after five in the morning. "It is too early to be up," I said to my dog, despite having been awake for the last hour thinking about Igor and the mess we found ourselves in.

Boris pawed again at the door and added a whimper for good measure. "Impatient beast. You are stubborn as Igor. Can't wait. Must get what you want no matter what.

Doesn't matter if I'm not what you need. You see it, you want it." I'd made it halfway down the steps and couldn't remember if I was talking about Boris or Igor. I was pretty sure at some point I'd switched from the dog to my friend.

The only thing I knew for certain was that I could hear Boris's food being shaken.

What the hell?

I made it down the rest of the steps, Boris well in front of me, to find Igor in the kitchen looking sheepish as he scooped a serving of food into Boris's bowl. "What were you saying as you came down the steps?"

"Huh?" Not a great deflection, but I needed time to come up with something plausible. I'd been muttering to myself, not expecting the man that had kept me up most of the night to be in the kitchen at this ungodly hour.

"You sounded upset, but hell, you could have been telling Boris he's a good boy since I can't understand what you're saying."

At least there was one small blessing for the day. "Annoyed to have Boris pawing at my door this early." I looked at the food in Igor's hand. "Now I discover it is your fault."

Igor's grin didn't hide his guilt. "I can't climb steps yet. I didn't want to wake you up by falling down or cursing. I also didn't want to get up the steps and have you yell at me for doing more than I should have."

It was too early in the morning for Igor logic. He was clearly too awake for his own good, and if I was going to be able to have a conversation with him, I was going to need coffee. Igor could stand there holding Boris's food for a few minutes while I worked on making myself, and maybe him if he was lucky, coffee.

Working through my routine, I had time to process Igor's words. "Why would you come up steps at this hour? And why are you worried? Since when have you cared about pissing me off?"

"I do not like upsetting you. I like... Your coffee, it is doing something wrong."

I whipped my head to the machine in a panic. Now that he'd pointed it out, I could hear the hissing and splashing and steaming of overly hot liquids hitting cool surfaces. "Fucking fuck. Fuckity-fucker-motherfuck!"

A towel appeared in front of my face. "At least we know your English cursing is up to par."

One towel was not going to be enough to clean up the mess of coffee, but it was enough that it wasn't dripping over the edge of the counter and onto the floor. There was going to be a massive mess, but that would be a problem for me to deal with later. Coffee in my mug was going to take priority over the coffee out of it.

Conversation ground to a halt while I ground new beans and started making more coffee.

Igor hovered just behind me, close enough that his breath ghosted over the bare skin of my shoulder. Close enough that I heard his soft questioning grunt over Boris's crunching of his kibble. "Are you sure this is a coffee conversation? We might need something stronger."

Maybe he was right. Maybe this wasn't a coffee conversation. Under normal circumstances, I would never consider liquor before dawn, but these weren't normal circumstances. Maybe the alcohol would help soothe some of my frazzled nerves. Decision made, I reached into the cabinet above the espresso machine and grabbed a cheap bottle of Irish whiskey. If I was going to mix it into coffee, there was no reason to go for the Redbreast I had stashed up there.

"Holy shit, Yurievich, you have held out on me. I didn't know you had that."

There was a reason for that. "Stay out of liquor, brat." I swung around to waggle a finger at Igor only to find him staring at me with wide eyes and parted lips, and was that a blush on his cheeks?

This was why we needed coffee before we talked. Not only was my brain sluggish from sleep deprivation, my dick was still interested in my dreams from when I'd managed sleep. In my current state, I couldn't figure out what was going on, and my brain felt like it was going to explode from the mixed signals it was receiving.

My tongue defied me and I tripped over my words as I laser focused on my coffee maker. "I-I must, coffee. Make coffee."

I was pretty sure I heard Igor chuckle, but I wasn't about to put more thought into it. My brain was not wired to work at this hour. Many of the players on the team had 4:00 and 5:00 a.m. workouts, but I was one who didn't roll out of bed until eight unless I absolutely had to.

At this early hour, it took all my focus to make two cups of coffee, which might have been for the best. For nearly three minutes, I wasn't able to think about Igor, the weird shit that had transpired between us over the last few weeks, or the awkwardness that had only grown since I'd walked out on him the night before.

That had been a dick move. I shouldn't have done that. I'd known as much as soon as my feet hit the steps, but the conversation had become way deeper than my brain had been willing to process and I'd needed time to sort everything out. I hadn't planned on him falling asleep while I was upstairs, and now that morning had arrived, it all felt a lot bigger and more ominous. At least I'd thanked him and checked in with him before I'd left.

I poured the foam into Igor's dry cappuccino and turned with both cups in my hands. On instinct, I almost handed him his mug, then remembered that he was still on crutches and pulled it back at the last second. "Patio."

It wasn't so much a question as it was a command and I didn't wait for him to respond before walking past him toward the door. Boris followed me but didn't wait for me to get the door fully opened before he plowed between my legs, causing me to teeter precariously on one leg before righting myself. Coffee sloshed over my hands and I let out a string of swear words even I couldn't make out.

"Are you okay?" Igor was by my side before the coffee hit the floor, using a rag he'd found on the counter to dry my hands. "Ice? Cold water?"

Shaking my head, I stalked toward the patio chairs. The crickets and frogs in the woods beside my house were nearly deafening, and I swore I could hear the mosquitos swarming to bite me. Before they could get me too many times, I turned on the ridiculous mosquito lights I'd purchased the year before. I doubted the fancy light things were worth what I'd paid, but if they kept even a few from biting me, they were worth the price.

With nothing left to distract us from the conversation off any longer, I sank into a chair and waited for Igor to follow suit. Before we could move forward, I owed him an apology.

"I am sorry about last night. I could have handled the entire situation better. The conversation, I had not been ready for it."

To my surprise and maybe relief, Igor started to laugh. "Stop right there. First, you asked me if it was okay if you left. Second, you left me with an unintentional gift, so thank you for walking away."

My mouth fell open and I stared dumbly at Igor as I tried to figure out the right words to use. I wasn't fast enough and a bug flew into my mouth, causing me to sputter and cough as I tried to get it out. "Blyad!" I spit, finally feeling the bug dislodge from my mouth. "Fucking mosquito!"

I could just make out Igor's face turning red as he tried to hold in his laughter.

"Laugh it up, asshole. Mosquitos, they eat me for dinner. I show them. I eat it for breakfast!" In all my blustering, I tried not to gag from the knowledge that a bug had been in my mouth.

Igor finally let himself laugh and some of the tension surrounding us eased.

"Shut up, idiot. You will wake neighbors. I like Alaina and Albert. They are nice and do not rat me out to homeowners association."

"You just told me to laugh!" Igor gasped between laughs, his face turning red from lack of oxygen. He sucked in a few more lungsful of air before finally sighing. "Okay, I think I'm better now."

It was sometimes like talking to a child when I talked with him. Then again, I was pretty sure most people would say we were both the same way. "Where were we?" At least I could try to get us back on track and not end up with a noise complaint before the sun had even begun to peek over the horizon.

The breath Igor sucked in was not to compose himself. It sounded resigned and he looked the same as he sat back in his chair, balancing his cup near his lips as he began to speak. "I said I was glad you walked away when you did. Well, not because you walked away but what you said as you did."

Try as I might, I couldn't remember what I'd said as I

left the room. Igor must have seen the confusion written on my face and took pity on me. "Most of it was in Russian and I couldn't make any of it out. But just before you made it to the steps, you said something along the lines of, 'If only he was submissive.'"

My eyes widened. It was hard to believe I'd said that to Igor and my first instinct was to find a hole to crawl into. I'd been telling myself for weeks that we would not work because he was straight and I was a Dom. Until the day before, I had zero intentions of ever telling Igor anything about that side of me.

The previous night, I'd realized I was going to have to talk to him about it. While my brain tried to work out how to go about doing that, my subconscious had taken over and decided for me. Now I needed to brace myself for his telling me that he was not a submissive.

"If you don't shut your mouth, you're going to swallow another bug. I get the impression you would not approve of that."

I snapped my mouth shut so hard my teeth clacked together. We both winced, but Igor pressed ahead after only a quick second's pause. "When I heard those words, something clicked into place."

That we were not right for one another.

"I went to my room and called..." He paused, conflict written all over his face before he continued. "A friend. I had suspected that he has a special relationship with his husband. What you said had pieces I'd not understood about myself falling into place. I asked him about his relationship with his husband. Will not go into the entire conversation, but he explained things to me. Made me realize something important."

He stopped there and my damned dick couldn't stop hoping that maybe, just maybe, he wasn't going to tell me that he could never be a submissive. When he didn't finish after a few seconds, I couldn't continue to wait in silence. "What did you realize?"

An uncomfortable laugh, almost a wheeze, came from Igor's throat. "That is what I was trying to tell you in the kitchen before coffee spilled everywhere. Yuri, I like to tease you. I like when you get frustrated with me. I like when you get annoyed and yell at me in Russian."

He was not telling me anything I hadn't figured out, but he also wasn't answering the question I'd hoped he would.

"I like driving you nuts. But what I don't like is when you actually get mad at me."

I had so many questions, but they were coming to mind too fast for me to voice a single one in English. Many of the words were not common in English, and I was struggling to find the right translations.

"My friend, he told me that there are Doms that likes submissives who do that. He called the submissives *brats*."

Had my chair not been against the side of the house, I was certain I'd have fallen backward out of it. It was too good to be true. It was too hard to believe that he meant what I thought he did.

Igor took a sip of his coffee, then dragged a hand down his face. "I did not understand it before last night. The thoughts were confusing. I did not understand why my dick got hard when you yelled at me. Or why I always want to poke the bear. I think that is the saying."

At least Igor was better at sayings than I was. I would not have come up with that, though thinking about it, at least that one made sense. Poking a wild bear would make them mad. Which meant that Igor liked to make me mad. *He'd admitted that he got turned on by it.* In the last thirty seconds, my body had gone from convinced I was not understanding what Igor was trying to tell me, to being convinced he was saying exactly what I wanted to hear.

"You... are you... Are you trying to tell me that you are brat?"

Igor nodded just as the first rays of sunlight poked over the trees behind him, creating a halo around his head that gave him an angelic look I knew was totally deceptive. "I think I am. At least, it makes sense. The way he described it. I have tried to see what makes my dick react, like leaving the cabinets open and leaving my crutches away from my bed. Then you get mad at me and yell and my dick gets hard."

Bugs be damned, my jaw fell open in shock at what Igor was admitting to me. "You did that on purpose?"

Igor looked bashful as he nodded. "Brats are submissive, no?"

I nodded, though I was sure the movement was

awkward. "Yes. There might be exceptions to the rule, but brats are usually submissive."

"That is what I thought. Now I know you are looking for a submissive, that makes you a Dom?"

My throat felt like it was filled with cotton as I tried to make an affirmative sound. Unfortunately, it came out more like Boris's squeaky duck with a broken squeaker, leaving me to sip my coffee while I nodded my head again.

Some of the confidence left Igor and I was certain that he was trying to disappear into the chair. "I know not every submissive or every Dom wants the same things and from what R... my friend said, even if people have compatible kinks, it doesn't mean that they will be a good match for one another."

I didn't know Ryder well, though I assumed that was who Igor had spoken to. What I did know was that they'd had a long conversation after I'd gone upstairs and he'd given Igor a lot of very good information. Beyond that, Igor had listened intently.

"Your friend is right on everything."

"Yes. And now I want to know, are you looking for someone like me?" Uncertainty creased his forehead and lips and the rapidly brightening sky let me see the fear in his light eyes.

There was no way I could keep him in suspense. He'd shown incredible bravery in bringing the subject up, well more than I'd managed to muster in the last ten hours, yet everything that raced through my mind sounded corny and ridiculous. I finally settled on the undeniable truth. "Brats are my favorite." The laugh that escaped me was somewhere between nervous and deranged, but I was unable to help it. This bubble of tension and uncertainty that we'd both been dancing around since Igor came home from the hospital had burst, leaving a peace that felt awkward and uncomfortable after so many weeks of the former.

A hesitant smile formed on Igor's lips, and his voice came out small and nervous. "Do you like *my* brat?"

I paused only for drama's sake. For four years, Igor had been my favorite pain in the ass. I knew he'd be my favorite pain in the ass even if I'd found a submissive before now. The answer was easy and immediate, but he could at least wait a few seconds in suspense. "I'm pretty sure you're my favorite brat."

CHAPTER 18

IGOR

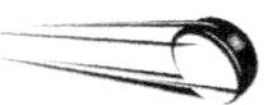

Had I just heard Yuri right? There was a distinct ringing in my ears, so maybe I'd misheard what he said. Except the way he was looking at me, the morning sun twinkling in his eyes and a smile on his face, I was pretty sure I hadn't.

Yuri shook his head, amusement dancing in his features. He hummed like he did when he was trying to come up with exactly the right words. Now that he'd told me I was the perfect brat for him, I had nothing but patience and was happy to let him take his time... at least within reason. I couldn't be expected to stay patient forever.

His mouth parted well before I'd run out of patience. Then he spoke, and I knew just how hard he'd considered his words as they came out in clear, though heavily accented, English. "I have told myself for weeks that you are straight. Yesterday—" He scrubbed his hands through his hair causing it to stick up at odd angles. "Yesterday at the parade, I knew I hurt you. I did not understand why, but I looked for you, and you were gone."

Frustration grew in Yuri, though I didn't think there was anything I could do to help ease it. "I thought I had lost you. When Marco said you were upset he kissed me, there was a few minutes there I thought I would throw up."

Guilt tightened my stomach, making the coffee I'd been sipping turn to sludge. The last thing I'd wanted to do was upset Yuri, but jealousy had gotten the better of me. I couldn't figure out what Yuri saw in me if *that* was who he wanted. I wasn't tanned or built like a swimmer. My skin was pale and burned more than tanned. My muscles didn't pop from my back or ripple in my legs. I wasn't built to propel myself *through* water; I was trained to walk *on* it. The only thing I might have had on him was my hockey butt. Nearly thirty years of squats and butterflies while stopping hundreds of thousands of hockey pucks had given me a tight, round ass... And holy shit, I'd totally checked that guy out while simultaneously comparing myself to him.

"You are the most important person to me, Igs. You are my best friend. I do not want to lose you. While we looked for you, my gut said I had upset you like Marco said, but my brain could not believe it. Igor is *straight*."

The last sentence made the guilt unfurl and I snorted a laugh. "*Was*."

At least the correction pulled a chuckle from Yuri. "*Was* straight. I could not understand why you would like a certain 'brown-haired, brown-eyed Russian goalie.'" He threw air quotes around the last half of the sentence. Even knowing what I did, I found it hard to believe that Marco had been the one who'd picked up on my crush on Yuri first.

His eyes dulled. Whatever storm was brewing inside him, he wasn't doing a good job of hiding it. "You told me you like me, and my head—" He mimed his head exploding.

After a resigned sigh, he continued. "Igor, I do not fall for straight guys. It is a recipe for disaster. Until yesterday, I didn't consider it a possibility. At the same time my head exploded, my heart broke. It was a dream and nightmare. All I could think was that the man—me—you discovered you have feelings for is not just looking for a relationship. You had no idea what I need from partners. I need more than connection, more than sex. And everything I know about you, you are pain in ass, not brat."

Things were making sense and I could understand the awkwardness and his reaction. If he hadn't dropped that little tidbit about hoping I was submissive, I'd have never known what he was looking for. I didn't know if I'd have discovered what I knew about myself had it not been for his unintentional slip.

"Last night I tossed and turned. Then wake up to my dog scratching at my door because you did not want me to be mad but what, wanted me awake?"

He'd been ranting so long I hadn't expected the question and sat staring awkwardly at him until my brain kicked in. "Yes. Awake. I wanted you awake so we can talk. My mind is too crazy."

"Your mind is crazy?" Igor shot me a look that made my stomach quiver.

I had to force myself not to raise my shoulders in an attempt to look smaller while at the same time my dick shifted in my shorts. Confusion mixed with unexplained nerves warred with arousal inside of me. My stomach flipped and my underwear got tight. "I am beginning to understand."

A smirk danced across Yuri's lips. "What do you understand?"

I'd said the words to myself, a thought more than a statement, but now I had to explain. "It is the look. The look that makes me want to push you harder, to see what will happen. It is not the same as when you get mad. It makes me all confused."

Yuri's head fell back, his laughter filling the patio and startling a bird out of a nearby bush. "And how is it that you know I am not mad?"

"Easy. You are mad when I eat bad food and get sick. You yell and call me a moron and do not speak to me for days."

"I take care of you."

"Begrudgingly." *Very* begrudgingly. And I always felt worse about making Yuri upset than the bad food made me feel. It was normally enough to keep me eating well for a number of months before a few drinks got in the way of my better judgment.

"You are an idiot." The sun caught the twinkle in his eyes and his big smile that showed his missing tooth let me know he didn't really mean the words, though his dry delivery would have had me questioning if the sun reflecting in his eyes hadn't softened his features enough for me to see the sincerity in his statement.

I found myself grinning. "Indisputable." And if I had anything to do with it, I was going to be *his* idiot.

Yuri wasn't going to be distracted by my smile and got the conversation back on track. "And why do you not want me mad at you?"

The waggle of his eyebrows and his infuriating smirk told me he knew exactly what he was doing, and he wasn't going to be happy unless I told him what he wanted to hear. Heat spread down my shoulders as I thought of the words he wanted to hear from me. I needed to tell him exactly why I didn't like it, but it was a lot easier to say in my head than find the words to say it out loud.

It took three separate tries between two long sips of coffee before I finally found a way to dislodge the words from my throat. "Because when you are really mad at me, my dick stays soft."

I didn't know what Yuri had been expecting or hoping to hear from me, but that clearly hadn't been it because he shot coffee across both the table and patio, then sputtered and coughed for another thirty seconds before sitting upright. His eyes were watering and his chest heaved as he caught his breath. "You really are brat." He hadn't laughed, hadn't grouched. His voice was awed and his eyes shone with disbelief.

The knowledge that we were moving in the right direction had pushed me through the conversations to that point. Even the last few minutes where I'd felt anxious and embarrassed hadn't been enough to deter me. It wasn't until Yuri finally accepted what I'd been saying all morning as truth that the weight of the conversation landed on my shoulders.

Everything was changing. *Had changed.* Not even a month before, I'd been the single, straight, retired professional hockey player getting ready to embark on a coaching career. Three and a half weeks before, I'd gone into surgery with nothing but a few lingering bruises from the season and a busted hip that needed repairs. I'd woken up to the same bruises, a throbbing pain from the repair, and my best friend sitting in the chair by my bed. I hadn't known then that in a half hour, my world would start to turn on its axis.

Yuri was crouched in front of me, his hands on my knees. "Igor. Igor. Are you okay?" He snapped his fingers in front of my eyes and I instinctively flinched, my focus snapping back to the patio where we were and Yuri's worried eyes studying me closely. "Are you okay?"

"That is a loaded question."

He gave me a knowing chuckle. "Feel the same. It is getting hot. We talk more inside where we can be comfortable."

I managed a nod despite the wave of exhaustion that had suddenly overcome me. Yuri didn't hesitate to take the lead, grabbing my hands and tugging me upward, then handing over my crutches. "Inside. We talk there." He gave a piercing whistle and Boris came trotting over from behind the pool house where he loved to sleep.

He grabbed both our coffee mugs and directed us toward the house, waiting patiently for me to make the single step into the house, then shutting the door behind us. Boris made a beeline for the treat jar, unwilling to let either of us forget to give him his prize for going out. I knew Yuri was distracted by everything going on when he didn't say a thing to the dog, just handed him two treats and kept walking toward the living room.

"I can't believe I've missed the signs," I said. Yuri hovered over me while I got seated and he propped a few pillows under my leg. He hadn't sat down before the air conditioner kicked on and he paused to grab a throw blanket off the couch to put over my legs.

"Missed what?" The adorable furrow on his brow made me smile.

"That you are a Dom. You are stubborn and a perfectionist. But you care. You give me medicine, feed me, get mad at me when I do not eat right or sleep enough or do too much. It is more than a friend."

To my surprise, a bright red blush stained Yuri's cheeks. "That is not because I am Dom. That is because I am me. I have my own.. things." His cheeks only grew redder as he spoke, making my curiosity climb higher by the second.

"What kind of quirks?" Had he really thought I wasn't going to ask?

He rubbed anxiously at the back of his neck. "I like to please. It is not just a Dom thing."

I encouraged him on with my hands when he stopped there. He definitely hadn't used enough words for me to understand what he was talking about or why he was embarrassed by it.

My gesture only drew a growl from Yuri before he finally sighed. "Fuck. You will make me spell it out." His hand waved vaguely in front of his body while he gathered his thoughts. "Doms like to help or please their submissives, yes. But I get an extra level of pleasure out of it. I do not want to be a table or a chair, but I like serving my partner. It is erotic and brings my enjoyment of caring for my partner to a different place. And when someone resists help, then finally lets me, it's a rush like no other.

"Like, you are so stubborn, but when you let me help you after being kozyol... like you say, my dick gets hard."

I held up my finger to let him know I needed a minute

to process. For a few seconds, I thought we'd had a translation issue, but the more I replayed his words, the more I was certain Yuri had told me he hadn't wanted to be a table or a chair. No matter what else he'd said, I needed an answer before I could respond to the rest. "Did you really say 'table or chair'?"

"Seriously? That is what you get out of that?"

"Oh, I have many questions, but I need to know that first."

Yuri gave me an exasperated look before finally nodding his head. "Yes. Service kink."

I was way too new to any type of alternative lifestyle to have heard of that before. "What is that?"

"I cannot believe I am talking about this now," Yuri said, more or less muttering to himself before finally addressing me. "It is different for everyone: server, couch, urinal. I am not sure I have a traditional service kink, but serving my partner brings me happiness and pleasure."

Keeping the surprise off my face as Yuri spoke was difficult and I hoped like hell I didn't sound as repulsed as I felt. "Urinal?"

I missed the pillow Yuri lobbed at my head. "Don't be ass. What is saying? Do not yuck someone's yum. It is not my kink, but I know wonderful people who enjoy it."

"Sorry." I meant the word. It hadn't been my intent to offend, but the statement had taken me by surprise. It was also a stark reminder of just how much I didn't know about kink, BDSM, and what I was discovering was a part of me.

"You will learn."

The finality of the statement, the way he was so confident in my abilities, had my heart speeding up with excitement. *I would learn.* Though I wasn't brave enough to ask more about Yuri's interests, I was curious enough to do so. "So, no urine for you?"

"Da. Like I said. I do not know what my *kink* is, or if it even *is* kink. I know that I get horny when I get to help someone." He adjusted himself, apparently done pretending that we were still keeping things strictly in the friend zone.

My gaze fell to the movement and I found myself surprised by the outline of Yuri's erection in his shorts. My ass clenched at the thought of it inside me, but not for the reasons I would have expected a few weeks earlier. I'd watched enough porn in the last couple of weeks to know that I wanted to have Yuri inside of me and I'd had plenty of time to daydream about that exact thing. I wanted him more than any of the porn stars I'd seen so far.

"I have helped you much since surgery. Many times after you insisted you do not need it."

It took a moment, but my eyes widened and Yuri let out a laugh that disturbed Boris from his spot on the floor. He made his way over to us and placed his head on the couch, looking between the two of us for pets. Yuri accommodated the request, never taking his eyes off me. "I have spent much of the summer hiding erections from you."

I focused on where this was going. Now that we'd figured out we were both what the other was looking for, we were doing an even better job of talking around the subject than we'd done for the weeks leading up to this. "That makes two of us." I couldn't shake how surreal it was to admit that to Yuri.

"Blyad! You say that after last night." He gave me a searching look. "You are serious."

The disbelief had left his tone, an understanding that hadn't been there before finally settling over him, and I nodded. "Yes. Serious. It is new, I know. But I am serious about this. My head might be confused sometimes, but my gut, it tells me this is right."

Yuri shook his head, more amused than in disbelief. "It is hard to believe this is real." He looked me up and down, allowing his thoughts to fully form before giving me a wry smile. "How is this real?"

I lifted a shoulder. "I have asked myself that a number of times recently. Usually when I'm watching porn, though." A yawn escaped me, my lack of sleep finally catching up with me. "Big conversations and no sleep are exhausting."

A strong hand landed on my thigh as Yuri hoisted himself upward. "Move forward." He gestured for me to scoot over and I obliged, not thinking much of it until he sat down behind me. He rested one leg down the back of the couch and the other on the coffee table. "Rest," he said, wrapping an arm around my stomach and pulling me so that my back was flush with his front, not giving me a chance to argue with him.

Everything about the position was different. I had always been the one in the back, my arm around my partner, my fingers usually grazing a soft breast. With Yuri, he was behind me, strong and steady, with one hand on my stomach and another draped over my shoulder. "You need sleep. Sleep, solnishko."

I nearly asked him what the word meant, but my eyes were heavy and I was afraid any words from me would ruin the moment. Instead of asking, I closed my eyes and let sleep take me.

CHAPTER 19

YURI

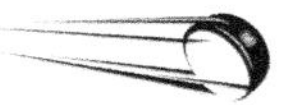

J*esus. Fucking. Christ.* How had I gotten myself in this position? Igor had been passed out on my chest for over two hours. My leg had gone numb nearly an hour earlier, but I hadn't had the heart to move him. I was going to have pins and needles from hell when he finally woke up.

I'd napped with him the first hour, but I'd been awake since, trying to figure out what to do and where to go with the information I now had. I was no closer to an answer than I'd been when we fell asleep, so we needed to talk to someone. The question was, who?

After another ten minutes of questioning myself, I came no closer to figuring it out and Igor was finally beginning to stir. He'd slid progressively down my chest as he'd slept and his head was now on my stomach, his mouth mere centimeters from my belly button, and every time he breathed out, goosebumps rose on my abs.

When Boris had dragged me out of bed at five, I'd thought I was tired, but after coffee and a short nap, I was wide awake. Igor, on the other hand, had clearly been exhausted. Aside from sliding down as he slept, he'd hardly moved. At least he'd hardly moved until he began to wake up and his hand moved from my thigh to my groin. I knew it hadn't been intentional on his part, his breathing was still too even, but my dick didn't know that and began to harden.

It was one thing to overtly show Igor that I'd been turned on by the admissions we'd made to one another over the morning; it was very different for him to *feel* it. That was exactly what was going to happen if his hand stayed where it was.

He finally adjusted and his head lolled downward, his mouth way too close to my dick for comfort. Then he parted his mouth, and the adorable sound of his light snore was forgotten when his breath ghosted over my already half-erect cock. If it hadn't known that Igor was asleep when he'd groped me, it definitely didn't know he was asleep as he kept breathing over my mesh shorts.

"Fuck." Despite biting my fist, my strangled groan sounded harsh in the quiet house. Not that I could stop it. It was that or thrust my dick into Igor's hand and inevitably hit his mouth. Each exhale he made sent my dick harder and harder until I was fully erect and trapped between him and the couch with nowhere to go and no relief in sight.

Five minutes later, with Igor still breathing on my cock head, I was ready to lose my mind. Then Igor stretched and his hand went from resting on my erection to gripping it. The moan I'd mostly staved off a handful of minutes earlier could no longer be held back and came out sounding both startled and frustrated.

"Wha—" Igor's word cut off before he had it fully out. I slammed my eyes shut in an attempt to focus on anything that would help me avoid coming in my pants, but his sharp inhale told me he knew exactly what he'd done. "Oh."

To my surprise, Igor didn't release my dick or make any attempt to move away—exactly the opposite. His hand stayed wrapped around me and he stroked downward. I didn't have to look at him to know it was an experimental stroke, though my eyes defied me and I opened them to look down at him. He wasn't looking at me, just staring intently at my erection under his hand.

The thoughtful hum he let out vibrated my stomach where he had my dick trapped, the sensation bringing me closer to the edge than I already was, and I let out a whimper. "Igor, you're gonna..."

His eyes flicked upward and he met my gaze with sleepy, lust-filled eyes. "Like this?" He stroked along my length again, the slick of the mesh, the heat of his hand,

and the pressure from his grasp all too much, and a chill ran down my body.

"Fuck. Too close."

Igor never moved his eyes from mine and repeated the movement. It was too much. I'd been close to coming before he woke up, but with the added pressure, his breath warming my dick, the hungry look in his eyes, and now the constant stroking, I knew I was going to come no matter what. My body tensed, my balls drawing upward, and tingles formed at the base of my spine.

"Igor." The word was as much of a warning as it was a plea.

I was going to come.

The heat turned into wonder and he worked me again, never taking his eyes off me. When his fingers ran over my mushroom head, I gasped and felt the first volley of cum begin to fill the space between my stomach and shorts. Igor continued to work me over with rapid movements eased by my cum.

I wanted to close my eyes and lose myself in the sensations, but Igor refused to look away and I stubbornly refused to break eye contact. An orgasm that I swore lasted longer than any other racked my body again and again, but aside from a few blinks, we didn't look away from one another.

When my orgasm finally stopped, my cock became overly sensitive and I flinched. Igor let go and finally looked down at my shorts. My eyes followed his and, just as expected, I could see I was a mess. There was no saving my shorts, and I was going to need a shower. His focus on my clothes only lasted a few seconds before his eyes flicked back upward to mine.

"You came." He sounded as shocked as I'd felt when he started deliberately stroking me.

I nodded. "You'd been edging me for five minutes before you woke up. I'd nearly come before you started trying to get me off."

His cheeks turned red. "Was... was that..." He took a steadying breath. "Was that okay?"

If that wasn't okay, there would have been something wrong with me. I didn't say that, though, because I could see the uncertainty and worry in Igor's gaze. There would be a day that he'd need to use words before he could get me off, but today wasn't that day. "More than. Thank you."

Igor blushed more at the praise than he had when he'd woken up and discovered my cock in his hand. I wasn't sure how I'd missed it for all these years and I didn't know how he'd missed it, but looking at him now, there was no question in my mind: Igor was submissive.

I reached for his face and ran my thumb over his stubbled cheek. "Come up here, solnishko."

He followed my lead, adjusting himself until he was eye to eye with me. "What does—"

Before he could finish the question, I leaned forward and brushed my lips against his. He responded with a startled inhale that quickly changed to a happy hum as I continued to press featherlight kisses to his lips, chin, and jaw. The more my lips made contact with his skin, the more relaxed his body became until he finally parted his lips when I made my way back to his mouth.

I took the opportunity to trace his lips with my tongue. Igor responded beautifully, his body shuddering at each new thing I did to him. When I finally placed my hands on his shoulders, I could feel the goosebumps that had formed on his skin while we'd been kissing. Pulling back to see if he was okay, Igor chased my lips, clearly wanting more contact.

"Are you okay?" I asked between light kisses to his lips.

Igor pulled back enough that I could see him. "Do I not look okay?" His words said one thing, but his voice said a totally different thing. I was pretty sure he wanted to call me a moron. Maybe I was, but Igor wasn't some nameless sub at a club—he was my best friend. We had a hell of a lot to still talk about and figure out, but I wanted him to at least know how much I enjoyed what we were doing and also needed to make sure he was okay.

"You have goosebumps."

Igor looked at his arms. "I also have an erection. Does that mean I am not okay?"

There was the snark that I knew from my best friend. It settled a restless part of my soul that I hadn't known was unsettled but left me with more questions. With any other partner, I'd know exactly what to say or do, but Igor was just peeling back the covers on a world he had never known.

It would be easy to get lost in my own head and my own worries, but looking at the earnest happiness on Igor's face, I was reminded that this was my best friend. He was stubborn and opinionated, mischievous and playful, and above all else, he didn't do anything he didn't want to do.

If he'd gotten me off, it was because he'd *wanted* to. Just like his admission about his erection. And that gave me the confidence to continue. "Do you need that taken care of?"

His head bobbed so forcefully, I worried he'd give himself whiplash. Then his hand went to the front of his shorts and he groped the erection fighting against the fabric. "Nyet!" I said sternly, inwardly smirking when his hand loosened and he looked up at me in surprise.

"You, solnishko, do not touch without permission."

He was too shocked at my words to ask about the name. "What?" The sheer level of shock on his face was enough to have me laughing.

I used my finger to close his mouth. "You have much to learn about submission." *And it was going to be fun to teach him.* "First rule, no touching your dick without permission from me."

Igor stared. The only reason his jaw didn't fall open again was because I hadn't removed my hand from under his chin. I could actually feel the added weight of his jaw as it tried to fall open. "Whoa now. That is my dick!"

Through his complaints, Igor's dick had remained just as hard as it had been before we started talking about this. "Two options. One: we talk about relationship and expectations now. Or two: I take care of that erection, then we talk." To emphasize my point, I ran my finger up the length of his dick and winked when his entire body shook. I was pretty sure I knew the answer before he managed to speak.

"T-two. Option two." His head fell back and he moaned when I wrapped my fist around his dick and balls.

"Good boy." I placed a kiss to the crook of his neck and slid my leg out from behind him. The process was harder than it should have been with my leg still mostly asleep. At least once he'd woken up and moved slightly, blood had started to flow back into my leg. There was enough feeling in it that I knew it would hold me upright as I adjusted both of us so that I was kneeling in front of him on the floor. The pins and needles were a bitch, but I had survived worse. Hell, the cold drying cum in my shorts was worse than the tingles in my foot and leg.

"Lift." I tugged at the waistband of his cotton shorts as I gave the instruction, leaving no room for him to question what I'd meant.

Igor lifted slightly. The way he leaned dramatically to one side, I knew that he was keeping pressure off his bad leg and a rush of pleasure washed over me. "You are so fucking good."

I hadn't known it was possible for someone's thighs to blush, but at my praise, I was certain Igor had blushed to his toes. *A brat with a bit of a praise kink.* This was going to be fun.

Igor's cock pressed against his underwear. It looked uncomfortable, trapped in such a small space. My suspicion was quickly confirmed when my fingers gripped the waistband of his underwear, and Igor nearly keened as I worked it clear of his erection and down his legs.

"Krasivo." It had been the first word to come to mind, followed shortly by the English translation. "Beautiful," I said to him as I took him in.

Had it only been eighteen hours since I'd been in the shower with him? It seemed like a million years removed from this moment. The day before had been a blur of activity and emotions. Too much had happened for me to fully enjoy the sight of a naked Igor. Long and lean with slim legs and arms, Igor was a natural hockey player. Strong muscles were hidden beneath tattoos on his arms, legs, chest, and back. His thick cock jutted out in front of him, angled slightly to the right at the tip and long and lean like the rest of him.

And I got to take him in.

"Is everything okay?"

I looked up to see Igor staring at me with worry. The last thing I wanted to do was make him think he had done something wrong or I wasn't insanely attracted to him. "Sorry, I got distracted by how gorgeous you are."

And there went his blush again, flaring back to life. With nothing to hide it, I watched it creep from his chest to his ears, turning his pale skin a rosy pink.

"Does this need to be taken care of?" I ran my finger over the tip of his dick as I spoke.

Igor inhaled sharply. "Fuck. Yes. Yes, it does."

"Mmm. Yes. So good for me." I changed my focus, using two fingers to trace the thick vein along the underside of his cock. It twitched and danced in response and Igor let out a moan of pleasure. "Fuck. Oh fuck." His gasp made me look up in time to see panic cross his face and his eyes go wide.

I pulled my hand back, fully expecting he was going to tell me it was too much too soon. "What is wrong?"

"Can I still cuss?"

The question took me by such surprise, I laughed. "That is what you are worried about? Not my hand on your dick?"

"What? Why would that bother me?" Now Igor was more confused and I felt guilty.

"I think lust has gone to your head. You can curse. I like hearing how you feel. You express yourself beautifully."

He fell back against the couch with a relieved sigh. "Thank fuck."

I really wanted to lap at the bead of precum at Igor's

slit, but first I had to know. "Why would you worry about cursing?"

Igor sat back up. "Because my friend gets in trouble when he uses bad words."

The next time I saw Malcolm Ward, I was going to need to ask him questions, but that was an issue for me to deal with later. Right now the man in front of me needed a reward for giving me an epic orgasm and being brave enough to tell me how he was feeling and what he wanted.

"You can use all the bad words you want." Igor was still processing my words when I leaned forward and lapped at his slit, pushing my tongue in to get everything possible out of it.

Igor fell back again and from the corner of my eye, I saw his fist move. I tracked the movement, my tongue still on his dick, now tracing the vein, and saw him put it in his mouth to muffle his moan. I sat back on my heels. "Do not silence your pleasure. I want to know how good I am making you feel. I want to hear you."

His hand dropped back to his side and I rewarded him with a kiss on the tip of his dick. His whimper turned into a groan of pleasure when I finally wrapped my lips around his dick and sucked him down. I'd practiced for years to lose my gag reflex. Igor's groan turned into needy babbles of praise and pleas that made all the work well worth it.

"Yuri. Fuck. Shit. Yes. How do you do that? So good. More, please."

I gave him more and swallowed him down, his dick sliding down my throat, and he gasped. The man was so responsive it was addictive. If he always reacted that way, I was certain I would frequently be on my knees for him. Then I hummed and Igor beat on the couch with his fists. "Y-Y-Yuri! Fuck, Yuri! My dick. Shit. Fuck. Yuri! Going to..."

I pulled off his dick and looked at him. "You must ask or wait to be told." Either could be fun, but regardless, I needed that control.

Shattering expectations once more, Igor nodded. "Yuri, please. Can I come in your mouth?" His dick twitched against my cheek. "Fuck, your mouth is amazing. I want so much more. Please. Can I come?"

His pleas were beautiful and after I'd come like a hair-triggered teenager during their first handjob, there was no way I was going to deny this beautiful man his release. I kissed his tip and looked into his beautiful, lust-drunk eyes. "You may come when you want."

Igor's entire body sagged with relief. "Can I come in your mouth?"

Dragging the answer out, I kissed his tight balls and the base of his shaft, working my way up. I'd made it all the way to the tip before I spoke. "I'd be offended if you did not." Then I wrapped my lips around his dick and sucked him back down.

To his credit, Igor lasted nearly thirty more seconds before he grunted. Even before cum hit the back of my throat, I'd felt his cock swell with his impending release and had backed off just enough so that I didn't choke.

"Coming!" He bellowed the word loud enough that I worried Seth and Mazdon would hear him from their house nearly a block away. I'd told him to be loud and he'd taken it to heart.

CHAPTER 20

IGOR

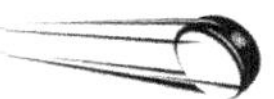

I'd barely had time to catch my breath and Yuri was standing up, pressing a kiss to my lips and using his thumb to wipe my brow. "I will be right back." He made it to the hallway before turning around and pointing at me. "Do not move. Your crutches are not near."

Even if I'd wanted to move, my limbs felt like they were made of cooked spaghetti. There was nowhere I was going to go any time in the near future. Hell, I couldn't manage to make a sound more than a grunt and settled on a thumbs-up to let him know I'd heard.

My eyes drifted shut as soon as Yuri was around the corner and didn't open until a warm cloth ran down my stomach. "Whoa!" I startled, realizing I'd drifted off while Yuri had been gone, and now he was back and cleaning me with a washcloth. The shock faded to awe at his attention. "Whoa."

Yuri looked up. "Okay?"

I was beginning to see that Yuri was going to be asking me that a lot. "Surreal. No one has ever cleaned me up after sex."

On his knees in front of me, Yuri appeared completely in his element. He'd lost his shorts between leaving and coming back. Yet even naked, he was relaxed and confident as he worked the cloth over my stomach, around my balls, and eventually wrapped it around my soft cock and cleaned me fully. "You deserve it."

The praise paired with the sheer sincerity of his voice had my stomach fluttering with an entire field's worth of butterflies. He was so open with the praise that it was easy for me to believe him.

"There." He stood and grabbed the shorts that he'd pulled from me earlier and shook them out before slipping them over my feet and working them up to my thighs. "Lift."

I nearly argued that I could do it on my own, but the determination in his eyes cut my protest off and I lifted my hips, acutely aware of balancing my weight mostly on my good leg. He'd foregone my underwear, but that was probably for the best since they'd been damp with precum when he'd pulled them off of me and by now they'd be cold and gross. Once I was settled on the couch, Yuri stood. His dick was already half-hard again and lying heavily against his thigh.

If he said anything after standing up, I didn't hear it

because my focus was completely on his dick. My thoughts bounced rapid-fire between thinking it was a perfect cock, that I was openly staring at a guy's dick, that I'd had it in my hand earlier, and that if there had been any questions about my newfound sexuality, they had been completely nullified as I sat there with my dick getting hard again despite having just come down Yuri's throat.

Yuri turned and I gasped. "Wait!" He stopped and looked back at me, his brow knit in confusion. "You are leaving?"

He gestured toward the steps. "Yes. To get shorts on. I told you that. *Someone* ruined my other pair. Will be right back. We have much to discuss."

Technically, he'd come in his own pants but I didn't think he wanted to deal in technicalities. "Don't get dressed on my account." I'd meant to think the words, but they'd come out clear as a bell.

A long finger waggled in my direction and Yuri's melodic laugh filled the room. "Oh no. Your distraction from staring at my penis says that I cannot be naked and have conversations with you."

Spoilsport.

Like he could read my mind, he shook his head and walked toward the steps. "There will be time for naked later. Now is time for clothes."

Highly overrated. Clothes could be worn outside of the house. Unfortunately, Yuri was already halfway up the steps and his dick disappeared with his ass as he turned the corner to his room. I'd been annoyed at my hip since before my surgery, but knowing I was unable to chase him up the steps turned my mood downright foul.

Yuri returned in a pair of loose sweatpants that hung low on his pelvic bones before I could do something stupid that would get me yelled at like trying to climb the steps. All I could do was question if this was better or worse than him naked. When he turned to head toward the kitchen, I decided that him clothed was worse than him naked, but him not being next to me was the worst of all.

Thankfully, he returned seconds later, glasses of water in hand. He held one out to me and when I took it, he sat down next to me and placed a pen and pad of paper that I hadn't seen before on his lap. "We must talk."

My nose crinkled. I'd known this was coming. Ryder had warned me that Doms liked to talk a lot and I guessed this was going to be one of those times. It didn't mean I had to like it. "Do we have to?"

Yuri glowered at me. "It is eight forty-five in the morning. I have been up for almost four hours thanks to you. We will talk and figure this out." He pointed between the two of us, then gave a resigned sigh. "You like orgasms. You like to drive me insane—you do that very well by the way. Me? I like stubborn brats, so you are in luck, but I also like control. I like to make decisions. I like punishments."

I'd noticed how he'd looked more closely at me when he'd said he liked punishments. I could only assume that he was looking for a negative reaction from me. Yuri knew this was new to me, but what he didn't know was that I'd had a hell of a lot of time on my hands over the last few weeks. Not being able to get up and go had left me with ample opportunities to look through porn sites and come to terms with the fact that I wasn't as straight as I'd always thought. My Internet searches had also led to countless rabbit holes as I'd scrolled porn sites.

Punishments, at least most of them, were far more interesting than scary. "What types of punishments?"

My direct question took Yuri by surprise and he stared blankly at me for a few seconds. "Nothing too extreme. A flogger or leather paddle, mostly my hands. I like seeing my hand prints on someone's skin."

I nodded. That wasn't too scary, not nearly as bad as the cock and ball torture I'd seen on one of my explorations. Trying to remember everything Ryder had told me the night before was harder with Yuri studying me than I'd thought. What had he said about punishments versus consequences? He'd said something about there being a difference, but my mind was drawing a blank, though that could have been because I'd gotten wrapped up in the idea of a paddle or a flogger. I hadn't seen a leather paddle, but it sounded interesting.

Yuri took my silence as an opportunity to start working things out. "We need to work on expectations and consequences."

"Are those fun or not?"

Yuri smirked, a hint of a wicked Dom coming through. "Depends on the infraction."

My nose wrinkled automatically. *Infraction* reminded me of the rules the dorm leaders had enforced in boarding school. They had never ended in anything fun either. It was usually banging erasers, scrubbing floors, or endless detentions. I was pretty sure that I'd found every rule to break during my tenure as a student. My brother had told me that by the time his son had started there, they had created rules from things I'd done that they hadn't had rules about before. I had learned every consequence the school had and then some, yet I'd known where the line was and I'd never crossed it to become expelled.

"What are you thinking about there?" Yuri was studying me again, though he looked more concerned than amused, and it left my stomach queasy.

"You said infraction. It reminded me of school. Consequences for breaking the rules never made my dick hard in my pants."

Yuri's eyes widened and his face turned red as he bit down on his lip to stave off another laugh. "Jesus, you do not hold back."

Shaking my head, I managed a shrug. "What is the point of holding back? You want me; I want you. You like brats; I am brat. You know me; I know you. Why hold back?"

"Maybe because this is so new to you. I do not want to overwhelm you in the first conversation."

"I watched a man get spanked on my computer. It was sexy and he liked it a lot. His dick was hard and he came while his... well, I guess it was his Dom, spanked him. His Dom told him he would be in a cage for the next week because he came without permission. That was hot too."

"So does that mean you're okay with cock cages?"

I looked down at my dick. It was already hard again. I hadn't had recovery time like this since my teen years, but I was pretty sure I would come in a few strokes if Yuri wrapped his hand around my length. "Not for a week. Few hours might be fun. Not more."

Yuri jotted a note down, nodding thoughtfully to himself. When he looked up, a subtle change had come over his expression. His eyes were focused and his jaw set in concentration. "I was serious. I want control of your orgasms."

My brain said *Hell no*, but my dick twitched with delight. "What if we are not together? I live there." I pointed toward my house. There would be a time when I didn't live in Yuri's guest room and we weren't spending all day, every day together.

"You will call or text."

I narrowed my eyes, thinking his words through. "How will you know I came if I don't tell you?"

Fire flashed in Yuri's eyes. That hint of strong-willed Dom had become a heaping serving in the blink of an eye and I had to fight not to hold my hands up in surrender. He might not have liked it, but it wasn't an unreasonable question to ask. "It is trust. It is respect. I will take care of you, give you what I feel is absolutely best for you. Orgasm when reasonable, denial if you need something else more. I promise to never take advantage of your gift to me, but that means it must work both ways."

The words hit me like a bag of cement to the chest, and air became difficult to take in. So much had been said in that answer, but my mind focused on the meaning more than the words. Had anyone ever put my needs first? Certainly not my parents, who'd sent me to boarding school the first chance they got. It hadn't been past girlfriends, who were more interested in what I could give them than what they could give me.

Was it too early to call Ryder?

Yuri was offering to put my needs first. To think about me and what I needed, not just what I wanted. And not just what he wanted. He was willing to give me everything I'd need, but I had to give him my orgasms... my submission. It was an overwhelming thought, but as I contemplated it, I realized that it was something I wanted. Hell, maybe I needed it.

Throughout our friendship, I'd given him a lot. A lot more than I gave most people. He was the one person I didn't argue with when he told me what I was doing was stupid. Sure, there were times I'd disagreed with him, even protested, but every food poisoning episode since I'd met him had been the direct result of Yuri *not* having a say in it before I'd made up my mind. I pushed, but never far enough to upset him, and I felt like shit every time I did.

I wanted to ask more about the denial and reward thing, but my mind latched on to his word choice at the end. My brain usually jumped around, so I wasn't all that surprised that I'd gone from one thought to another as quickly as I had. What did surprise me was that I'd only just picked up on the last sentence.

"Gift?" What did that mean?

The only thing I saw on Yuri's face was pride. Pride in me. I wished I'd seen that look before because I was pretty sure I would have figured my shit out a lot sooner. "Yes, gift. Submissives, you"—he pointed at me like I needed clarification—"give the Dom a beautiful gift. Gift of submission. It is the Dom's job to not abuse that."

I couldn't quite wrap my head around what he was saying. Ryder and I had talked about a lot the night before, but this was new to me. Yuri must have seen the confusion on my face because he nodded. "As the submissive, you give me only as much as you are willing. You tell me how much, to stop, where *your* line is. It is *my* job to respect that and not cross lines. Submissives are in control, always."

"But you can deny me what I want?" How did this work? Why had Ryder made this sound so effortless, but I was struggling to wrap my head around Yuri's carefully chosen words?

"I can deny you what you ask for if I think that is what

you need... or maybe even what you want. But if you do not agree, we have a word. It stops everything without question."

Something pinged in my brain. "Like that game? I say a word and get out of jail free?"

He let out a truly amused chuckle. "Basically, yes. We talk about it. We see what went wrong." He tapped the notebook in his lap with the pen he was holding. "See, I have been taking notes since we sat down."

While I couldn't read it from my position, Yuri had scratched notes all over the paper. I hadn't known we'd said that much, much less talked about that many noteworthy topics.

"Spanking, flogging, paddles, yes. You like porn. Cock cages, maybe. Consequences, yes." Placing the notebook back on his lap, Yuri looked over at me. "Unsure of orgasm control." Then he looked down at my dick. "But dick says otherwise."

There was no point in hiding my shock. We had talked about all of that so naturally I hadn't really thought of it as having a serious conversation, though Yuri clearly had.

"Yes, see, this is why we talk. You are surprised at how much I have learned. You are so new to this lifestyle, you cannot know what you do not know to ask."

That was a deep thought. "So a word stops it all?"

He nodded without hesitation. "In its tracks. No questions. I say to do something, you cannot or do not want to, you say the word. It stops. We talk. We move on."

"Will you deny often?" I couldn't believe the question had come out of my mouth, I'd already decided I liked the idea, but the reality was a little frightening to think about. I didn't know if I'd like it in practice, but Yuri was so earnest, so open, that it would have been foolish for me to not give it serious thought.

Somehow, Yuri didn't laugh at my question. "Domination for me is not about denial. It is about mutual respect and taking decisions out of your hands. You hear that I want to control your orgasms. What I want is to take one decision away from you. If I make easy decisions for you, you have more left to make big decisions." He paused, obviously reaching for words he was struggling to find, but I was happy to wait him out. The more he spoke, the more my pulse slowed.

"You ask, Yuri, can I come? I take time and think about it. What time is it? Should he be doing something else? Does he have plans? Has he respected rules today? Is he tired and should sleep? I will give you answer taking all into consideration." He found my eyes again and I knew he desperately wanted me to understand what he was saying. "I make small decisions: orgasms, bedtime, chores. Everything is clear and you do not have to make so many small choices. Then when big decisions come your way—who starts in net, a different job offer, an unexpected change in routine or schedule—you have more focus to give to that. Clearer mind to think. And I am still here to talk to about big problems."

I sat in stunned silence. It made sense in some crazy way that I'd never expected. His words, his ideas, his plan, it was all crystal clear. There was only one thing that had filled me with fear and panic, and it hadn't been Yuri's control of my orgasms. "I will not be going anywhere without you."

CHAPTER 21

YURI

Igor had been out of his depth and confused for most of the conversation. He'd gone from indignant about his orgasms to thoughtfully pondering the pros of what I'd told him my overall goal was. But then I'd tried to explain to him what I meant by big decisions and had used a job offer as an example. I had only meant it as an example of something stressful, never meaning to cause him stress in the moment, but that was exactly what I'd done. I'd seen the way his pupils dilated and his breath had caught and no matter how I'd tried to soften the end of the thought, he'd been caught up on the job offer.

What I hadn't expected was that Igor had translated *job offer* to moving away. Not just moving from Nashville, but more importantly from me. Until then, I'd thought there was a chance that Igor had been experimenting, or maybe I was a convenient single man that he knew and trusted. He'd convinced me that he wasn't completely straight, but I hadn't fully understood how invested he'd become in *me*.

Looking at him beside me, horrified at the thought of going somewhere without me, I discovered just how serious his feelings were. And in return, just how invested I'd become in him. While I'd thrown the idea out as a potential big decision, it had also caused me more stress than I'd been willing to admit to myself. At least until I'd seen how it had impacted Igor.

I knew I needed to keep the conversation on track, but the emotions swirling in my stomach, heart, and brain were inevitably going to impact the direction of our conversation. "And that is why we talk. There is no such thing as too much talk for me, not when it comes to this." I gestured between us for emphasis.

As his friend, I had always made time for Igor. Moving forward as his boyfriend, his Dom, I would never make a decision that didn't take Igor into account. My English made communication hard at times and I'd learned early on that making time to talk was the most important thing in any relationship but most especially in one that had any degree of power exchange. Knowing that I was talking to my best friend about entering just that type of relationship with him, I knew communication was going to be the single most important part for us.

Nervously raking his hands through his hair, Igor no

longer looked as stubborn or petulant as he normally did. A vulnerable innocence radiated off him that I wished I could take away with reassurances or action. Except we hadn't finished our conversation. I didn't have what I needed to know how to help him. The only way I could help was to push forward and hope that I didn't put my foot in my mouth in the process.

Pointing back at my notebook page, I tried to redirect the conversation. "That is why we must talk today. I need to know what are hard limits. What makes your dick say yes, your brain say no, or a combination of the two. Then we have a..." Fuck, there was a word for what I was looking for and I couldn't find it. "We have a plan written out to follow."

"Blueprint?" Igor supplied and I snapped my fingers. Finally, I hadn't fucked up a description so much that it made no sense.

"Yes, blueprint. My notes here, they tell us how we will communicate, how we will work out problems. What will work and not. If in a day, week, year, or ten years, we discover something does not work for us, we talk and make changes."

"I like that." Igor's voice was so small that I had to question if he knew he'd said the words out loud. He looked more in awe than upset, and I was going to take it and run.

"Great. Then let's talk about expectations."

His nose wrinkled again, but he didn't argue with me, instead giving a nod. "What type of expectations?"

This could be fun. And part of me really wanted to tease him more, make unreasonable expectations just for the reaction, but the logical part of my brain knew that was a terrible idea. For now Igor was not in the right place for jokes. Maybe if he wasn't just discovering submission, jokes and teasing would have worked, but what he needed was clear boundaries and honest communication and agreements from both of us.

"Let's start with food choices."

It was a light topic and would hopefully be easy to agree on. It also drew a resigned yet slightly amused groan from Igor. "You are taking away my favorite foods."

Not bothering to sugarcoat it, I nodded. "Not all of them. Just the ones that make you sick."

"And how will you do that?" He hadn't issued a challenge, more asked a question, and I was happy to oblige.

"By making an expectation that you clear all restaurants by me before you eat at them."

I should have known Igor wouldn't agree without any discussion. "What do I get when I agree?"

Shrugging, I looked down at the list. "Well, we already know you like blowjobs."

Igor flushed, though he managed to nod his head in agreement.

"But if you listen well, maybe you can earn a spanking and an extra orgasm when you get home."

Questions flew across Igor's face faster than I could keep up with. I hoped he was going to ask about a spanking as a reward, but he wasn't ready to go there just yet. "What if I don't agree when you say no?"

"Then we talk. We talk about why you decided to not listen. The consequence will depend on how often it happens and why it did. Maybe extra chores or no orgasm. Maybe spanking—not for fun—or flogging. That is why we are working on this now.

"And this part is really, really important. If I am ever really mad at you, this list will not be used. No one should ever be touched in anger. Ever. If there is a time that one of us is really mad, we will talk it through like..." I trailed off for a moment trying to figure out what to say. This was not a place to fuck up my words. The only word I cme up with was simple yet fitting. "Like partners . After we have talked and calmed down, if you still need a consequence to recenter yourself, then we can talk again."

I paused to see where Igor's questions were. There was no way he didn't have questions; I just needed to wait him out. Thankfully, I didn't have to wait long. "Some people need to be spanked to feel better?" He couldn't keep the surprise out of his voice and I knew that if that was his biggest worry, we were in good shape.

"People need all sorts of different things. Just like I need to be able to not only help my partner with decisions, I also need to be able to *do* things for them. That's where my need to serve them and be useful really comes into play. Your making me work to do things for you might drive me mentally insane, but the physical reward when you finally let me is what makes it all worth it for me."

Something I'd said resonated with Igor because he nodded his head. "Okay. Let's keep talking."

And we did. We talked for nearly two more hours until both our stomachs began to rumble with hunger and Igor looked exhausted again. We'd covered topics ranging from reasonable sleeping hours to healthy eating and expectations around communication. Some of the conversations were awkward, others were funny, but as I shut the notebook, I knew we had a good starting point for our relationship.

It was still strange to think about it like that, but that was exactly where the conversations had led us. "You still need to come up with a safeword."

We'd covered those in our talk and I was leaving it up to him which system he chose. I'd had partners who used stoplight colors and ones who used a random word. For me, I tended to use a combination of the two. The traffic light system worked great for scenes that built slowly to a point that *red* might be needed. However, if something came up suddenly, I stuck with *tunec*, the Russian word for tuna. It was a food I'd never liked and there was no way I'd forget the word. It was definitely the best thing for me when it came to needing things to stop immediately.

Igor click-clacked behind me as he thought. I'd put

two grilled cheese in one of the pans before he finally spoke. "Queue."

"*Q*?" I asked, turning to study him while trying to figure out why he had chosen a letter as his safeword. Maybe I hadn't heard him right.

Igor nodded emphatically. "It's such a weird word. Queue here, please. I remember the first time I heard it when I played in the AHL. I had just moved to Canada, and one of the assistants said to queue. I asked four times what that meant before one of the guys on the team figured out that I did not understand what it meant and explained it to me. Why not just say *line up* or *wait here?* Why do they need some weird word for it? And why does it have so many damn letters?"

I shook my head, though I couldn't fault his logic. "Works for me." I didn't have a chance to say anything else before Igor was engrossed in texting someone. He stayed glued to his phone until I slid a plate of food in front of him, and even then he kept staring at the phone.

"Solnishko, phone down. When we eat, we do not stare at phones."

At least my words made him look up from the screen, but he seemed more confused than ready to comply. For emphasis, I pointed at his phone. "Down, please. Meals are a good time to connect and talk. Cannot connect if someone is staring at a phone."

While he didn't put the phone down, he did back out

of the conversation he had open. "I'm talking to a friend. We're discussing today."

I understood just how important having an understanding friend would be for him, but I also wasn't willing to budge on my stance. We stared one another down for a few seconds, though my patience was much greater than Igor's. His light eyes were easy to read, every thought and possibility flashing as he debated between arguing, relenting, or some combination of the two. In the end, he sighed and put his phone on the table, turning it over so the screen was facing downward.

"Thank you."

Igor's lips pursed, letting me know just how conflicted he was with what he'd done. I wanted a brat to keep me on my toes and I knew Igor would be perfect for the job. I was going to have to utilize my patience and let him find his footing. "You're welcome."

He poked at the small side salad with his fork and I sat back, content to let him think for now. I'd eaten three bites of my own salad before his voice finally broke the silence. "Should I have argued more?"

Amusement bubbled inside me, though I hoped it didn't show on my face or in my voice. "I believe you did exactly right there. I know there will be times that you argue. Maybe to get a punishment, maybe because you're testing limits and boundaries, or maybe to get my attention, but this is new to both of us. I would be surprised if you had defied me so quickly."

Before Igor could respond, I knew I needed to clarify the statement and make my wishes clear. "I want a brat, Igor. I need someone who is not going to follow without argument all the time. I like the push and pull. It makes the submission so much more gratifying for me. I like when you argue and push, so do not always agree if it does not feel right. However, I understand that it will take time for you—for both of us."

Igor relaxed and went back to his salad. Ten minutes later, his plate empty and in the sink, he looked over at me. "Can I go back to my conversation now?"

Pride and arousal zipped through me. Whether he knew it or not, Igor had looked to me for permission. "Yes. Thank you for asking." Igor's cheeks tinted pink and he turned quickly to pocket his phone and hobble off toward his room, leaving me to once again wonder how no one had picked up on his submission before.

It was only eleven and we'd put in a full day. I pulled up the time converter on my phone and noticed it was seven in the evening in Russia, late enough that Danil would be home and early enough that Babushka would still be awake. I pressed Danil's contact number and listened as the line rang.

"Yuri! My long-lost brother. I thought you disappeared!" Danil's fast-paced Russian words were a balm to my soul. It was the first time all summer I'd had a chance to relax and think about where I would have been if I'd not been in Nashville with Igor.

"I have been busy. The phone works both ways. You can call me, you know."

Danil gave a boisterous laugh and I heard Babushka in the background asking who he was talking to. "Yuri, Babushka." Then he turned his attention back to me. "There is a parade this evening through town. I came over for dinner and to keep her inside."

We both chuckled, our familiar banter returning like we weren't over five thousand miles apart and hadn't seen one another in over a year. We talked about his work, my summer, and Igor's recovery. I filled him in on the Pride parade and listened to the awe in his voice at how open the city had been to it. One year, I hoped that I could talk Babushka and Danil into moving here with us. Danil would love the city. Even the conservative state I lived in was night and day compared to living in Russia.

Twenty minutes in, I heard a *thwack* and Danil yelped. "Ouch, Babushka! What was that for?"

In my mind, I could see her finger shaking at Danil as she scolded him for hogging the phone before her warm voice filled my ear. "Yuri! My sweet prince! How are you, solnishko?"

"I'm good, Babushka." The smile on my face and in my voice was impossible to hide, and I took a moment to burrow into the big couch in the den.

"And your friend?"

"He's good. Finally moving more. It's been a slow recovery. Slower than he'd like."

She gave a thoughtful hum in my ear. "But I am sure that you are keeping him in line, no?"

"Yeah. It's a full-time job, though."

"Yes. But you are up for it. You like order and rules."

Oh god, she was talking about it. I tried so hard to keep conversations like this at bay, but I'd walked into this one. "Bab—"

I didn't have a chance to finish her name before she clucked her tongue in my ear. "Do not try to silence me, child. I know these things. Are things going well for both of you?"

How did she know these things? I hadn't even said Igor's name and we'd only been talking for a few seconds. "Things are well."

"Are you treating him well?"

"Babushka..." I dropped my voice to a warning tone as I said the word. I loved her, but she needed to stop.

She blew a raspberry into my ear that made me wince. "Child, I raised you. I have not said anything since you started talking about him. Since you moved to Nashville, it has been Igor this and Igor that. Every conversation is about him. I know you have feelings for him. I haven't said anything all this time but this summer, when you stayed there to be with him, I thought you'd finally come to your senses. Have you not? Has he not? Has he hurt my solnishko? Do I need to fly over there with dinner rolls?"

Somewhere between horrified and in disbelief, I found laughter. "Babushka! Stop it!" I had to pause to catch my breath. "You do need to come here, yes, but leave the dinner rolls at home. Well, you can bring them if you want but make sure they are fresh. No stale rolls need to be thrown here. It is very, very new, but we're figuring things out."

"Well, that is good. I'm glad to hear that you have pulled your head out of your ass."

Danil was cackling in the background while I rubbed my temples. It was clear where I'd gotten my stubbornness from. Hopefully, Igor appreciated it as much as I appreciated my babushka's. Heaven help us if the two ever found themselves in the same room.

CHAPTER 22

IGOR

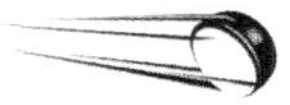

"I hurt so bad." Ryder flopped down on the couch beside me, flinging his forearm over his eyes and sighing loudly. "I hate training camp."

Looking over at my friend, I could tell he was sore. There was a nasty bruise on his thigh and a big scab on his elbow that had started to heal but still looked painful. "How much longer do you have?"

He yawned. "Another week. And we're not even at full contact yet!"

Being able to drive to Malcolm's house today had been both a breath of fresh air and surreal. I'd driven myself to PT for the first time since my surgery, Indy finally giving me the all clear at the end of our session the day before. From the stadium, I'd driven to Ryder's place instead of back to Yuri's.

Technically, I was free to move home, finally able to

safely climb steps and move with a single crutch or a cane. My leg was still sore, but it was getting better by the day. I should have been ecstatic to head back to my house. I'd been lamenting not being able to go home for nearly seven weeks. But now that the time had come, the last place I wanted to be was alone in my home. Which was why I'd called Ryder and asked if I could stop over.

It turned out that he and Malcolm lived in the development that connected to ours. The homes were bigger and slightly more spaced out, and most of the married couples on the team lived there. And while neither were married, both Coach Cunningham and Coach Bouchard lived in the same neighborhood, so I was familiar with it. I hadn't expected the huge garage attached to a house that was basically the size of a small car dealership showroom, though. Ryder had met me outside the garage door and led me through to the house as he pointed out all his cars, a huge grin on his face as he'd done so.

My head had been swimming with thoughts about the day and moving forward, so most of what he'd said went in one ear and right out the other. He'd directed me straight into the house and I wasn't sure if he'd invited me to sit on the couch or if I'd taken it upon myself to take a seat. Now that I'd sat down, it didn't matter much as I wasn't sure I'd be getting up again, not because I was sore but because I was pretty sure the couch had swallowed me whole. At least it was a comfortable place to die.

"I know the pain of training camp all too well and I don't get checked into the boards. Training camp is hard."

Ryder's eyes twinkled, little flecks of hazel shining in his otherwise brown eyes. "But now you're the coach!" His mouth parted as he realized something. "How is that going to work? You're Yuri's coach, but he's your Dom!"

I shrugged, honestly not sure, though it was far from the first time the thought had crossed my mind. "We're still figuring things out. Did it take time for you to figure things out with Malcolm? I never had a problem pushing Yuri's buttons before, but now I feel like I'm second-guessing everything. He keeps telling me that being myself is perfect for him and to stop overthinking. I just can't stop worrying that I'm going to mess it up."

I couldn't decide if it was good or bad when Ryder pursed his lips and thought for nearly a minute. "When Malcolm discovered I was little, he figured it all out before he ever brought it up with me. It was so natural. That doesn't mean that it was seamless. It took months before I was able to tell him when I needed to shut my brain off for a bit. Before then, he always initiated."

After slipping up and revealing that Malcolm was his Daddy, Ryder hadn't talked directly about their relationship until now. All the new information had my brain tripping over itself in an attempt to keep up with his thoughts. His cheeks turned red as he spoke, I guessed much like mine did every time I tried to talk about submitting to Yuri. "Then at the end of regular season play, it was all too much to process. I finally admitted to myself that Malcolm loved every part of me, however I was feeling at the time. It didn't just have to be him that initiated playtime."

His eyes fell to the corner of the room and a soft smile played on his lips. My eyes naturally followed his gaze and fell on a table with wood train tracks, a few rugs with roads, and buckets of cars and trains. I finally figured out what playtime meant for Ryder and knew he was trusting me with a very special part of himself. While I had questions, I wasn't here to pepper him for information about *his* life; I was here for clarity on *mine*. The questions about him could wait.

Not pressing Ryder for information about his personal life and focusing on mine had me tossing my arm over my eyes the same way Ryder had a few minutes earlier. "I don't feel like we're moving forward. It's so awkward!"

"You like impact play, right?"

I lifted a shoulder. "I'm not completely certain, but I think so. I've watched a lot of... call it research... lately, and I can definitely say that it interests me. I've never been spanked before, though. It's on the list of rewards and consequences that Yuri made."

Ryder wiggled in his spot, giddy with excitement. "Ask him for a spanking!"

I knew I'd heard him right but at the same time, I was certain I couldn't have heard him right. "What?"

"You need to break the ice. Tell him that you need to get out of your head."

"With a spanking?" I hadn't gone down this particular rabbit hole before, yet I was having a hard time finding fault in Ryder's logic.

Ryder was ready to argue his point. "Yes! Lots of submissives need and like the physical release of being spanked. It lets their mind clear and recenter. You haven't been talking to Yuri about your concerns and now they've gotten bigger than you can handle on your own. You need to tell him that."

"Ugh." My head fell forward with my groan. "What if he's mad at me?"

The look Ryder gave me was filled with a giant unspoken *are you serious,* but the words he said were filled with compassion. "If Yuri is anything like Malcolm or a halfway decent Dom in general, he's going to be way more proud of you for talking with him and telling him what's on your mind. Even if it's weeks late."

"I know, logically, Yuri will be happy if I talk to him. It is more that I like the idea of Yuri happy. I do not like him upset. Fun spankings sounds sexy. Punishment spankings sound... not." *Where is the line between fun and punishment?* I was finally finding a voice to put with the fears I'd been harboring for weeks.

Ryder just shrugged. "Are you really supposed to *like* it? Like you said, fun spankings are just that. They are to make you horny, for foreplay, or sometimes to get you both off. A consequence spanking is meant to give you—and Yuri—a chance to work out what's wrong in a safe, consensual, and agreed upon way. They really shouldn't be sexy. They should, however, bring you closer together. Honestly, I don't think this is really a consequence anyway, at least not the way you're describing it. It sounds more like a way to connect and get things on track. Would it help if I told you some people call them therapeutic spankings?"

"Therapeutic spanking?" My eyes and voice rose in unison. *Actually, that might help.*

"It's a release. It's meant to allow you to let go. Some people just need a way to get out of their heads. From what I've read, they tend to hit differently." He chuckled at his joke. "Sorry, that was just funny. I meant that they are made for releasing emotions. Tears, yelling, massive emotional release, it's all really normal and honestly can be super healthy."

I'd done enough agonizing therapies to know that sometimes the ones that hurt the worst were the ones that helped the most. Reframing my view on them, a therapeutic spanking didn't hold the same weight as a consequence. It didn't seem scary. I liked thinking about it as a way to connect. Maybe what we both needed was a healthy release of everything we'd pent up for the last three weeks.

"That doesn't sound as bad." I even managed a smile as I thought about it. "And I think Yuri has talked about something like that. He said I might need or ask for one. It didn't make sense at first. I think I understand now."

Ryder nodded, his brown hair flopping into his eyes before he pushed it back. "You have to talk to Yuri first, though. It's really important that you get all those thoughts out."

Groaning because I knew he was right, I found myself nodding. "He harped on communication a lot that first day."

"Uh-huh. Malcolm's big on it too. And routines. He really, really likes routines." He stifled a yawn and glanced toward the clock on the wall, then back to me. "If he hasn't picked up on the fact that things have been weird, then he's going to feel guilty too. If he's anything like Malcolm, he's going to feel like a bad Dom for not detecting that you've been struggling.

"This is all so new to both of you, maybe he's been trying to give you space, or has been expecting you to be kind of confused, or maybe he's been trying to take his cues from you and not push too hard too fast. Knowing that it's something you have thought about and understand and—at least on some level—want, I bet he'd oblige."

"I really hate that you're probably right. But that means needing to get up, which could be hard on this couch."

"It's the best part of it! It's like a constant hug."

A door opened in the front of the house and Malcolm's deep voice called out. "Hey, baby, I'm home."

"In the living room! Igor came over after his therapy session today."

Malcolm came around the corner, tired and obviously happy to be home. "That explains the unfamiliar car." He studied Ryder and a silent conversation passed between the two of them before Malcolm finally shook his head and turned away. "Five minutes."

Ryder rolled his eyes, though the smile on his face said he wasn't actually upset. "That's my warning."

"Warning for what?" I probably shouldn't have asked, except curiosity had gotten the better of me.

"Nap time. Malcolm takes it very seriously." Ryder wiggled toward the front of the couch and I followed suit, grabbing the cane I was using to help dislodge me from the cushions that had engulfed me. Ryder noticed my struggle and gripped my other arm to pull me forward. "Isn't it wonderful?"

He was so sincere that I couldn't help but smile. "That's one word for it." My accompanying wink took any bite from my words. It really was a comfortable couch and if I ever wanted to be trapped, it would be the place I'd pick.

We slowly made our way to the door, Ryder talking the entire way. "You have to get out of your head. I bet you'll find exactly what you've needed to let go of those remaining doubts. You've been so worried about upsetting

Yuri you haven't been yourself. If you bite the bullet and actually talk with him, I think you're going to see that you've built up a scenario in your head that's way worse than reality."

Malcolm came out of an office and wrapped his arm around Ryder's body to press a kiss to his head. "I don't know exactly what the two of you are actually talking about, but I can tell you that Ry's giving you good advice. You can't hide things from your boyfriend, especially if your boyfriend is your Dom. Talking to a friend is great, but you really should be with Yuri, talking to him."

I wrinkled my nose, mostly in acceptance that I was going to have to go to Yuri's house and talk. Why did feelings have to be so complicated? And why did Ryder and Malcolm have to live only a few blocks from home? There wasn't going to be nearly enough time to sort my feelings out between here and there.

"Fine, you're right. I guess." My groan was absolutely defeated. "Talk later."

Ryder opened the door and waved me goodbye as I made my way down the few steps on their porch and to my car. "Text when you're allowed to."

I waved back, promising to let him know how it went, then sank into the driver's seat of my car, wondering if Yuri would actually not allow me to text for a while. Would I be able to accept that? A pesky voice in the back of my brain was telling me that I would, especially if it made things go back to normal. Another rather logical voice told me that I had my safeword if I needed it.

Shaking my head at myself, I turned off Ryder's street and directed my car out of the neighborhood, taking the next turn into ours. A few more turns and my home was in sight. Logically, I should have parked in my own driveway, walked up my own front steps, and entered my own house for my first official day home since I'd walked out the door on my way to the hospital nearly seven weeks earlier. Except as I drove by my driveway, my house felt like just that, a house. A place where my belongings were.

My car parked itself in Yuri's driveway of its own accord. His garage, his front door, his familiar windows and familiar trees, and his familiar dog sitting in the familiar bay window looked way more like my home than the one I'd paid for. I took a moment to breathe, wondering if I could really walk inside and ask Yuri to spank me to get me out of my head.

Ryder and Malcolm had made more sense than I'd cared to admit to myself and deep down, I knew they were right. We had to figure out a way past this awkward place we'd been at for nearly three weeks. And maybe that was why Ryder and Malcolm were right. I needed this.

Ryder was so certain it would help and things would be fine, I'd found myself hoping he was right. If they weren't, it was better to figure it out early on anyway. At least I could tell myself that for now.

With newly discovered clarity, I shut the car off and

got out, making my way to the front door as quickly as my gait would allow. I'd told Yuri I would go to my house after PT, leaving me in this uncomfortable place where I didn't know if I should walk in or knock on his door. There were too many questions and not enough answers, and that nearly paralyzed me with indecision.

I finally took a deep breath and raised my hand to knock just as the door swung open, and Yuri and I both yelped in shock.

CHAPTER 23

YURI

Igor teetered on the top step for a second, nearly falling backward before I reached out and grabbed him. He looked as though he'd just seen a ghost, though I probably didn't look any better myself. The last person I'd expected to be on my porch was the man I was going next door to see.

"Come in," I said, taking his free arm and leading him into the house and directly to the couch in the living room.

Boris was clearly excited to see him as he walked around wagging his entire backside waiting for Igor to sit on the couch. My dog had fallen in love with Igor, leaving me second best.

"Are you okay? Did something happen at therapy? Did you hurt your leg driving?" Fuck, I'd beaten myself up the last three hours for not taking him to therapy that morning. Indy had sworn he was fine to drive and Igor had assured me he was feeling good as well, so I'd relented and regretted it ever since.

"I'm not hurt. Therapy was fine."

His words were too clipped, too formal, too rehearsed to settle my nerves. If I was being honest with myself, it was that carefulness that had me so on edge. It had been there for weeks, simmering just below the surface, but hadn't come to the forefront until Igor pulled out of the driveway that morning.

Things weren't right. He was being too careful, too planned, too... I couldn't find a word or an action that fit what he was; I just knew it was off. More off than he had been since we had talked about consequences and rewards. He'd still be a pain in my ass, but not in the same way my best friend was a pain in my ass. And nowhere near the pain in the ass that earned a spanking. Usually just enough to earn a growl or stern glare.

It had been such a subtle change that I hadn't picked up on it right away. It hadn't been until the last few days that I'd realized he hadn't pushed me to the point I was more than exasperated with him.

I'd spent the morning trying to put my finger on what was up and how to talk to him, but he clearly had something to talk to me about first. The man in front of me was... anxious, almost antsy, but I knew that wasn't the right word and it took me a moment to figure it out.

"You are nervous."

The sound that came out of Igor was like a balloon

deflating, and then he nodded. "I went to talk with Ryder today. He and Malcolm pointed stuff out."

I didn't like the sound of *stuff*, though I was happy he'd been able to talk with them and I wasn't convinced that it was all bad things they'd talked out. The truth was Igor thrived with routines and schedules. His laundry was done, he had been working on coaching plans in the evenings, and he had plenty of time to relax and play a game or chat with Ryder. He was eating better and not waking up exhausted. He'd even made a routine with Boris in the evenings, the two going on walks every night. It had started out just to the corner and back but had progressed to around the block and the night before, they'd been gone an hour.

But that hadn't made things right, either.

There was a lot I wanted to talk to Igor about. After three hours of thinking, I'd had plenty of time to work my own thoughts and feelings out and had a plan on how to talk to him, but I knew he wasn't going to be able to focus on what I had to say if he had his own thoughts bouncing around in his head.

"Would you like to talk about that *stuff*?" The sentence sat like acid on my tongue. What if they'd discussed ending what we were just starting? What if Igor was doubting his sexuality? Thirty-five years thinking he was straight, only to discover he was attracted to men might have been too much to process once we'd really gotten to the cuddling, kissing, handjobs, and blowjobs of the previous weeks. He'd always been an eager participant, but maybe I'd read the signs wrong.

Igor nodded slowly, gathering his thoughts for a number of seconds before finally speaking. "Yeah. It's just all confusing in my head and I don't know where to start."

I gave him a few more minutes to sort out his feelings and just when I thought I'd have to prod, Igor blurted out a sentence so fast, my ears didn't immediately process it. "I think I need to be spanked."

When the words finally sank into my brain, I knew my shock and confusion had to show on my face. "You think you need to be spanked?"

His cheeks turned bright red before he gave a near imperceptible nod.

Until then, I'd been convinced he was trying to find the words to break up with me. Somehow over the course of the morning and his discussion with his friends, he had come to the same conclusion I had. I'd been heading over to talk to him about exactly that when he'd shown up on my doorstep.

I swallowed thickly, trying to control my libido's immediate happy dance. "What makes you say that?"

Igor adjusted on the couch, his movements so much smoother than they'd been a few weeks earlier. "I have been torn and I didn't talk to you about it." He shook his head, disagreeing with himself. "Actually, I did not fully understand my feelings until Ryder and I talked today. I might not completely understand still."

That sounded ominous, but I proceeded carefully. "Talking is important." *I'd wanted to talk to him too, except this was taking priority.*

"Ryder said as much." He blinked at me, his pale eyes showing confusion.

"It is new to you. Everything is new: Boyfriend, submission, domination. Questions and concerns are normal for any new relationship that has power exchange. "I only figured out today that you have not been completely yourself. You are... Igor, but reserved. I miss my pain in the ass that makes me want to scream. I am sorry."

Igor puffed up, confidence returning to him as I spoke. He even managed a small laugh when I'd told him I missed his driving me insane. "No. Do not apologize. I knew I was struggling, but I had no idea how to talk about it or what my struggles really were about. Not until I talked with Ryder."

Now that he'd started talking, words were coming out more easily. "I keep worrying that I will push too far and actually upset you. Spankings sound fun in theory, but I realized it is not the fun spankings I am worried about. I know you said spankings will never happen if you are mad at me, but I do not know where that line is."

His words were making sense. "It can be big and overwhelming. And you have never been spanked before."

Igor nodded emphatically, his eyes lighting up the same way they did when he was happy and excited. "Yes. That!"

"You say was. Did something change?"

"Something did. Ryder told me to think of it like therapy, not a consequence."

Ryder was a very smart man and I was thankful Igor had him to talk to. Igor's thoughts kept going and no matter what I wanted to say, I was going to let him finish.

"He said that they are different than ones that are meant to be erotic. They help people recenter." Igor lifted his eyes once more to meet mine in a silent plea for me to understand what he was talking about. I wished he could have seen his face when he saw my smile—it stopped his thought in its tracks. "You know about them?"

If possible, his bashfulness had flared back even stronger than it had been when we'd sat down. "I do. But I think Ryder explained them much better than I could." I reached out to hold his hand. The distance between us had begun to feel too great and I needed to touch him.

With his hand in mine, I took a moment to gather my thoughts before speaking . "I had come to the same conclusion earlier. Well, not quite same. I just realized something was off. I didn't know exactly what, but you do not drive me insane like before. I had thought role play, let me spank you because you purposely did something wrong. Maybe, then you would tell me what was wrong." I gave an uncomfortable shrug, knowing I hadn't explained my thoughts well, but hoped like hell Igor understood.

His laugh came out a half gasp, half laugh, and all

disbelief. "Yeah, I think Ryder did a better job explaining that."

"Brat."

The playful, mischievous smile I was so accustomed to on Igor was back on his face. I hadn't taken him across my lap, hadn't begun to redden his perfect ass, and he was already lighter. It was a stark reminder that we needed to talk more often, especially while we were both figuring things out. I loved how Ryder called it therapeutic. That was exactly what Igor needed at the moment. He needed a release and the ability to know that all was okay.

"Do you think you can make it up the steps today?"

After studying the steps and actually giving it thought, he nodded. "I think so. It will take me time."

"Do you want me to walk with you?" There was no way I was going to leave him to walk up the steps by himself if he had any doubt in his mind that he was completely capable of the journey.

"You don't need to walk with me, though I think I'm going to always want you to walk *with* me."

There were so many emotions and feelings to work out, so many hurdles left to cross before either of us were ready to broach the topic of love, but those words told me we'd get there sooner rather than later. I'd loved Igor as a friend for years. He'd been the most important person in my life since I'd signed with the Grizzlies. It wasn't going to take much to turn my platonic love for him into an all-encompassing love of not only my friend but my boyfriend.

Simply knowing that he'd thought about his needs and our needs enough to talk with Ryder about them pushed my feelings about him to the brink of love, however premature it might be.

"I'll always walk with you, Igs." I stood and held my hand out, marveling at his lack of hesitation in reaching out to me and allowing me to support him on the way up. Igor from a month ago wouldn't have thought about taking my hand or letting me help without a fight. This wasn't the same placating way he'd been allowing me to do things for him either. This was my boyfriend, my submissive, giving me a part of himself without thought or hesitation and the action sent my heart soaring.

"Thanks." He leaned forward and gave me a kiss, a smile tugging at his lips as he did so. "Is it wrong that I'm actually looking forward to this?"

"Not at all." We walked up the steps together, me right behind him as he made steady progress. I thought about running back downstairs for a bottle of water, but there was an untouched one on my nightstand from the night before and I decided that it would do. I didn't want to leave Igor for even a minute. It was time for me to take that worry away from him.

There was a fine line between too fast and too slow as I moved us toward the bed. In an ideal world, I'd be able to sit on the side of the bed and drape Igor's body over my lap. The position was so much more vulnerable and easier to let go in than lying nearly flat on the bed. Unfortunately, Igor's hip was still healing. Bent over my lap was a recipe for a pinch or twinge that would pull him straight from pleasure to pain. Igor needed to let go, and while the physical vulnerability might not be there, the fact that he was letting himself be so open with me was enough for me to be confident that he'd be able to get what he needed.

I toed my shoes off, then bent to remove Igor's. "You do not need to do that for me," he said, instinctively stepping away from me.

On my knee looking up into his face, I cocked my eyebrow. He hadn't realized it, but it was the first time in three weeks that he'd resisted me in any way. I wasn't going to point it out to him, though I was beyond excited by the development. "You are right. I do not need to, I want to."

He didn't argue more, just moved toward the bed and sat to allow me to remove each of his shoes. I compromised and didn't untie his laces, no matter how much it drove me insane that he didn't tie them right, and set his shoes to the side of the bed. Once we were both standing again, I took his waistband in my hands, giving him plenty of warning that his pants were about to come off.

While Igor didn't stop me, I did notice his breath catch when I had his pants down. I left him in his underwear and shirt. He would lose his underwear in short order, but I had no intention of removing his shirt; this wasn't meant to be sexy or lead to fun. If all went according to plan, sex would be the last thing Igor would be thinking about when we were done.

I fully expected him to sleep hard for a few hours when this was finished.

Reaching for his underwear, I paused for a moment. "Do you remember your safeword?"

Igor swallowed twice before he finally got his voice to work. "Queue."

"It's really important that you remember that and use it if you need it." I removed his underwear as I spoke. "I'm not going to stop if you say no or to stop. You need to use your safeword."

He didn't seem to notice he was now standing in the middle of my room, naked from the waist down. "Will it hurt that bad?"

"It is not so much hurt. I am not out to make you bruised. It is more that the emotions can get a bit intense. You might tell me to stop or yell *no*, but that is not what you mean. It is okay to yell, to beg, cry, or do all three. I will worry if you stay silent."

Igor looked far from convinced and I knew that if we waited any longer, he had a very real chance of making this moment even bigger in his mind. I climbed onto my bed, thankful for the firm mattress and comfortable headboard, and settled myself on a pillow. "Come here please, Igor." He followed the request faster than I'd expected, though he moved carefully until he was near enough to me that I could finish positioning him.

With him spread across the bed, his ass propped up on my legs and his soft dick nestled between my thighs, I ran my left hand over his backside. “Are you comfortable?”

He nodded, his face buried in the bed.

“Does your hip hurt at all?”

That time, he shook his head.

“Okay, then we start. You have your safeword. Use it if you need to.” He’d just begun to nod his head when I brought my hand down for the first time. It wasn’t enough to hurt, just enough for him to feel it. Igor let out a yelp of surprise that morphed into a hum.

The question about if he would like spankings was already answered, though this one wasn’t meant to be fun and I knew that once pushed, the feelings would change quickly. I didn’t give him a chance to find a predictable rhythm or pattern, working to warm the globes of his ass quickly and efficiently.

With both cheeks sufficiently pink, I began to pick up the intensity and with it, Igor’s little wiggles stilled and his hums of pleasure became hisses of pain. I concentrated on his cheeks, sometimes allowing my hand to slip to the underside of his ass where the skin was more tender. I wouldn’t make contact as hard there, but each time Igor whimpered.

His skin had gone from creamy to pink and was beginning to bloom with deeper red patches when I began to spank him harder again. The little whimpers he'd given periodically turned constant but he didn't ask me to stop. The first time he made more than a whimper, I could hear the strangle in his throat as he tried to hold back.

Giving him a harder spank, my hand warmed with the force I'd put into it. He was so close to letting go and I was determined to get him there. "It's okay, solnishko. Let it out." I forced my voice to stay steady, coaxing him to let go.

He shook his head, stubbornly refusing to make a noise, but his gasp was strained and I could hear how exhausted he was from holding it in. The impacts hadn't been enough to hurt Igor, the odds of his skin staying red for more than an hour or two slim to none, yet he was already teetering on the edge. A little more encouragement and he'd get there. It was just going to take patience on my part.

"Stop fighting it, Igor. You're doing great."

Igor thrashed, pushing against the hand I had around his waist. "No. No, no, no, no, no. Don't, stop."

The hardest thing I'd ever done was continue spanking him, knowing that his pleas weren't related to his pain level but his will to hold on to the control of his emotions. He rocked his body over and over, each time the force becoming less intense, and there was less distinction between his words until the *nos* and *stops* ran together. At that point, I adjusted the angle of my hand, striking him on the lower side of his ass, and the first sob escaped Igor.

My heart broke for his cries as I continued spanking him, not as fast, not as intense, but continuing the sharp contact. "No. No. Please..." He hiccuped between words, snot and spit choking him for a moment. With the sentence out, his body collapsed onto the bed, the remaining tension leaving his muscles as he sobbed into the bedspread. "Th-thank-thank you."

The spanks turned into soothing circles. "There. So beautiful. You are okay." I adjusted Igor on the bed so that I could hold him as he cried. I pushed his bangs from his sweaty forehead and dried his tears and wiped his nose with a tissue, holding him close as he let everything out.

CHAPTER 24
IGOR

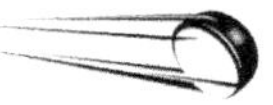

The world came back to me slowly. For a few minutes, I had no idea where I was, what time it was, or even when I'd fallen asleep. I tried to open my eyes to find them swollen and my nose stuffy as memory gradually returned.

I was curled in Yuri's bed, a firm weight around me that I knew instantly was Yuri's arms. His chest was pressed to my back, but he'd taken care not to press against my ass. A minor adjustment confirmed that the skin was still sensitive but nowhere near as bad as I'd expected while I'd been draped over his lap as he'd spanked me.

The thing that struck me the most was the weight I'd been carrying around for weeks had been lifted from my chest. Even through my stuffy nose, I could breathe more easily and could already admit Ryder had been right.

Yuri's hand ran through my hair and his lips pressed against my shoulder. "How are you, solnishko?"

"Are you ever going to tell me what that means?" I asked, deflecting for a few extra seconds.

His body vibrated against my back as he laughed silently. "I think not, nyet. Are you feeling better?"

"I am. I don't know how that works, but it does. You were right. Both of you."

As though a loud noise would burst our bubble, Yuri gave a quiet chuckle. "Yes. You have wise boyfriend and friend. Are you hungry? You have been sleeping for almost two hours now."

My eyes went as wide as the swelling would allow them to. "Two hours? I've been sleeping for two hours?"

"You crashed hard. You didn't even move when I put lotion on you."

I knew my cheeks heated with Yuri's words. The thought of him putting lotion on my sore backside while I slept was both embarrassing and overwhelmingly sweet. "Thank you," I said into the pillow more than to him.

"You are very welcome. Are you up for going downstairs and talking some while I make us a late lunch?"

"More talking?" I wasn't trying to whine, but I couldn't help it if it came out as one.

Yuri just laughed. "Yeah, we must figure out how to get you back to yourself. I love the last few weeks—orgasms, cuddles, time together are nice—but I miss my pain in ass."

And truthfully, I'd missed myself. The neatly folded piles of laundry in the living room in my house were not my normal. I did laundry as I ran out of outfits I wanted to wear. I chose game day suits by what was still hanging in the closet and not in the overflowing dry cleaning bag in the corner. My dishes weren't normally done and my bed was never made.

"Does that mean I can stop making my bed?" I asked as we started to get out of Yuri's bed. I hissed when my ass dragged across the sheets. No matter how soft they were, it was still something against my very tender skin.

Yuri sat up quickly and scrambled to my side. He was still wearing sweats and a T-shirt while I was naked from the waist down. "Was I too hard?"

The genuine worry in his eyes twisted a spot in my chest that I'd never had twinge like that. It took my breath away for a few seconds and I had to work to get the right words out of my mouth that would reassure Yuri but also explain how I felt. "It was not too hard. I can't believe I'm saying this, but I needed that. It actually helped. Other than this." I gestured around my swollen face. "And it's not really painful, it's... tender. I know it's there and I'm not used to it."

Yuri relaxed and tension I hadn't known he'd been holding eased from his shoulders. "The goal was not to hurt you."

"I'm not hurt. I know the goal wasn't to hurt. Ryder said that it was to get me out of my head, and it worked.

Honestly, I don't know if it's even that tender. I've had bruises hurt a lot worse than this."

Yuri slid off the bed and walked into his closet, returning a moment later holding a pair of his sweats. "You will fit my pants. You were at the gym in yours. I do not want to put them back on you." Without waiting for a response, he bent to feed my legs into the pants. When he'd worked them up to my knees, he looked up at me, a soft smile on his face. "I like you, Igor. I like all of you. But I like most when you are all you. Not a... a..." He paused long enough for me to stand and for him to work the pants the rest of the way up my legs.

He snapped his fingers. "A censored Igor. That is the word, no?"

My smile grew as I nodded at him. "Yes." It was easier to talk than to think about being dressed by Yuri. In the last few days, he'd done so more than once, and I was beginning to understand that it was one of those things that brought him pleasure. If putting clothes on me brought him happiness, I wasn't going to tell him no, no matter how awkward it was to sit here while someone dressed me.

"Bed must be made each day," he said suddenly as he secured the drawstring around my waist.

"What?" Had I really heard him right?

Yuri thrust my cane into my hand and motioned toward the door. "Lunch. Bed made. Unmade bed is..." He didn't finish the sentence, but he did shudder and I guessed that was all he was going to give me.

"You will just get into it again that night. Why make it?"

Yuri growled, making the frustrated, annoyed sound that had found its way straight to my dick so many times after surgery. The last three weeks he hadn't made that noise and I'd almost forgotten my body's response to it. Except as soon as he'd made that noise again, it'd proved to still have the same effect on me. Damn, I'd missed that sound and my body's reaction to it.

I must have made a noise because Yuri chuckled. "Glad to see things are back to normal. You will make your bed because it is rule."

It was a good thing Yuri was walking just in front of me because I scrunched my nose up in silent protest. "Do not make faces at me, Igor. Bed gets made."

How the hell did he know I'd made a face?

"Define *made*." I needed to know the definition to know if I was going to mess up or not. Were we talking military style, or blankets picked up off the floor, or something in between? There were a lot of definitions of made, and I needed to make sure we were on the same page. I was not about to make the bed with military creases if all he wanted was the comforter I'd inevitably kicked to the ground in my sleep picked up.

If the way Yuri rubbed at his temples was any indication, I was getting under his skin. Pride shot through me.

This was what had been missing. I wasn't even trying to irritate him, yet I was doing a damn good job of it. And he couldn't punish me for making sure I understood expectations. *This was perfect.*

We made it to the kitchen and Yuri pointed to the chair at the island. "Sit ass down."

Fighting a smile, I complied with his order, propping my cane between my knees then leaning forward. "You haven't answered my question."

Yuri turned from the fridge and narrowed his eyes at me. "Blankets pulled up and flat, minimum. I do not expect beds to look like hotel. I do expect presentable."

That sucked. Making beds was stupid, and I didn't care if I sounded petulant. "Making the bed is so pointless."

The look Yuri shot me made my whining totally worth it. But then his expression changed and he lifted a shoulder as if to say *whatever.* "Make bed, get reward. Don't, earn consequence. Your choice." He turned back around, his head disappearing into the fridge.

And why was it that my body couldn't decide how the fuck to react or which outcome would be better? At this particular juncture in time, a reward sounded just a bit more appealing, but that was mostly due to the fact that my ass was still warm from earlier.

With the reminder, I wiggled in my seat to find that the soft fleece of Yuri's sweats sent wonderful tingles through my body, making my dick take more interest in the conversation.

"Behave."

"Your back is to me!"

He didn't bother looking at me when he stuck his middle finger in the air. "I know you enough."

The raspberry I blew out was confirmation that I had been as predictable as he'd expected. "I can't decide which I should go for."

"How about you go for not standing in corner."

The gasp I let out hadn't been for the sake of drama; he'd actually shocked me. "Is that seriously something you'd do?"

Yuri laughed, pulling packs of lunch meat and cheese from the fridge. "I cannot spank you again today."

"Can rewards be sex?" I was shocked the words had come out of my mouth without my brain even filtering them. Sure, I often lacked a filter, but I hadn't even been thinking about sex just then. At least I hadn't been aware I'd been.

Yuri set the ingredients on the counter and stared at me for an uncomfortable few seconds. "We have had sex."

I rolled my eyes. We'd had this conversation before. Yes, we'd technically had sex. I'd heard his lectures, but I wasn't talking about frotting or hand jobs. "You know what I mean."

Food was forgotten. "I do. I know what you mean, but that is a big step when you have not done that before."

"I've had sex before, Yuri! I'm not some forty-year-old virgin!"

There was a chance I'd said the words too loudly and maybe slapped the counter just a little too aggressively because Boris jumped beside me and Yuri blinked in surprise before finally speaking. "Have you ever had something in your ass?"

Did a finger count? Probably not, so I shook my head, deciding honesty was the best policy and would probably get me further. "Not more than a finger, no."

Yuri dug the heels of his hands into his eyes, groaning and shaking his head. "You will kill me." His words said I was driving him crazy, but his tone said it was crazy with lust. "You have tried, though?"

I was suddenly shy to admit that, yes, I had, and lifted a single shoulder. "A few times in the shower."

The noise Yuri made in his throat was unmistakable arousal. "Be good, get rewards."

"What does that mean?" I tried thinking back to our conversation about rewards, consequences, and expectations. "I remember a lot of consequences for not following rules."

"My solnishko, rewards are as fun as consequences. Sometimes, they are same."

I mimed my brain exploding. It wasn't the first time I'd done it, it likely wouldn't be the last, but I was pretty sure something was getting lost in translation. "More words."

He returned to the fridge for condiments, then came

back to the counter and laid everything between us. He gestured for me to make a sandwich for myself and I reached for the bread and a knife, waiting for Yuri's explanation. Much like in everything, Yuri was not quick to answer, spending time gathering his thoughts while he began to assemble his own sandwich.

"You like spanking. You got hard at first, before consequence really set in. While you were on my lap, I knew where I was taking you. I knew when to go harder and how to take you to next level." He placed two pieces of cheese on his sandwich before continuing calmly, like we were discussing the weather. "I know your body. It is my job to know you. All of you. That means knowing when to push more and when to back off."

My crazy Russian goalie took my breath away at every turn. There had never been a person in my life who had tried to know more than what I gave them about me, but Yuri had studied and learned me like he did the teams we played. He'd known exactly when to push and when to stop, even when I hadn't known where those lines were. In the moment, all I'd known was that emotions had rolled through me like summer storms rolled across the plains in Kansas.

The storms would build and transform as I watched them come toward the training camp. That was how it had been while draped over Yuri's lap this afternoon. The storm inside me built and transformed before finally slamming into me and blowing my self-control away as easily as the storms had blown leaves from the trees. When it was over, I was left as depleted of emotion as the sunny skies that followed the storms were depleted of rain.

"I can take you to places you have never been and pull you back from the edge before you go over. Behave for me, solnishko, and your pleasure will never be so great." He lifted a shoulder. "Misbehave and your consequences can be just as infuriating as pleasurable."

Was any of that an answer? I didn't remember what the question had been. Yuri had taken my brain and jumbled it up, making me forget everything but what he'd just said. "I… I…" I shook my head, trying desperately to form a sentence. "We're talking about how to get your fingers or dick in my ass, right?"

He burst out laughing, any attempt at seriousness lost when he tossed a pickle in my direction. It landed on the slice of bread I'd only managed to spread mayonnaise on. "Yes, idiot. But how we do it is up to you."

"I ask you before I go out to eat. I make my bed." I forced myself not to shudder at the thought of making my bed. "What else earns rewards?"

"We have found something that motivates you to behave. Should have thought about this much sooner."

Maybe he should have. Maybe it wouldn't have taken us five years to figure out that we were attracted to one another. Maybe it wouldn't have taken me until this summer to realize I'd been missing something in my life. I refused to allow myself to dwell on what I'd missed and instead focused on what I was now gaining.

"What else earns me sex?" It wasn't like Yuri had deprived me. I'd had more orgasms in the last three weeks than I'd had in the last three months, but there was a closeness that came with penetration that I'd missed. There was something special that came with that type of connection that I'd just begun to realize I desperately needed.

"Your mind is stuck." At least he didn't look upset or annoyed with me. "You will earn rewards, I am sure. You will earn consequences too. Let us see which you will like more."

CHAPTER 25

YURI

Igor writhed on the bed in front of me as I slowly pushed the dildo into his ass. In the last two weeks, we'd made progress and I knew that I could easily slide into him with the amount I'd played with his ass. And damn did I want to do just that. The only thing keeping me from doing so was that we'd discovered Igor had a hair trigger when it came to prostate orgasms.

There was yet to be a time that I'd touched his prostate more than three or four times before he came.

Besides, we hadn't made it here as a reward.

"You went out after therapy without telling me." I twisted the dildo just enough that I knew it would push against his prostate. I knew I'd found the spot when Igor moaned loudly and threw his head from side to side while gripping the bedsheets.

"I, I, I." He was nearly whimpering. I'd been at this for

twenty minutes, fucking him with the toy, always slowing down just before he came, and he was clearly getting frustrated. "For-for-forgot!"

My hand left the dildo and I stroked up and down his erection, watching as goose bumps rose on his arms and legs and taking pleasure in the way he whimpered as precum dripped from his slit and down his shaft. "You did not make the bed when you got up this morning."

Igor only groaned. He'd been the last to wake up. I'd gone for coffee with Tapio early that morning, hoping that I'd be able to convince him to make my babushka's cake. He'd taken one look at the recipe and his eyes had gone wide with shock before he'd shaken his head slowly.

So maybe I was a little frustrated and more than a little homesick, and maybe Igor had pushed just a little too far today. But he was Igor. Pushing limits was normal for him, and since he had me wrapped around his finger, I had been letting him get away with most everything, always choosing to focus on the good.

I had a feeling we both needed this denial session for different reasons. Given that he'd made it as long as he had, I was planning on sinking into him to come. What I wasn't sure of was if he was going to get to come or not.

For his part, Igor couldn't decide if he loved or hated what was being done to him. He'd gone between apologizing and begging for more, and I'd been giving him more, exploring where his limits were. I was pretty sure I'd figured out where to stop, at least until he screamed out in what I thought was pleasure.

"Fuck, Yuri! Gonna—" He grunted and bit his lip hard enough that I knew he was going to draw blood. I didn't force him to finish the sentence and gripped around his erection and balls, squeezing hard enough that his dick pulsated without coming.

When his body sagged against the bed, I patted his balls. "Good boy." He sucked in a sharp inhale before letting out a pleasured whimper. *He'd liked that.*

"Please. Please, Yuri. I want to come. Please, sir."

And holy shit, hearing that word come from Igor's mouth sent my need to be in him higher than I'd thought possible. "Not until I say."

I left the dildo in Igor's ass but propped it in with a pillow and reached up for his hand. "I have given you rewards for good behavior, solnishko." I plucked at his nipple with my blunt nails, pulling a needy moan from Igor.

"Orgasms. Yes, orgasms good." He bobbed his head rapidly and arched his chest upward when I plucked at his other bud.

"Many orgasms. But you also come when not told to." I lifted an eyebrow as though I was expecting a response.

"Sorry," he said in a hurry before closing his eyes and drawing on some reserves he'd been hiding somewhere. "I haven't come today. Maybe you can spank me?"

"Brat. You would like that too much." That was how

he'd come two days earlier. Yes, I'd been trying to deny him, but he'd come before I'd finished his twenty spanks. Likely because he'd been doing as much humping of my legs as whimpering for me to stop. I needed to remember the cage I'd bought for him. Unfortunately, that wasn't an option right now, but I did get an idea.

"I'll make the damned bed. I'll share my location with you. Just please, please, let me come!"

I pulled the dildo from his ass and set it on the nightstand by my bed. "I will make you deal. If you get up and stand with your hands on the wall, feet spread apart, and do not come for the next ten minutes, I will let you come."

I really hoped he would make it ten minutes. I had been hoping to feel his channel around my cock for days, but the man was impossible to keep from coming.

Igor gave me a searching look, trying to figure out what I had planned. "Remember what I said? Consequences not always fun, but can be very rewarding?"

He nodded slowly. His face said one thing, but his twitching cock said another. "Yes..." He stood up, his hip finally at the point he wasn't limping as badly and he was moving smoothly. There was an effortless seduction in his movements he had no idea he possessed. I continued to marvel at just how naturally submission came to him and that he'd never discovered it before now.

With less than an inch between us, we were eye to eye, allowing me to see the battle between nerves and arousal raging inside him. I kissed him, hoping to kiss the worry from him. His body and lips softened in unison, leaving him to chase my lips as I put space between us.

"Hands on the wall. Legs apart, ass out." I waited to turn around until Igor complied and I made the trip to my closet as fast as humanly possible.

Igor liked to joke that I was obsessively organized. I never expected him to be as obsessive with organization and it worked for him. I just so happened to like walking into my closet and barely needing to glance at the shelf to find what I was looking for. Item in hand, I returned to the bedroom.

Igor hadn't moved more than to place his face against the wall. Given how flushed his body was, I was willing to bet the cool paint felt heavenly against his skin. He heard me approach and turned his head in my direction. "Why am I here?"

His cock hung between his thighs, a bead of precum dripping to the floor beneath him. "Safeword?"

"Queue."

I kissed between his shoulders, Igor's muscles trembling beneath my lips. "So good. So proud of you."

His body went shockingly still and he blinked over at me, searching my eyes for any sign that I was lying to him. I knew then that I hadn't told him enough just how amazing he was. It was easy to forget he was still so new to submission, especially with the cocky confidence that he often displayed.

Igor showed the world he was capable and fearless.

Pucks flew at him at over ninety miles per hour, and he didn't flinch. He went through surgery and PT, bitching repeatedly about the pain in his body but never once telling Indy he couldn't do what she asked. He was often the loudest in the room, ready with a joke or a jab to lighten the mood, yet under all of that, there was a submissive who needed reassurance.

I met his eyes before nodding my head. "You might have earned the paddle, but after, you are going to get the best reward." I kissed his shoulder, the side of his neck, and used my finger to angle his chin my way so that I could kiss his lips. "You have been so good. You have listened so well tonight. You have tried so hard to follow all rules. And you responded to me without question."

He whimpered when I stepped back, the space between us finally allowing him a moment to gather his wits about him again. "Wait. Paddle?" His eyebrows crept up his forehead and his mouth parted in surprise.

"Yes." I ran the smooth leather of the paddle up Igor's thigh and over the round globe of his ass. His muscles tensed, his body betraying his hesitancy, but his back arched into the leather. "Twelve swats."

"Twelve?" His eyebrow rose in question. "That is an oddly specific number."

I fought laughter at his statement. "Twelve. You have left towels on the floor in bathroom four days, despite being reminded every day before shower. That is four. You told me you would do dishes last night."

"I did!" With his protest, his hands nearly left the wall to make his point. He caught my inclined head and my eyebrow raise and quickly replanted his hands back on the wall.

"You put them in the sink, poured soapy water over them, and left them. I found them this morning, had to do them while you were gone."

His skin heated at my words, a beautiful blush creeping down his back, but his response lacked apology. "To be fair, you never said *how* to do them."

Given that he was arguing about the technicalities of how dishes should be done, rather than that he didn't deserve a swat with the paddle for the way he did them, I had a pretty good idea most of it was for appearance's sake. I moved the paddle from his ass and used the side to trace his spine. Igor squirmed and whimpered and another drop of precum hit the wood floor between his feet.

"Brat. You know how to do dishes. Do you need thirteen swats for arguing?"

That time I saw the worry in his eyes. Something in my voice had finally set him on edge and he shook his head rapidly. "No. No, sir."

"Then you should not argue, solnishko."

He groaned, so I continued. "Six is for coffee cup left on table outside yesterday morning. Seven is for my time cleaning up the mess Boris made when he broke it."

The nervous tension in his shoulders and back and

true remorse in his eyes over that one was enough to almost make me take back the seventh. "I'm sorry."

His genuine apology and the worry behind his gaze let me know the mistake had been a true mistake. "I know. This will help you remember to pick up your dishes, even if they are cheap old mugs."

Igor let out a relieved breath and his shoulders relaxed. "Not a special mug then?"

"Not special, no. Dollar store mug years ago." He had honestly done the thing a favor, but I wasn't going to tell him that.

Something about the mug had Igor ready to accept the consequence. His head had bowed downward but he managed to look up at me through his light lashes. "That is seven. five more. Why?"

I lifted my fingers. "Bed this morning, shoes in hallway." That one counted for two. It should have counted for three since I'd nearly broken my leg on his tennis shoe as I'd turned off lights the night before. "You were late for therapy this morning. And finally, not letting me know you were going out after."

To my surprise, Igor balked most at the last item on my list. His mouth hung open for a moment, and then he stuck his bottom lip out in a pout before finally protesting. "You already punished me for that one!"

"Oh, sweet Igor. You forget what I told you. You be good, you get rewards. You do not listen, you get consequences. Both have potential to be rewarding, just one you must work harder for. You have pushed buttons lately. Now you must work hard for your reward, but I know you can do it."

He tilted his head upward, his eyes nearly even with mine but refusing to meet my gaze, and he sighed. "You promise I have earned a reward?"

The reluctance and disbelief in his voice made my heart squeeze. "Promise. I am so proud of you right now. You will have a reward one way or another, but it will feel much better if you have not come first."

I knew he'd guessed correctly when his eyes flew open and he sputtered. His voice cracked when he finally found words to put to his thoughts. "Y-you mean... are you really? You're going to fuck me?"

"I cannot wait to sink into you, solnishko. You have earned it, especially tonight. You have waited to come. You have taken all the teasing. Twelve swats." I tapped the flat of the oiled black leather paddle to the fleshiest part of his ass cheek. It wasn't anywhere near a swat but enough to let Igor know I was getting ready and give him a chance to feel the leather as it made contact with his skin.

I had no intention of going too hard on him, especially given this was his first time being paddled. When it was done, he'd wear red splotches from the three-inch strip of leather. His milky flesh might even show little dots from the red stitching along the edges of the paddle. I wanted him to feel it, to find out if it was something he liked—all signs were pointing to his loving it—while also making sure that he wasn't too sore for me to finally get the reward I'd been craving for weeks.

Igor drew in a sharp breath that turned into a moan when the paddle stayed in contact with his ass. After a few seconds, he nodded before blinking at me through hooded eyes. "I understand, sir. I need this to help me remember the rules."

Jesusfuckingchrist. My dick twitched as violently as my heart beat against my ribs. His words, his submission, the gift he was so eager to give me hit me deep in the chest and forced me to take a few deep breaths of my own to regain my composure.

Igor adjusted to widen his stance and pushed his ass farther from the wall, preparing himself for contact with the paddle. Pulling the paddle back at arm's length from him, I swung it downward, landing the first swat on the spot I'd rested the paddle on a moment earlier. Igor let out a startled hiss but pressed his ass back to prepare for the next swat.

"One," he said without prompting, his shoulders squaring with the wall for the second swat of the paddle.

I delivered the second to the other side of his ass and watched as a pretty pink bloomed where it had struck. "Two." Igor swayed his ass side to side before planting his stance. "I'm ready, sir."

The third swat landed just below the second and Igor gave a moan. "Three." I delivered the next two before he had time to react. "Four. Five." He dropped his head and sweat began to bead along his hairline and across his shoulders.

"Harder, p-please. I-I can take it. I-I-I need you to remind me to follow the rules."

I obliged. The next three swats took our total count to eight. With the ninth and tenth, I swore I was paddling my own heart. I could easily give him more and harder and knew Igor could handle it, but the way my heart thundered in my chest at his sounds and the way he counted and practically begged for more, I wasn't sure my heart could take it. He was everything I'd ever looked for in a lover: strong, confident, and cocky.

The eleventh was delivered low on his ass but not as hard as the last three. The punishment was winding down yet my emotions were continuing to climb higher. Somehow, my perfect complement in every way had been living next door to me for nearly five years. I'd worked with him every day and talked with him even more frequently.

When I landed the last swat to the opposite cheek, Igor counted it, his voice breathy and I was pretty sure more lust-filled than it'd been when I'd been edging him on the bed. He wasn't afraid to push, wasn't afraid to tease, and had loved the paddle more than I'd have ever imagined. And those butterflies that had filled my stomach and chest couldn't be mistaken for anything but love.

I was in love with the man in front of me, with his red ass, his cock dripping precum on the floor, and sweat rolling down his back. He was infuriating, stubborn, sweet, and caring, a little bit of a pain slut, a lot bratty, and he held my heart in his hands. He didn't know it and I wasn't ready to tell him yet, especially not while he was pressed against a wall after being punished, but I was completely in love with Igor Ozols.

The paddle got unceremoniously dropped onto the chair to the side of me, Igor far more important than a piece of leather, and I reached out to run my hands down his back, over his ass, and back up his sides, guiding him to stand as I did so. "Perfect. So beautiful." I kissed his shoulder and cheek, then guided him to the bed. He was still hard as a rock, my own cock throbbing in time with my heartbeat, but his glassy eyes and heaving chest told me now was not the time for sex.

Now was the time to curl up in bed and hold him until he was back to his normal bratty, horny self. Until then, I'd take the time to let him feel just how much I loved him.

CHAPTER 26

IGOR

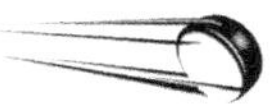

"Did I miss it?"

Fuck, my throat felt like there was sand in it.

Soft lips pressed against my shoulder and I could feel Yuri's chest vibrating against my back as he suppressed laughter. "Miss what?"

My ass was tender, but I wasn't sure if that was because of the edging, the paddling, or Yuri fucking me. I really, really hoped I hadn't missed him fucking me for the first time.

"You fucking me."

"Ozols!" I didn't know if that was shock or repulsion coming from him. All I knew for certain was that he wasn't amused. "I will never take advantage of you. Maybe one day, in future, we will negotiate that. I will never enter you without your knowing and fully aware. A good Dom, hell, a good boyfriend, would never have sex with someone who is too far gone to consent."

I had to clear my throat because it wasn't getting any easier to talk. "Subspace?" I'd read about it over the past few weeks, but it had always struck me as something I would neither want nor be able to reach. I had a fear of not being in control of my body and the way it had been explained online had been like a trance that made thoughts and actions difficult. Besides, every blog I'd read, the author had said they reached that space after highly emotional, painful, or intense scenes. I had no interest in being pushed that hard. It had sounded deeply uncomfortable to me, but whatever space I'd been in between the spanking and now had not felt scary.

He sighed and rolled me so that I was facing him and pressed a kiss to my lips before finally leaning back and pressing a bottle of water into my hand. I drank greedily while he began to explain the meaning of the word. "Subspace. Intense emotions or play can lead to it. A lot of people describe it as dreamlike. It is different for everyone."

Pressing my lips together and narrowing my eyes, I tried to recall exactly how I'd felt before waking up. *Dreamlike* was a good word for it, a much less frightening word than trance. My limbs had felt both like feathers and lead weights, every movement difficult like my arms and legs were detached from my brain. It had also been hard to think, much less talk.

Yuri had told me I was perfect and beautiful and I'd wanted to respond, but my mouth hadn't been working with my brain. There was just one thing plaguing me. "But it wasn't hard or extraordinarily emotional." At least I hadn't thought it had been.

Yuri smiled. "Everyone has a different threshold and triggers that send them into subspace. It wasn't intense in pain, but it was intense both in time and sensations. You must have triggers around sensations."

The way he'd so casually explained it, I struggled to understand why I'd ever been leery of reaching subspace or why my reading had made me uncomfortable with the idea. It surprised me that I liked knowing I could hit that place again. For a little bit, everything had gone hazy and all I'd wanted to do was please Yuri and be good for him, a far cry from the person who usually liked to drive him insane. For at least a short amount of time, it had been nice... not that I'd want to please him all the time. Which was convenient, since Yuri liked it when I pushed back.

The fog had mostly cleared while we were talking, and with both my thirst and questions satisfied, I was able to turn my attention to more pressing issues. Like the fact that my dick was still hard and Yuri hadn't fucked me.

I wiggled free of the blankets, my cock happily showing its sustained interest. "So, since you were such a good and respectful Dom earlier, do you think you could be a good and wicked boyfriend now?"

Yuri's answering laugh was just as wicked and calculating as I'd hoped. "You still want my dick in your ass?"

"Fuck yes, I do." My thoughts worked before Yuri could begin to move off the bed, and I reached out and grabbed his arm. "I don't just want it—I need it." I hoped he could see and hear the sincerity in my voice because I wasn't able to find the right words to tell him that I needed to belong to him. I needed to belong to him like I'd never needed anything before.

There was no question in my mind that I'd like it. There was no doubt he would make it perfect. What I both wanted and needed was to feel him and let him take that last piece of me that he hadn't taken already. I hadn't said it, wasn't ready to say it, but I'd given him my heart in that alleyway in Nashville, surrounded by old brick buildings and a dumpster. I'd known, as I'd told him my feelings, that my heart was already his. It might have happened before then, but that had been the moment I'd known I would fall apart if he rejected me.

I'd had so many firsts in my life: first lust, first love, first kiss, first fuck. This was something I hadn't experienced before, and it was something I could give to Yuri and most importantly *wanted* to give to him. And I wanted it to be him, not some other guy, not some other fuck. I'd had meaningless sex before and I could get that anywhere. What I wanted now was someone I trusted, cared about, loved, to give me something I'd never had before. I wanted this first to be with him.

Yuri sat up slowly, my declaration hanging between us for a few long seconds before he leaned down to kiss me. His lips brushed mine so gently I almost didn't believe it had happened, the contact no more than a butterfly landing on my arm. It was when he pulled back that I could see how much he'd appreciated my statement. His eyes had softened to a light velvet brown, and I was pretty sure I saw a hint of moisture in them that hadn't been there before.

"I want to be in you so bad, Igor." He kissed the tip of my nose, then stood. "I will make this good for you. I promise."

Was it possible for my heart to literally beat out of my chest? His words had it trying its damnedest to do just that.

His eyes never strayed from mine as he moved around the room, grabbing supplies from the nightstand and stripping his clothes off before climbing back onto the bed and grabbing a pillow. I'd expected him to kneel between my legs but to my surprise, he lay down and used the pillow under his hips. "Come here, solnishko. Let me make you feel so good."

He stroked his dick a few times, each stroke making his tip disappear behind his foreskin before reappearing and glistening with even more precum than before. My body vibrated with an energy that risked knocking me right off the bed.

"Come here, over my hips."

"Me on top?" I'd thought of this so many times, but I'd never imagined me over him.

Yuri nodded. "Yes, on top. It will be easier for you to control. You can go how you feel best, especially at first."

That made sense, and I straddled him, for the first time feeling his dick along my crease. It pulled a full-body shudder from me I couldn't hide.

Yuri held up the bottle of lube as well as a condom. I took the lube and poured it onto my hand before reaching behind me and slicking his cock. "You are sure?"

We'd talked about using condoms or not. We were tested regularly throughout the season and had both been tested shortly before the playoffs. We'd both tested negative then and hadn't been with anyone else since.

"More than sure." This was my way of showing Yuri just how serious I was about him. I didn't have sex without condoms. I'd always been adamant about that with past partners, no matter how long we'd been together. With Yuri, I didn't want a barrier between us, even one as thin as latex.

My confidence waned once his dick was lubed. "Uh, do I need to... to stretch myself?" I was proud of myself for asking the question, but my embarrassment was painfully obvious if the heat in my cheeks was anything to go by.

"Take it slow." Yuri reached one hand between us, guiding his dick closer to my hole. "I stretched you pretty damn well earlier. You should be loose still. But go slow. A penis is different than a dildo."

The chuckle that escaped me at his comment had my body relaxing faster than I'd expected and he slipped inside of me unexpectedly. My laughter cut off and turned to a moan as my body adjusted to his girth.

Yuri moved his hand from his dick and placed both of his hands on my hips. "That is it. Slow. Do not hurt yourself."

He hadn't been kidding that the real thing was not the same as a toy. He felt thicker than the toy and he didn't slide as easily in my ass.

"Down more. Move slowly."

"What? You're not fully inside me?" My brain struggled to work out how that was possible.

He answered my question with one of his own. "Do your balls rest on my stomach?" He lifted an eyebrow in challenge, and only then did I notice that, no, my balls were nowhere near his stomach. "Relax, solnishko. You will be fine."

"What does that even mean?" The question distracted me for all of point-oh-one seconds as I sank down a fraction of an inch farther.

Yuri rubbed circles on my hips with his thumbs. "It means—"

I was thankful for the distraction when I felt his dick slide deeper inside me. Before he had a chance to finish, something changed and I no longer felt like I was being split in half. Far from painful, the sensation had turned pleasant and now I wanted more. "Oh. Ohhhh." My slow, halting descent turned into a smooth, fluid motion that kept going until my balls really were resting against his stomach.

We both let out sighs of relief when I had taken his entire length in me. While I saw stars bursting in my vision, it was Yuri who looked like he was having an out-of-body experience. His lips remained parted and his breathing was so steady I almost thought he'd fallen asleep until he cracked his eyes open and his lips turned up at the corners.

Then I noticed his legs start shaking under me and realized I needed to move. As I used my thighs to lift slightly off his body, twin groans escaped us. Until that summer, I'd never imagined myself perched atop another man while riding his dick, yet as I moved and felt his dick sliding in and out of me, every ridge and vein hitting another sensitive spot, I couldn't figure out why I'd never considered it before.

"Fuck. Igor." Yuri's words came out with a heavy Russian accent, leaving me almost unable to make out my name on his tongue. Knowing my movements had reduced him to nothing more than single-word sentences had both my confidence and need growing.

I lifted until I felt like if I went farther, he'd slide right out of my ass, then sank back down faster than the first time. Pleasure sparked along my entire spine, new sensations awakening with every movement. When my ass rested against his thighs the second time, I rolled my hips in a circle, trying to take in everything I could about the experience.

His dick hit my prostate mid-circle and I gasped, too surprised to vocalize how good the contact felt. Rocking forward and backward, I quickly discovered I could hit my prostate over and over again with his cock. I was content to continue until Yuri smacked my hip.

"*Idti*." I had no idea what he'd said or what he meant, but looking at his eyes and hearing the desperation in his voice, I decided he wanted me to move.

"Too much?" I asked, halting my rocking and adjusting enough that I could resume my up-and-down motion.

Yuri shook his head. "Too much, not enough. Ride me, solnishko. Make me come."

The desperation and need in his voice brought a renewed urgency to my own orgasm and I started moving again. With my new discovery fresh in my mind, I added a rock to my thrusts and before long I was gasping as loudly as Yuri.

"Yuri," I said, my voice coming as a breathy plea. "I need—"

I hadn't finish my sentence and Yuri's hand was already coming around to jack my dick. With his attention focused on my cock, I leaned back slightly, resting my hands on his thighs, and worked his cock up and down as fast as I could.

A string of Russian words spilled from Yuri, so broken

that I wondered if he was uttering actual words. I didn't focus on that too long, my dick and mind too focused on how he was making me feel. "Fuck, yes. Yes, Yuri. Gonna, I'm gonna—*Fuck!*"

Yuri's dick in my ass and my rapidly building orgasm had consumed every reserve in me, to the point I hadn't bothered with English, instead reverting to my native tongue, not noticing until I'd screamed the last word over the sound of my ass slapping against his stomach and thighs.

"Come for me, solnishko." He twisted his hand around the tip of my cock at the same time I rocked his dick into my prostate. Cum burst from my dick before I knew what was happening. With my eyes slammed shut, fireworks exploded behind my eyelids and everything went white while my ass contracted over and over again around Yuri's cock.

Somewhere in the distance, I heard Yuri let out a primal noise just before I felt his dick pulsate inside me. The feeling was so unexpected, my eyes shot open. My vision took a moment to refocus, though when it did, I was greeted with one of the most beautiful sights I'd ever seen.

Below me, Yuri's lips were parted, his chest heaving and sweat beading on his fine chest hairs. His eyes had turned to pools of liquid chocolate and his cheeks were flushed. I'd seen Venice, Paris, and Rome, but I'd argue that none of them were as beautiful as Yuri as he came inside of me.

The thought was nearly enough to send me into a fit of laughter until I felt his cock pulsate once again. I gasped, my ass already tender but not sore and my dick totally spent while Yuri emptied inside of me. I'd never felt closer and more connected to a person in all my life. That thought alone was enough to take my breath away the same way my powerful orgasm had a moment earlier.

Yuri gave me a lazy smile. "Perfection." Unlike the Russian interspersed with broken English that he'd been uttering, the word was in crisp, clean English.

I could only nod, my voice too filled with emotion and my heart threatening to say something inappropriate. After swallowing a few times, I finally parroted his word back. "Perfection."

"Up, slowly. I will get cloth to clean you."

As I started to lean up, his softening cock moved just enough that his cum began dripping out of me. I winced at the unfamiliar sensation. "Weird." I sat up more, trying to clench my stretched and sensitive muscles to keep as much of it inside me as possible.

Yuri chuckled, forcing his dick to slide out of me unexpectedly, and a large glop of cum slid from my ass and dropped onto the space between his legs. My face screwed up in disgust while Yuri laughed harder. "Sex is dirty, but you are beautiful with my load dripping from your ass."

He sat up and ran his finger along my crack, gathering some of his release and pushing it gently into my hole.

I moaned, wondering if it was possible to recover as fast as I wanted to. Objectively, nothing about his words or actions should have been sweet or sexy, yet I couldn't help but feel that they were both. Deciding I wasn't in the right frame of mind to fully analyze any of it, I collapsed onto the bed beside Yuri, content to let him pepper my shoulders, jaw, and lips with light kisses.

The cum sliding from my ass could wait so long as I continued to get the attention from him.

He pulled back all too soon for my liking, declaring it was time to clean up. While I wanted to argue that the kissing was better, my brain wasn't ready to make words, so I settled on a grunt of displeasure and watched as Yuri disappeared into the bathroom.

CHAPTER 27

YURI

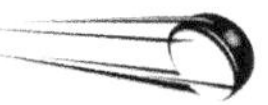

"I will kill Igor."

Seth blinked at me, unsurprised by my outburst as I skated toward the bench. "I think we all expected that to happen well before the end of day two."

We'd started training camp the second week of September. I'd expected there to be some awkwardness—we'd gone from being mostly alone all summer while working on our relationship and respective roles to being thrown back into the real world. A real world where we were no longer teammates but coach and player.

Our talks the last few weeks had revolved around making sure that Igor knew not to treat me differently than the other goalies. The problem clearly was that I hadn't told him to not be a total idiot. The first day I'd played it off as new coach jitters. Once we'd gotten home last night, he'd been back to his usual bratty self and the spanking he'd earned for not doing the dishes—again—had been a little more pleasurable for me than normal. I'd thought that he'd gotten it out of his system.

I was wrong.

Not only had Igor treated me the same as any other player, he'd critiqued and criticized all of us to the point I was expecting the call-up to skate off crying.

I shook both my catcher and blocker off, then pulled my helmet off and leveled Seth with a stare. "He has let position go to his head."

Seth smiled while shaking his head at me. I could tell he thought this was funny. Then again, we hadn't told anyone but the other coaches that we were dating, so he had no idea how infuriating this was to me. Thankfully, our coaching staff had taken the news well, to the point our assistant coach had mentioned that he'd always suspected we were together. The statement had made Igor turn bright red, but the questions had mostly stuck to logistics.

I'd never been so thankful for Ryder and Malcolm as I had been that day. Nashville's football team wasn't normally on my radar, especially with our seasons overlapping so much, but since they—and the football league—had already dealt with a player-coach relationship, it had forced other organizations to realize it was a possibility and the hockey league had already had an action plan in place.

After squeezing half the contents of my water bottle into my mouth, I sagged against my stool by the door. With fifty pounds of gear on, there was no way I'd fit on the bench with the other players, so I'd gotten used to my little spot.

"My legs feel like porridge." I unintentionally muttered the words out loud, and Seth turned his head away from the scrimmage happening in front of us.

"It's the second day of training camp. Of *course* your legs will feel like that. Mine are barely holding me up right now. I can't wait to get in that ice bath in the back."

I shook my head because this was different than any year prior. "I mean, stuff my school served in Russia. It is —" I tried to think of how to describe it in English. Before I could explain that it was a very watered-down version of bland porridge that tasted like wet cardboard smelled, Igor's voice broke through my thoughts, causing me to look over to the far side of the ice where a group was practicing shots on our call-up. My eyes settled on our goalie prospect, Nate Kowalski, in time to see Brax finish a trick shot that would never happen in a game and would be nearly impossible for anyone to block.

"Kowalski! You protect the net! You must try."

Glowering at Igor, I pinched the bridge of my nose as I stood and grabbed my mask and reached for the door, leaving my blocker and catcher on the floor. "Pray for idiot. He is going to get piece of mind." I had been out for no more than two minutes and I'd intended to stay out longer, but the look on Nate's face was enough for my Dom to rear his head. Igor had been on a power trip long enough; he needed to be put in his place.

Stepping back onto the ice, I was reminded just how long I'd been in net the last couple days. My legs felt heavy as cement but also like they couldn't support my weight. Before skating off a few minutes earlier, I'd started contemplating making a bed in the crease. At least I'd have gotten to lie down.

My lips pursed and I growled in frustration as I reached behind me to shut the door. "Fucker. I can't wait to get him—"

Seth leaned closer as I ranted. I'd have said I couldn't wait to get home to put the man over my lap, but Igor's voice scolding Nate again had my words cutting off and me skating harder toward the group as I called out to the goalie. "Take break, Kowalski. You earn it."

Being called up from the AHL for the first time was never easy. Nerves and fears were never far from the surface, and my idiot boyfriend was going to break the newbie before he got a chance to get his feet under him.

"Everyone take break. Need to talk with Idiot."

The veterans breathed a sigh of relief and motioned for the tryouts and call-ups to follow them. Nate looked nervously between us, but with another encouraging nudge from our team captain, he followed. Brax paused beside me for a second to pat me on the shoulder. "Go easy on him."

My scowl had him chuckling and glancing at Igor. "Sorry, dude, you done pissed your bestie off."

Igor tried to scowl back, but now that everyone had skated away, I could see a vulnerable side of him that he usually reserved for when we were alone. "What are you doing, Igor? Do you want to make them hate you?"

His mouth flapped open and shut a few times before he finally shook his head. "You told me to not treat you differently."

For as utterly infuriating as he'd been the last day and a half, I already found myself trying not to crack a smile. "I meant do not make me work *less* than the new guys. I did not mean for you to work us like mules. There is balance!"

Igor scrubbed at his face, Coach Ozols and my bratty submissive nowhere to be found when his eyes met mine. "I think this was a mistake. Maybe I am not cut out to be anyone's coach."

Reaching out, I pushed at his shoulder, resisting the urge to pull him in for a kiss and tell him I could take all the confusion away. "You will be a good coach. But *you* could not have stopped the shot Brax made. It was unfair shot, wouldn't be legal in a game, and Brax was showing off. You laugh, you do not yell."

Igor's head hung low and I stopped fighting the urge to comfort him. I lifted my mask and pulled him toward me, kissing his cheek and holding him close before speaking quietly in his ear. "You treat me like player. You help me with form, you critique position, posture, flexibility. You do not berate for missed goal. Put yourself in Nate's shoes."

I tapped his ass harder than was casual but soft enough that I hoped any onlookers would not pick up on my reminder for him to behave. As I finally pulled back, the silence on the ice was deafening. When I'd skated over to Igor, there had been a scrimmage being played on the other half—blades cutting into ice, sticks slapping the ground, and men yelling for a pass or for help. Now that our conversation was over, none of those things were present and I certainly hadn't heard a buzzer.

"It is very quiet in here."

Igor nodded, looking rather pale. "They are looking at us."

Of course they were. I turned on my skates and saw the entire team plus all of our recruits staring at us. Even those I'd dismissed so I could have a talk with Igor were standing along the boards staring at us. I gave Igor a searching look, trying to ask him if he was okay with what I was about to do. He understood enough to give me a barely perceptible nod, so I turned back to the team and took a deep breath.

"Attention, please. Igor and I need to tell you that he is sorry for being asshole last two days."

Bouchard and Cunningham snorted laughter at my comment, though the rest of the team couldn't figure out what to make of my statement.

Igor pushed on my shoulder. "Stop it. You tell me I will

scare off the newbies." He rolled his eyes, a little glint of my bratty sub dancing in his gaze.

I made a show out of sighing. "Ugh, fine. We are also together."

"What?" Seth's screech drowned out all the other murmurs from the team. "I practically live next door to you two *and you didn't tell me?*"

"Down, tiger," his boyfriend, Maz, said, skating to a stop next to him. "I'm honestly more interested in what the press is going to say when they get a whiff of this. It's, like, in the water or something at this rink."

"Quick! Everyone dump out their water!" Toby, our team's veteran ball of energy, called. I couldn't believe that we actually had two new full-time roster players as well as two trying out who were younger than Toby and his best friend, Jean-Luc. They'd both been with us for three years and had only just celebrated their twenty-first birthdays. We'd finally acquired a few draft picks as well as two guys from a college team who were younger than they were.

Jean-Luc looked at his water bottle, tilting his head this way and that as he studied it closely. "Well, too late for me." He took a long drink and exaggerated a satisfied sigh at the end, sending the rest of the team into laughter.

This was why I loved calling Nashville home and the Grizzlies not only my teammates but my friends. No one stayed mad at one another for long. We talked shit out and worked through our problems. I'd heard rumors that it hadn't always been this way, but for as long as I'd been here, it had been much more than a team. We were family. It was unlike any team I'd played with before, and I hoped that I would never have to play with a different team again.

Igor interrupted my musings by clearing his throat. When I looked over at him, a faint pink blush stained his skin and he was visibly uncomfortable, shuffling from skate to skate. "I am sorry, though. I will work harder to not be such an asshole." He looked over to Eric and our tryout, Gavin. "I'm really not as bad as I've been the last few days."

I nodded my head. "He is nice. Power got to his head."

Cunningham clapped his hands, grabbing attention around the rink. "Good practice, guys. On that sappy note, let's wrap it up for the afternoon. We'll pick up here tomorrow on fresh legs."

"Thank fuck," I said, breathing a sigh of relief. I really wanted out of my skates and my gear. I hoped Leslie could work some serious magic on this stuff before the next morning because I was pretty sure it had gained ten pounds of sweat over the day. I did not envy equipment managers at all, but Leslie was fantastic at their job, and if anyone could do it, it would be them.

In the locker room, I stripped the rest of my practice gear off, seriously contemplating throwing it away instead of taking it home to wash. My nose turned up in disgust as I threw it into my bag. "Gross."

Seth wiggled my way as he shimmied out of his own

soaked compression gear. “You and Igs? Seriously? How have you not killed him yet?”

Seth was all smooth lines and lean muscle. Not that I had bulk to me, but there was a certain sensuality to him that most of the guys didn’t have. His boyfriend was bulkier with a coarser beard and had actual chest hair where Seth was smooth as the day he was born. I’d never asked, nor did I need to know, why he was as hairless as he was. I knew if I asked, I’d probably find out way more about my friend than I ever needed to know.

Friendships needed boundaries.

“How has Maz not killed you yet?” I asked, turning the question back on him.

Pink filled the apples of Seth’s cheeks and he batted his lashes at me. “He has ways to keep me in line.”

I was thankful I hadn’t had anything in my mouth because I would have choked on it. Lacking anything to choke on, my mouth flapped open and shut as I tried to come up with what to say to that. Finally, I shook my head clear of the fog and waggled a finger at him. “Too much, Johnson.”

“Are you trying to kill Yuri?” Maz asked, coming up and slinging an arm around Seth’s bare shoulders, totally uncaring of the sweat or his stench.

Seth turned his fluttering eyes on his boyfriend. “I would never.”

Maz faked a cough. “Bullshit.” He coughed again. “Go get a shower.” He pecked Seth’s cheek, then smacked his ass with the towel he'd had slung around his shoulders. Seth yelped and scurried to the showers, grabbing a kit of shampoo and bodywash as he ran.

"How does food sound?"

"Not until I am showered, but I could definitely eat after today. Coach Idiot worked off lunch."

Maz laughed at my word choice. "He's never living that down, is he?"

I shook my head. "Igor, idiot, sounds close."

"Well, your idiot is welcome to join us."

"Igor, turn down food?" We both laughed, but it turned out the joke was on us when Igor gave me sad eyes and declined the offer.

"I need to go home. Rest. There's much to think about for tomorrow."

Until the three of us were pulling out of the garage in Seth and Maz's SUV while Igor headed home in mine, I hadn't seriously considered that he wouldn't be joining us. We turned in opposite directions, and I watched my car disappear around the corner that would lead to the highway and back to our neighborhood while we headed toward a local burger joint just outside of the crowded part of downtown. We'd all rationalized that we deserved it after the practice we'd been through.

My phone buzzed with an incoming text just as we'd placed our orders.

***Igor**: I'm at the grocery store. Can I grab a pastrami sandwich at the deli?*

The question made me equal parts pleased and suspicious. It wasn't like him to be so specific with his meals. He usually just asked if he could eat at a certain place, not get a specific meal.

***Me**: That's fine. Can you pick up milk while you're there? We're out.*

***Igor**: Milk. Got it. See you at home.*

"What's got you smiling like an idiot over there?"

I hadn't realized I was smiling, but once Maz said as much, I could feel my cheeks aching. "He calls my place home. I like it."

Seth *awwed* and batted his eyes, causing Maz to smack his shoulder playfully. "You're such a sappy romantic."

"I know. But this is coming from my tall, dark, and handsome Phantom. I know a thing or two about romance and romantic gestures."

We'd all heard the story of how the two met and I had to admit it was a sweetly sappy story, though I couldn't help but tease them. I pretended to gag. "You kill my appetite and I am hungry."

I questioned my teasing when they then turned the tables on me, peppering me with questions about Igor, how we'd finally hooked up, when, and how we'd decided to get together. The line of questioning took us straight through our meals and out into the parking lot. They managed to ask me more questions than I'd thought possible as we drove back to our neighborhood, and once we were there, they invited me in for a drink.

While I usually abstained from drinking during training camp, I also usually abstained from big greasy burgers and cheese-covered garlic fries as well. I'd already indulged in the latter, so I didn't think a single drink was going to be the end of the world. Before we walked in, I shot Igor a text letting him know I was at Seth and Maz's house and told him to come over if he wanted.

One drink turned into two, turned into watching some film of the training camp and discussing who we wanted to see end up with permanent spots on the roster. We ended up talking for over three hours before I finally admitted that I needed to get home and start thinking about a very light dinner. The walk would at least help some of the heavy lunch to digest a little more to make room for a salad or at least some water.

I'd made it around the bend on my street when I knew things weren't right. Parked outside my house were two Nashville fire trucks, the fire chief's SUV, a police SUV, and an ambulance. My stomach dropped to my toes and I forgot all about the heavy meal in my stomach and my stiff legs as I ran the last three houses in an all-out sprint.

My feet had just crossed the boundary between Igor's house and mine when the front door opened and three firefighters and Igor stepped onto the front porch, all of them laughing.

I could just make out Igor's voice but not what he said, then laughter from others. They appeared on the front step, all smiling.

I couldn't decide if I was happy or pissed. "What happened?"

One firefighter patted Igor's arm. "Good luck." He turned to me and shot me a smile. "Might want to teach your boyfriend how to turn off your alarm system before he decides to do any more baking."

My face fell and my eyes widened in shock. "Baking?" Igor, baking? I had to have misheard him. "Igor does not bake."

He baked less than I did, and that was saying something.

CHAPTER 28

IGOR

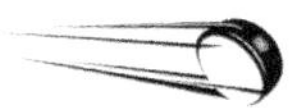

There had been no doubt I'd been an asshole the last two days. Once Yuri had called me out on it, I'd felt terrible. I'd visited the hotel Gavin and Eric were staying in to apologize to them for being a total idiot, promising to be better for the rest of the week. They'd taken my sudden appearance well, both smiling at the fumbled disaster I'd made of things the past few days but easily passing it off as nerves.

Two apologies down, I knew I had to make things right with Yuri, and that was going to be harder. Even if he forgave me as quickly as Gavin and Eric had, I knew I wasn't going to forgive myself as easily. Guilt roiled in my gut and sat like a lead weight. I hadn't been trying to be such a bear to everyone, and I definitely hadn't meant to nearly make the newbies miserable.

It didn't matter that I was his coach; Yuri deserved a

lot better than what I'd given him and the team. The disappointment in myself and knowing I hadn't been a good coach or boyfriend was threatening to eat me alive. When I'd gotten back home, I'd nearly paced a hole in the floor while I thought of what to say or do to let Yuri know that I'd try harder from here on out, but my mind was utterly blank on what said, *I'm sorry for being a hardhead and bad boyfriend.*

After Boris watched me pace for ten minutes, we both got antsy and I took him for a walk around the block. We were fifteen minutes into it when I remembered the korolevsky cake that he always talked about. It had been well over a year since Yuri had last had it, and I couldn't imagine it being as difficult to make as Yuri made it out to be. I'd helped my own great-grandmother bake as a child. If I could get back to the house and find the recipe, I was certain I could make it.

Yuri always spoke so fondly of the cake, so having it again would show him I was willing to put in the work to do better... right?

It took another fifteen minutes of searching through the folded pieces of paper on the counter—making sure not to disturb the neat organization Yuri had them in—before I found the recipe. I picked it out immediately, not because of the meticulous handwriting or the little heart at the bottom that was clearly not in Yuri's penmanship, but because it was the only fucking thing written completely in Cyrillic.

"Fuck. Fuck. Dammit." I cursed the words on the page, trying to make out any of the ingredients. Then I remembered Yuri had translated the name to Royal Cake and I was able to do a search for it on the Internet. If I hadn't remembered that, I never would have figured out Королевский Торт meant korolevsky.

Looking at the pictures of the recipe I'd found, I realized I'd had it growing up. My great-grandmother, having left Russia as a child, had made it a few times, though she'd called it a king's cake. She'd died when I was eight or nine, but I still remembered the layers of rich cake, sweet caramel-colored icing, and melted chocolate she always poured on top of it. Breaking through the layer of solidified dark chocolate had always been my favorite part of the cake. She'd let me make it with her one time and I could remember her hands wrapped around mine as we iced each layer, then neatly stacked them on top of one another.

Pocketing my phone, I turned to Boris. "Be good. I'll be back."

I hadn't bothered looking at the list of ingredients until I got into my tiny red coupe. "The fuck?" I asked the windshield. "Where do I find these?" Caramel sauce, poppy seeds, tart cherries, hazelnuts, sour cream, and dark chocolate chips, along with about fifteen other ingredients. I was half expecting to see a kitchen sink listed before I got to the end.

After another search to see which store had everything

I needed, I pointed my car toward a boutique grocer a few miles away. Twenty-five minutes and fifty dollars later, I was convinced it was called a king's cake because only a king would be able to afford it. After that shopping trip, I didn't think baking the cake could actually be harder than finding the ingredients.

I'd placed the items in my car, still shaking my head at the absurd price of the ingredients, and shut the trunk in time to see Blaise leaving the store with a small bag in hand. For a brief second, I wondered if his bag had cost as much as mine, then shook the thought from my head and acknowledged him.

"Blaise, what are you doing here?"

He blinked at his name and looked around to see who'd addressed him. "Igor? What are you doing here?"

"I asked first."

Blaise looked around, a slight pink staining his cheeks. "I ran out of an ingredient for dinner. Now, why are you here?"

"I need to make an apology cake for Yuri."

"Oh... Yeah, Imil mentioned today was... awkward." Blaise gave me a relaxed smile. The season was still young, but he hadn't seemed as anxious as he had in previous seasons. Maybe it was his new promotion to Director of Hockey Operations, or maybe it was that he'd gotten more comfortable around the insanity we called a team. I wasn't sure what it was, but I liked him relaxed and smiling more often, instead of being an anxious ball of nerves.

Holding my fingers up, I placed my thumb and forefinger close together. "Just a bit."

His answering laugh was worth the discomfort of the day. "I'm sure you will work out the kinks quickly."

Literally and figuratively. "I cannot take more days like yesterday and today. I feel bad for being an idiot."

"I'm sure Yuri has already forgiven you. Eric and Gavin are good guys too. They'll soon see you're really just a goofy ball of energy. The season is still new." With that, he held up his bag. "I better get back and make dinner for us before my phone blows up with texts wondering where I am. Good luck with your cake. Don't be too hard on yourself."

He got into his black sedan and left before I had a chance to ask who *us* was. The thought kept me preoccupied until I got back home and into the kitchen, where my focus turned completely to the recipe on my phone.

An hour and a half later, with smoke billowing from the oven, a smoke detector screaming in the background, a house alarm I couldn't figure out how to unlock to tell the operator *not* to call nine-one-one, and a dog flipping out because of the smoke and noise, I was ready to admit baking the cake had been harder than finding the ingredients.

A more pressing concern was how to get the smell of burnt batter out of the house. Opening the windows wasn't helping, and the molten abomination that was supposed to be the cherry layer of the cake was continuing to ooze down the side of the pan and onto the bottom of the oven. Parts of it were turning black, parts were still bubbling and oozing, and there was something that looked suspiciously like lava growing from the center of one of the globs of bubbling mess. I really hoped it was just a cherry bursting, or I'd discovered some new form of science that created actual lava from cake batter.

With two pot holders, I pulled the cake from the oven and dropped it onto the counter.

"Mr. Yurievich, we are calling emergency services on your behalf. If you are in the house, please leave immediately."

I rolled my eyes at the alarm system as I pressed every button again. "What the fuck is wrong with this piece-of-shit panel? I. Do. Not. Need. Emergency. Services." There was a chance I was screaming at the piece of technology on the wall. "Just need something to fucking work right!"

I glanced back into the kitchen and the bubbling, smoking mess in the oven had me shaking my head in disbelief. "Maybe a scientist. Can this useless piece of shit call a scientist? I think I made a new discovery."

Given that the cherry cake was continuing to bubble over the sides of the pan where it sat on the counter, I had to believe I'd made some sort of discovery. What else explained the excessive amount of batter that had destroyed the oven and was now destroying the kitchen as it continued to grow. As I'd slid the cake layers into the oven, I'd been wondering how the hell the small amounts of batter were going to create entire layers of cake.

"What did I do wrong?" I asked the smoky kitchen.

"Mr. Yurievich, help is on the way. ETA, two minutes."

"*You stupid fucking piece of useless goddamned technology. What is the point of a communication button if it doesn't fucking work?*" I pushed each of the kitchen windows open and opened the back door, then turned the ceiling fan on full speed in hopes of clearing some of the smoke from the room.

The exhaust fan was doing something, so maybe adding more fans would help.

Smoke poured from the windows and door and I was finally able to see again seconds before the most obnoxious smoke detector ever created stopped screaming that there was smoke and to exit the house. The silence was short lived, though, because soon I heard the sound of the fire truck coming down the street.

So much for a nice surprise. *This* was not going to be a nice surprise.

I walked to the front door, Boris on my heels, in time to watch the fire truck pull up out front. Firefighters jumped from the truck, their focus fully on the suspected fire, and I could see their surprise when they saw me on the front steps shaking my head.

"Sorry." They probably wouldn't be able to detect my embarrassed blush through the flush on my cheeks from the heat in the kitchen. "I could not turn off the alarm. The house alarm panel is cursed and I could not get it to connect to the two-way thing."

The firefighter who appeared to be in charge looked me up and down, an eyebrow raised in question. "No fire?"

I shook my head.

"That's a lot of smoke." He gestured toward the doorway behind me where a trail of smoke had begun to follow me out of the house.

"I cannot bake. There is a new science experiment on the counter. It is..." I trailed off as I tried to figure out how to explain the epic disaster I'd created. "Easier to show than explain." I gestured for the man to follow me, and within a few minutes, there was an entire department of police, fire, and paramedics in the kitchen looking at the mess I'd made.

"What exactly were you trying to make?" one of the paramedics asked.

"A Russian cake for my boyfriend. It is his favorite and he wasn't able to go home this year for his grandma to make it for him because he was taking care of me after surgery. I thought it would be a nice surprise." I looked around the kitchen and sighed. "It is going to be a surprise when he gets home but not the kind I wanted."

The paramedic actually laughed. "Probably not. That oven's going to need to be power washed after this. I think you might have messed up the baking powder."

"I messed up something." I looked over the destroyed

kitchen. "At least my house is just next door. We can stay there until it airs out."

A firefighter nodded his head. "Probably a good idea."

As I walked to the front door, the reality of the ridiculous situation finally sank in and I began to laugh at the entire day. "No more *I'm sorry for being an idiot* cakes. I really am sorry to bring everyone out here."

The people around me laughed as well, all agreeing that I would be better off ordering something from now on. The paramedic even jotted down the name of a Russian bakery on the other side of Nashville. We made it back to the front porch still chuckling just in time to see Yuri sprinting up the front yard looking panicked.

He looked me up and down, terror filling his voice and eyes. "What happened?"

A firefighter clapped me on the upper arm. "Good luck." Then he turned his attention to Yuri. "Might want to teach your boyfriend how to turn off your alarm system before he decides to do any more baking."

Yuri's panic transformed into wide-eyed shock as he looked between the firefighter and me. "Baking?" He shook his head in disbelief. "Igor does not bake."

The guilty look on my face when he glanced my way had him blinking at me in shock. "You tried to bake?"

Men and women passed us on their way back to their vehicles. I could hear them chuckling about the disaster I'd made, but I couldn't find it in me to care what they thought. My attention was focused solely on Yuri. "I wanted to make you the cake Babushka makes you."

"You tried to make korolevsky?" Yuri's eyebrows went so far up his forehead they nearly disappeared into his hair. "You cannot bake cupcakes!"

"I definitely cannot make korolevsky. Something went wrong. One of the paramedics said maybe too much baking powder? I don't know." I'd been leading him into the kitchen as I'd spoken, fully expecting Yuri to be irate at the absolute disaster his kitchen had become while he was out. "I'm so, so sorry."

As an added *fuck you*, the cursed cake bubbled again, another cherry oozing out of the pan and onto the counter. I grimaced, bracing myself for Yuri's ire.

The anger never came. "My sweet solnishko, you baked me korolevsky?"

Not expecting the gentle tone of his voice or the soft expression on his face, I nodded slowly. "Tried to. Definitely did not bake it." I looked at the disaster again, needing to fight the urge to cry in defeat. The cake had bested me, much like the rest of the day.

Yuri gave a sharp shake of his head. "That is the sweetest thing anyone has ever done for me."

"Did you hit your head while you were with Seth and Maz?" I'd destroyed his kitchen and he was calling it *sweet*? I wondered if the paramedics had left yet—there was a real chance the shock of the mess had given Yuri a stroke.

He turned to me, taking my face in his hands, and

pressed a gentle kiss to my mouth. When he pulled back, a huge smile had formed on his lips. “You big idiot. You are so sweet. I cannot believe you even tried! Come, solnishko. We will clean mess later.”

I was convinced I’d misheard him. I had to have been mistaken, but Yuri wrapped his hand around mine and tugged gently, guiding me toward the living room. It still smelled, but it wasn’t nearly as bad as it had been ten minutes earlier. The firefighters had left the front door open and smoke had passed through the screen door with ease. The house was going to get uncomfortably hot soon since the weather hadn’t cooled off enough for all the windows to be open, but that issue felt small compared to what had happened since I’d put the cake layers in the oven.

At the couch, Yuri turned and settled himself on the edge, pulling my hand downward. When he didn’t immediately direct me to sit beside him, I sank to my knees, simply happy to be off my feet. A few weeks earlier, the position would have been uncomfortable, but the months of therapy had finally given me my mobility back and the position wasn’t a strain.

“Thank you.”

Despite the words being delivered tenderly, my head shot up in disbelief that he’d meant them sincerely. When I only saw a genuine smile as he tilted his head toward me, I found myself questioning what he’d meant. “For nearly burning down the kitchen?”

"No, idiot," he responded with a chuckle before placing his hands on my shoulders and directing me to lie on the couch. He adjusted me so we were lengthwise on the cushions, our feet tangled together at one end while he hugged me to his chest at the other. "For trying. That is..." He trailed off as he tried to come up with words. For once I was happy to wait him out. "The sweetest thing anyone has ever done for me."

"I wanted to let you know that I am sorry. And I'm even more sorry now that there's such a mess to clean up."

Yuri waved his hand like it would magically fix the kitchen. "I call cleaners in morning. Kitchen is not important." He tapped my nose. "You, solnishko, are. Thank you. Thank you for thinking about me, about my cake, about my home. Thank you for being a pain in ass with huge heart. I did not stay here over the summer to fall in love with you, but I am happy I did."

"Happy about what?" Had Yuri meant that he was glad he'd stayed the summer or that he fell in love with me? Those were two very different things with very different meanings and until I figured it out, I didn't know how to respond.

He tapped my nose and I watched in awe as his cheeks flushed red while he worked out what to say. I'd just begun to accept that he'd meant happy that he'd stayed here when he finally spoke. "That I fell in love with you. So happy you took the chance to tell me how you felt. So happy you are here to burn cake in oven and destroy my kitchen. So happy you are my solnishko."

I was more convinced than ever that the word meant idiot, but if he said it so lovingly every time, I'd be his idiot until the day I died. Wrapping my arms around his chest, I laid my head flat against his ribs and could hear his heart thudding in his chest. "I love you too." Lifting my head, I smiled at him, hoping I got the next words right. "Thank you for showing up. To the hospital. To doctors' appointments and PT. You show up every day for me and show me how much you care for me. How much you love me."

Laying my head back on his chest, I rocked my groin against his, our erections grinding together and eliciting twin moans from us.

Yuri reached down and swatted my ass through my pants. "Brat. Trying to be sweet and you are horny."

Was I ever not?

"I think you're the most impressive score in my stats."

Rolling my eyes, I reached up and tweaked his nipple, earning me another swat. "You're a goalie. You do not have goals!"

"See, best score!" He kissed me again. "Always the best score."

By that logic, he was also my best score. I couldn't find fault in his logic.

EPILOGUE

YURI

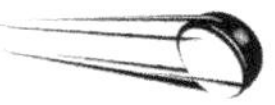

December

"Where is Idiot?"

Seth looked up from placing his good luck bear in his bag. We'd finished the last game before our holiday break, and I'd expected to see Igor in the locker room. Except he was nowhere to be found. When I thought about it, I hadn't seen him since warm-ups.

"I don't know." Seth sounded guilty, but without more information, I couldn't begin to figure out why.

"Coach!" I called to the back of the locker room where Cunningham and Bouchard had taken up court with Toby and Jean-Luc while they watched a video of a play from the second period.

Both coaches looked up to meet my eyes. Neither said anything, so I repeated the question I'd asked Seth a moment before, though I chose not to call Igor an idiot.

Bouchard shrugged. "He's not here?"

He sounded guilty too. What the hell?

"Oh, he told me to let you know that he needed to run home right after the game. Said to tell you nice work, but he'd see you when you got back."

"What? That makes no sense! We drove together!" I turned to Seth. "Can you and Maz drive me home? My idiot is... idiot."

Seth just nodded. "Better hurry with your shower. We're leaving soon." Maz was already out of the shower and putting his suit back on.

"Blyad!" These men were infuriating. Why were they my friends? I rushed through a shower, then changed and ran out to the locker room without drying my hair.

Maz looked me over. "Great. We have to finish shopping for the team party tomorrow but we can drop you off first."

I groaned. It was all Igor had talked about for weeks. My solnishko had a weakness for all things Christmas. His parents had never been big on traditions or celebrations. It hadn't been until he'd moved to America that he'd ever celebrated Christmas, and all these years later, he was still determined to make up for lost time.

The team party got more insane as the years went by and this year promised to be no different. If anything, I was expecting more insanity. Thanks to a colder than normal fall, the rink had been up for over a month already and Igor had been at the craft store multiple times a week for longer than that. I was starting to question if there would be a single Christmas craft left in Nashville. Though now I thought about it, he'd been suspiciously quiet about this year's theme, which made me even more nervous.

I'd pulled Eric's name during the Secret Santa drawing. As the only other goalie on the team, we'd had enough conversations over the first few months of the season that buying him a gift had been easy. There was a pair of neon orange foam earplugs to block Igor out—an inside joke after training camp—and some weird and apparently rare trading card he'd been looking for all season. I wasn't even ten years older than him, but I was having a hard time figuring out why the weird cartoon thing was so valuable. It was some purple thing that looked like a cross between an orca and a stingray, but instead of a tail, it had something that looked like scissors coming out of its ass.

Whatever the draw, Eric had been looking for it all season and when it had finally come up, he'd refused to spend the money. It made a perfect gift for the new goalie.

We pulled into our neighborhood less than fifteen minutes after leaving the arena, then spent a few minutes snaking through the streets until we reached my block. Maz pulled into the driveway and I climbed out of the car, realizing immediately that every light in and out of the house was on.

Seth shook his head and tried to stifle a laugh as he took in the abomination that had become my front yard. "I'm used to Ig's place looking like Christmas Depot puked on it, but he took over your house this year too. I'm glad we don't have your electric bill."

"You have not seen inside. It is worse. I made him get LED bulbs. Maybe that will help."

Maz cleared his throat, his mouth turned up in amusement. "Keep telling yourself that, man."

I opened the door and began to step out of the car. Seth craned around and shot me a beaming, mischievous smile. "Have a good night, Yuri."

Yup. That was weird. I returned his smile. "Thanks. You too."

No matter what, I was glad to be home and away from the odd people my team had turned into that afternoon so I could figure out why my boyfriend had left me stranded at the arena mid-game. Hell, why weren't Cunningham and Bouchard annoyed at his sudden departure? I knew I was missing something, but fuck if I knew what.

I twisted the key in the lock and opened the door at the same time I yelled into the house. "Igor!" His name had barely left my mouth and I knew something absolutely was not right. First, there were voices in the kitchen. Not just *a* voice, not just the radio, but *people* talking. Second, my house smelled amazing. Not Christmas baking or Thanksgiving dinner good, but good like *home*. Like walking into my babushka's house on Christmas morning.

There were so many smells, I was having a hard time picking them out. The unmistakable smell of yeast and various savory meats made me miss Babushka's pirozhki.

I swore there was also the smell of mushrooms that reminded me of gathering them with Danil as kids. We'd bring them home by the bagful and Babushka would preserve them, and then every Christmas Eve, she'd make this creamy mushroom soup that warmed us from the inside out.

If that wasn't enough to have my senses overwhelmed, there was the distinct smell of salmon, dill, and onion of kulebyaka. I hadn't smelled anything so amazing in my house in... well, ever. I'd never smelled *home* here before.

I made it all the way to the wall that separated the cooking space from the hallway before I recognized the voices in the kitchen. Igor was laughing at something my brother said. My brother, Danil. He'd never been in my house. I was nearly afraid to believe that my ears were not deceiving me, and all the while my eyes filled with tears because deep down, I knew it had to be him.

Then I heard Babushka's voice chastising my boyfriend in Russian as he tried to steal something from a plate. "You will have time later, little rabbit. Wait for dinner." *Zaychonok*, it was a word I hadn't heard since my childhood when she would call me that as I ran through the house bouncing excitedly. It fit Igor so well—he was so damn impatient, so excitable, I could see him as a rabbit almost more than my solnishko.

I swore my feet couldn't move fast enough to get me to the kitchen. If they weren't there when I turned the corner, there was a chance I'd break down. I didn't have to get to the wall because Danil was turning the corner while telling Igor he was going to go grab something out of his bag.

"Danil!" He didn't call me on the tears pouring down my cheeks or the way my voice broke when I said his name. He didn't even harass me for pulling him close, patting his cheeks and arms to make sure I wasn't dreaming. His big smile couldn't hide his own tears as I pulled him into a hug. "What? How? Why are you here?" I asked in Russian, nearly afraid to let him go.

He pulled back enough to wipe the tears from his own cheeks. "Your boyfriend can be very persuasive. He has been asking us to come for three months."

Igor stood just behind Danil, chewing on his lip and blinking owlishly at me. All of the insanity of the day was beginning to make sense. "Solnishko." I stepped back from Danil and pulled Igor into a hug as I whispered into his ear. "I don't know if you deserve a spanking or a mind-blowing orgasm for this."

"Why not both?" He kissed my cheek. "You have missed your family. I know you want them here. It is Christmas time, a time for miracles."

All I could do was nod because Babushka was in my

kitchen, drying her hands on a towel and walking toward me. All five foot three of her, in the same damned apron she'd always worn in her kitchen at home. "My sweet prince," she said, gesturing for me to bend to give her a hug.

I complied readily, too overcome by her in my kitchen to do anything but hold her tight. She carded her hands through my hair as she shushed me. "Do not cry, my child. Do not cry." She repeated that over and over again. "My beautiful solnishko."

Igor's voice was what finally stopped the free-flowing tears. "Wait, why does she call him an idiot?"

My head came up from my babushka's shoulder to stare at my boyfriend in confusion, a confusion that was only matched by Danil's. "What?" we both asked in unison.

"Solnishko."

I started to laugh, but Danil remained confused. "It means sunshine."

Igor looked between Danil and me, then to Babushka, and back to me. "You mean for the last six months, you've been calling me your *sunshine*? I was convinced it meant idiot!"

Danil looked at me for clarification, but I was too caught up in laughter to explain. I couldn't believe that Igor had thought I was calling him an idiot for months. "Do not misunderstand, you can be idiot. I call you idiot sometimes because that is what I called you in training camp. Igor, idiot, sounds alike. I call you *solnishko* because you are sunshine."

"Gross." Danil faked a gag, only to be smacked on the arm by Babushka. "Ouch!" We all knew the yelp was for show, but it still made Babushka give a satisfied nod of her head.

"Be nice! Your brother is being sweet!" She shook her finger at him as she spoke in Russian. She couldn't speak many words in English, but her comprehension was better than many people I knew from home. I had no doubt she'd understood most of what I'd said to Igor. "You have much time to torment Yuri. Do not make him send us back home before you start your job."

"What?" I looked between Babushka, Danil, and Igor. "What job?" I asked in Russian, then turned to Igor and asked him the same but in English. "What job? What are they talking about?"

Danil grinned. "My company, they opened a new headquarters in New York. Since it is much easier to get to New York from here than it is to get to London from Russia, I asked about moving to the US for work. They agreed."

Igor nodded rapidly. "Apparently, there is something about your grandma not being able to stay home alone due to politics and dinner rolls."

"Mochi perkhoti." Babushka pretended to spit on the floor, not that I could blame her for the sentiment.

I at least tried to help Igor understand the dinner rolls

by explaining about the parades. "We would rather keep Babushka out of jail. It was hard enough to keep her out the first time it happened. I'm not sure what they would do with repeat dinner-roll-throwing offenders."

Igor blinked at my grandmother before breaking into a smile. "I think this is just the start of a beautiful friendship." Then he turned to me with a guilty look on his face. "I might have offered them my house."

I didn't answer right away, instead looking over at the house that had been mostly vacant for six months. We'd talked about what to do since we were paying two mortgages on houses next door to one another while living only in mine.

Igor had been opposed to giving up his house, insisting that he didn't want to lose the rink in the winter. That had left us with two homes, one sitting vacant.

After pressing another kiss to Babushka's cheek, I stepped back and motioned for Igor to come toward me. "You planned all of this?"

He gave a tentative nod.

Remembering all the weirdness from the team this afternoon, I poked his shoulder. "How many others were in on this?"

That time, he hesitated and lifted his shoulders like he wasn't sure how much to say. "Um, the team?"

"The *entire* team?"

He nodded slowly. "It was not easy to duck out of the game today. I went to the rink with you. As soon as you were busy, I ran to the airport to get them. Dropped them off here, ran back to the rink for warm-ups, then hurried back here to help get the house ready."

"Idiot!" It probably wasn't possible to call someone an idiot with as much love as I'd had in my voice. I kissed the breath out of him, both of us panting and swollen lipped when I finally pulled back. "I love you so much."

Igor grinned widely. "I love you too."

Babushka cleared her throat. "Dinner is ready. Then cake. Little rabbit told me he tried to make it for you."

Igor hadn't understood Babushka's words, but my wide-eyed shock when I turned to him must have given something away because he was already grinning before I said anything. "You asked her to make korolevsky?"

He nodded. "And, if you'll notice, the fire department did not show up this time." He leaned in conspiratorially. "I think she's a witch. She made it look way too easy."

That was my babushka. She was a master in the kitchen. Anything from breakfast to dessert, if it could be thought, she could create it.

Pulling Igor close once more, I whispered into his ear. "That answers the question of a spanking or an orgasm. All the orgasms for you."

He held his arm up to signal a goal. "Score!"

~*~

Up next in the Nashville Grizzlies Series: *Assisted*, coming winter 2023. An assistant coach and the director of hockey, what could possibly go wrong?

Cameos in *Scored*:

Seth and Maz: It's the book where the Grizzlies first made an appearance. A sexy encounter at a Halloween party leaves Seth fantasizing about his masked Phantom while Maz can't keep his mind off Pretty, the man in the gorgeous lingerie an high heels that stole his heart. When Seth and Maz discover that not only do they know one another but are teammates too, things are bound to get awkward. Discover how the two manage to keep things hot both on and off the ice when you pick up Seth now.

Trevor and Brax: The charismatic team captain wasn't in the market for a Daddy, but when his old teammates son needs a place to stay as his career with the Grizzlies gets started, Trevor finds everything he never dreamed he'd have. Pick up Traded to follow the two though an awkward, funny, and oh-so-sweet discovery of who they are both individually and as a couple.

. . .

Ryder and Malcom: Want to know more about Malcolm, Ryder, and the first out NFL players? Pick up Surprise Play today and find out how the two discovered the pieces they were missing.

Want more? Check out my entire backlist here: https://readerlinks.com/l/2406807/linktree

KOROLEVSKY, AKA RUSSIAN ROYAL CAKE, AKA THE CAKE THAT BROKE CARLY'S FOOT

Let's start with the basics: Here's the link to the recipe that started this entire ordeal. https://letthebakingbegin.com/russian-royal-cake-korolevskiy-cake/

Don't say it, I know, I know. "Carly! You based so much of this book on Korolevsky, and you've spelled it differently than the recipe did!" Yes, you caught me. I did. Remember way at the beginning of this book, I mentioned that Russian is a complex language with multiple ways to spell the same word? This is one of them. The recipe I used spells it with an *iy* while every other mention of the cake I found is simply *y*. For the sake of, well, I don't even know what... I think I was just exhausted by that point, I changed the spelling in the book to reflect the *y* spelling.

Okay, onto the cake process!

Let's break this down. Famous last words: "50 minutes." I knew before I started this cake that there was no way in heck this cake would take fifty minutes. Heck, it took me trips to five different stores as well as two Amazon order just get the ingredients to my house!

Then came the baking... of four cakes. As well as mistake number one. There's a little * somewhere in the recipe (or maybe in the author's life-story) about how you should bake the vanilla—walnut and poppyseed—cakes immediately, BEFORE starting the chocolate cakes. Well, I missed that part.

What happens if you do not bake them immediately? Well, quite simply put, the become sticky layers that do not rise... so have fun cutting them in half (But I managed that, more on that later)

While they were in the oven, much time was spent cleaning the disaster that had become my kitchen, my mixer, my daughter, and myself, through the process of making not 1, not 2, not 3, but FOUR separate cake layers. Flour, cocoa, baking powder, if it was in the cake, it was on the counters, the floors, and us!

Then came the fun part, removing the layers that had not risen (major disappointment there) from the pans, letting them cool, then splitting the fuckers in half. NO SMALL

TASK! While they finished cooling, I set to work making the icing that turned into a buttery mess that produced way too little icing to actually cover the cake.

Pro tip: double the icing recipe.

I don't think I mentioned that I couldn't find Dolce de leche at the store here, so I had to make it by boiling sweetened condensed milk in little jars on the stove for HOURS. Side note here, I did eventually find dolce de leche at the Mexican grocer down the road. As it turns out, I liked the one I made way more, so I used the instead!

With all the layers iced and in the fridge for the night, I finally sat down for the first time in about 8 hours, only to discover that the foot that I'd been babying for five weeks was in so much pain I couldn't move it. Time to admit that it wasn't simply muscular, it was actually a stress fracture that required a boot for a few weeks. Thankfully, I'm almost completely better now!

The next day dawned early and very rainy and I was in the kitchen, mixing up *more* icing so that I could *finally* eat this cake. Cake fully iced, I meted the chocolate drizzle as directed (and it worked!) and poured it over the cake. Then pretended I knew what the hell I was doing and "piped" some decorations on the top with the very little bit of icing I had left.

The finished project was admittedly gorgeous and weighed no less than eight pounds. I'm totally pulling a number of out my ass, but I was shocked at how heavy this eight layer Russian Royal cake weighed!

Final verdict: DENSE... RICH... a little dry—though I'm guessing that was because I messed up and waited too long to put the cakes in the oven—and all together amazing! The cake was fantastic and one day, maybe in a year or so, I'd like to try again, but I think I'll use this recipe instead... it looks a lot easier!!

A Note from Carly

Dear Reader,

Thank you so much for picking up *Scored.* Yuri and Igor's story is one of my favorites, but boy was it a challenge from start to finish. Up against a deadline, school ended in May and I remember thinking on the last day of school. "Oh. Fuck. There goes work for the next three months."

Truer words have never been uttered from me. From mental health crises, to doctors dropping the ball, we experienced so much more than any family should every have to deal with the first two months of summer break. Then August rolled around and I naively thought that I could see the light at the end of the tunnel. Little did I know, that was simply a little fleck of gold glitter in the middle of the tunnel. It had probably gotten lodged there sixteen year ago during an ill-advised crafting project... anyway, I've digressed.

My sister-in-laws three year battle with metastatic breast cancer was coming to an end. While not unexpected, it was obviously heartbreaking for my husband. He was called the first week of August and asked to get to California as quickly as possible. He dropped everything and was on a flight the next day... Homecoming: TBD.

He ended up there for a month. A month of me being mom to four kids while trying to work and get them ready to go back to school. I ended up navigating four airports with four kids at the end of August to fly out to California after my sister-in-law passed and back. We were there for a week, and of course school had started, which meant catch up time with four kids. It also meant more lost work because I had come home while Mr. Marie stayed for a little longer to be with his sister's kids and her husband while they began to adjust.

All this is to say that Yuri and Igor's story, while I loved writing it, was written painfully slowly. It has been wonderful being back at my computer the last few weeks, feeling creative energy flowing through me and excited to see where the next books take us.

If you've followed me for anytime, you know that hockey is a passion of mine, I have two kids who play and spend hours, days, and weeks at hockey rinks. My schedule literally is filled with hockey practices, games, or scrimmages. If I'm not carting a kid to a practice or game, I'm heading up to watch the Cleveland Monsters—our local AHL team—play! Even with my love of the sport, I still learn new things about the game every time I start writing!

I truly hope you enjoyed reading Igor and Yuri's book as much as I enjoyed writing it. Please take a few minutes to *leave a review of Scored*, as an independent author, reviews are invaluable. Even a short review can help others find my books. Thank you again for reading *Scored*.

Peace, Love, and Happy Reading,

Carly

About the Author

Carly Marie has had stories, characters, and plot bunnies bouncing around in her head as long as she can remember. Today, she is a USA Today Bestselling author, lover of all things romance, and avid reader.

Carly spends her days writing sweet, kinky stories about men who love each other and her nights as a wife, mother, and chauffeur. She spends far too much time reading books, in hockey rinks or driving between them, and far too little time cleaning her house.

Carly lives in Ohio with her husband, four kids, three cats, and has lost count of the number of chickens in the backyard. The numerous plot bunnies that run through her head on a daily basis ensure that she will continue to write and share her stories for years to come.

Keep up to date on all the latest by following me at:

Mailing List:Carly's Connection

Website: www.authorcarlymarie.com

instagram.com/carlymariewrites

amazon.com/author/carlymarie

bookbub.com/authors/carly-marie

goodreads.com/CarlyMarieWrites

Printed in Great Britain
by Amazon

23452911R00219